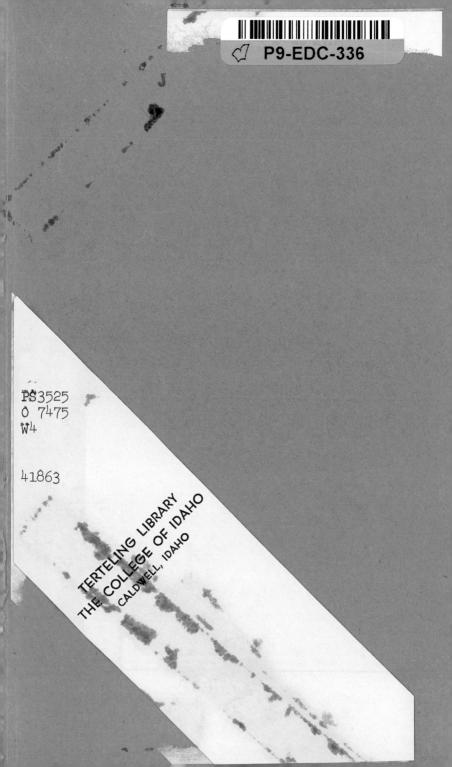

Books by **Wright Morris**

What a Way to Go   1962

Ceremony in Lone Tree   1960

The Territory Ahead   1958

Love Among the Cannibals   1957

The Field of Vision   1956

The Huge Season   1954

The Deep Sleep   1953

The Works of Love   1952

Man and Boy   1951

The World in the Attic   1949

The Home Place   1948

The Inhabitants   1946

The Man Who Was There   1945

My Uncle Dudley   1942

What a Way to Go

*The story of Pygmalion points to a ceremony
of a sacred marriage in which the king wedded
the image of Aphrodite, or rather of Astarte.
If that was so, the tale was in a sense true, not
of a single man only, but of a whole series of
men. . . .*

JAMES GEORGE FRAZER

*I remember well the time when the thought of the
eye made me cold all over.*

CHARLES DARWIN

Wright Morris
What a Way to Go

New York *Atheneum* **1962**

For **G. H.** *and* **D. H.**

What a Way to Go

one | Death had spared Arnold Soby—as it had also deprived him—of the academic wife who gave teas to freshmen, saw that the wall flowers at the parties were watered, and played cards in the foyer while the seniors danced. He was not, however, that Bachelor of the Arts who had never sunk his teeth into the apple. No, Soby knew the bitter-sweet taste, and the lingering smell of life. That it had proved gratifying was implied in the way a little of it proved sufficient for a lifetime. He did not cultivate romantic affairs among the campus wives who were ripe for cultivation, or use his vacations to dig for buried treasure in the sands of Acapulco or Martha's Vineyard. Not that this didn't cost him something. He was considered more than reasonably safe. When the Foreign Affairs Club planned its trip to the UN it was inevitable that the girls would ask Soby, who had no interest in the subject, to be their chaperone. He was safe, acceptable, and he was also good fun. He would see that they were taken to the Modern Museum and to lunch at the Met. If there was a questionable foreign movie to be seen, they saw it. They preferred to be herded around by Soby, or clustered under the drip of his umbrella, and dusted with the ashes, as well as the sparks, of his inverted pipe. He sometimes looked, he invariably smelled like a man. Allowing for the seasonal flaking of the skin around his earlobes and his eyebrows, the consensus was that he might be square, but he was cute. He had learned to live with it and felt no need to wear Bermuda shorts.

The slogan of the Rawley Centennial Fund Drive—
The Times change, and Rawley changes with the Times—did not apply to Arnold Soby, one of its more durable ornaments. Soby, never Arnold Soby, nor Professor Soby, nor Dr. Soby. His superiors—in a manner of speaking—used the term with a certain affection, as if they had placed a hand on his head and pronounced the word son. The younger generation, for much the same reason, added the word *old*. Take Old Soby they would say, meaning that one could easily do worse. Not that he was old, quite the contrary, he did not age so much as he dated. One could imagine him at the wheel of any car with its top down, a Kelly Springfield tire, unused, in nickel plated clamps on the running board. One had to imagine it, however, since he did not drive. He played respectable tennis in the style of a man who had played mixed doubles with Suzanne Lenglen, and been struck by a smash from the racket of Borotra, the bounding Basque. At teas, weddings of students, and cocktail parties he wore flannels the color of piano keys. A colleague once described him as the only Rhodes scholar who came home at Christmas without an accent. Twenty-five years later, crouched under a slicker at the annual Hamilton-Chase classic, Soby heard the voice of the girl behind him, muffled by large bites of hotdog, explain why she was taking a poetry seminar. "I don't know about the Wasteland," she said, licking

her fingers, "but *he's* cute."

Soby *cute?* Under the slicker all that appeared was the inverted bowl of his pipe, a Soby trademark rain or shine. When he arose, ten minutes later, to join in the singing of the Alma Mater, one had the impression that he was all legs. Even more so a few minutes later, crossing the grassy quad on his way to his rooms, his trousers rolled on the gartered calves of Mr. Prufrock, his eyes above the level of the crowd gathered waiting for taxis, where, as if seeing people off personally, he would remove his hat, bow.

Was that what the girl had meant? His bowing, his formal air, the way he stood half tipped, like some fabled bird, was partly his temperament, partly a problem of scale. His cap on, he looked something more than his forty-seven years. The cap off, as it was in class, or in more favorable campus weather, there was something of a youthful Alec Guinness trying to pass himself off as one of the elders. The impression was largely due to his hair. It lay flat, and grew forward to conceal part of his forehead, not unlike the heads of small fry, after a swim, and certain Roman Senators. The lick at the front, just before it was trimmed, would be lightly powdered with green chalk dust from the absent-minded sweep of his hand. Rather large ears, inclined to be hairy, the bridge of his nose somewhat bruised by glasses and the thoughtful way he stroked it with his fingers when bored. Blue eyes, very pale, sometimes looking like holes in his head. How often it was said, "If only he would do *something* about his teeth!"

Well, he did. He grinned more than he smiled. *Something,* alas, was to have them pulled or capped, which he soberly stated as his intention—when he found the time. Publicly, he admitted that false teeth might ruin his smoking since they were not designed to clamp down on a pipe. Privately, there was the problem of pain, since he was a physical coward, and the notion, however vague, that he would be losing more than his teeth. Never mind what. All in all not much of a figure, but something in his scale, his reserve, and his voice on the tape machine in the library, reading selections from the modern poets, suggested a man who had surprised people once, and might do it again.

When Soby spoke, as he did on occasion, of the sunny sensuality of Greece, Rawley girls put down their pencils and took mental notes. Part of a freshman's matriculation at Rawley was the tale, something of a classic, of Soby's love affair with Sophia Demos, a Greek girl and Rawley sophomore. The daughter of the prosperous owner of a chain of Chicago restaurants, what Sophia knew of Greece, sunny or otherwise, she learned from Soby. Dark, her almost scowling face a partial clearing in a wild mat of hair, Sophia's eyebrows were not divided, in the usual manner, at the bridge of her nose, but formed a bushy hedge over her eyes. Large boned, fond of dangling earrings and bracelets that clanked on her arms as she gestured, Sophia's stride was that of a woman who crossed a field with the plow invisible behind her. No one thought to call her pretty, or less than extraordinary. No apparent time seemed to separate her from the voyages of Ulysses, and the murder of kings ill advised in the ways of love. When she crossed the Rawley campus it was lit up, for a moment, with the light of Greece. So much was implied, if not exactly stated, in the service held at her death—a light had gone out and Rawley was the darker for it. With her brother, an unreconstructed Ajax, whose interests were not at all academic, she had been returning from a weekend with her family when his souped-up Ford struck an underpass embankment while racing the train that passed, a moment later, over their heads.

She had been the bride of Soby for just seven months. No question that he saw her through the lenses of a stereopticon viewer, and the file of cards featuring views of Athens and the isles of Greece. Not that she was not sufficiently Greek, merely that he had lacked sufficient time to know her. She remained as near, and as far, in the sense he had of *knowing*, as the morning she appeared in his office with a cluster of grapes, one hand full of the chewed pits and skins. All that Soby filed under psychology, as it concerned the human personality, had no more part in her make-up than features in the faces of Cycladic dolls, the head not as yet prepared for such innovations as eyes. She gazed at him, from grapes to death, with a serene and impersonal affection, without sentiment or any interest whatsoever in what made Soby *tick*. So much for the spiritual, the immaterial side of their seven months together.

On the material side, what Soby came to know of the clear and sunny sensuality of Greece, he learned from her, but most of what he learned he preferred not to admit. Not that he was a prude. Not after the first two or three nights. Weeks after she was gone the drag of her nails was still visible on his back, and the grip of her fingers in the soft flesh of his arms. *That* Soby would admit to, if pressed, but what he refused to admit to himself was that their most intimate relationship was the most impersonal. One could only put it in the manner it came to him. Her nails—seldom so clean the problem of infection was not present —at the moment they dug into his flesh were indifferent to whose flesh it might be. Not that Soby admitted this, understand. Not for some time. The window of their apartment opened on to a field, and just beyond it, through a stand of trees that were barren in the winter, one could see the lights of the Hamilton dormitories. That window often stood open and Arnold Soby, as he listened to his wife's breathing, saw in his imagination a man not himself, an anony-

mous lover, crawl in and out under the mask of darkness, faceless and nameless as the passion he came to
gratify.

All of this Soby knew, but the young man who
arose in the morning chose not to admit it. What did
love have to do with such forces, such nameless lusts?
Nor did it help that he read, in a book of stories his
wife thought they should translate, of Greek maidens
who were staked out in a field at night, like cattle, to
be ravished by the fellow bold enough to take them.
Even the satyr, half man half beast, was somewhat
ornamental for such a passion, although the leering
smile was unmistakably appropriate.

Then it was over: with his wife's broken body he
went to Chicago, the near-north side, where Mr.
Demos and his family lived above a restaurant where
fruit wrapped in tissue paper was piled in the window, and a Cadillac sedan covered with a tarpaulin
sat in the back yard. After the funeral they rode up
and down the drives in Lincoln Park. Sophia had her
mother's figure, her father's dark face with the single
bushy brow shading the eyes. They spoke no English.
Soby never saw them again.

The times changed, and Rawley changed with the
times. A school that once dismissed girls for painting their lips now supplied the ivy chapel, the Ham-
mond organ, for the marriages of students who spe-

cialized in what was locally known as the seventh-month child. Soby supplied silver spoons to many of them. In his damp office in the library basement he kept a small kitty, as he called it, for emergencies, and doled out Spanish sherry with his free advice. With Soby they were candid—a charitable term for what they came to tell him—and in return they would remember to ask him about his work.

His work? Oh yes, his work. Shortly after the death of his wife he had begun a work. The problems seemed to lie less in the material than in the manner Soby would dare to admit it. The Wisdom of the Body, as he humorously described it, its causes and its cure. If there were young ladies who came to him who felt their experience in these matters was wider, they nevertheless broached the subject even at the dances he chaperoned. What did he *mean* by such wisdom? Concealing his teeth behind his characteristic smile Soby would wag his hand at the jitter-bugging couples, given over, if one could judge by their actions, the archaic blankness of their expressions, to a wisdom that was *not* of the mind. Did he mean to imply that sort of thing was wisdom? Only in a manner of speaking. They would have to wait—as he would—till his researches were complete.

This project had been forgotten by Soby, as well as most of his colleagues, until his sabbatical in Italy was cut short by the war. He was in Florence, waiting for a plane, when he happened to pick up a book about Venice. Or rather about Death in Venice. Quite possibly he picked it up because he had failed to get there. How explain the impression it left on him?

The story, very German and romantic, if not actually a bit morbid, concerned a cultivated man, a writer—not unlike Soby—who came to Venice for a change and relaxation. A strange thing happened. He was seized with a ridiculous passion for a beautiful boy—or the boy's sublime beauty. Not the usual sort of thing, however, since it was the immaterial beauty that enslaved him. But a slave he was. Worse, he began to think and act like a fool. His nights were given over to hallucinated dreams. Only the seasonal pestilence, which carried him off, prevented him from doing something outrageous in public. But all of that was incidental. It was the poor devil's dream that impressed Soby. Novels are full of dreams, and Soby was full of novels, but this dream impressed him as something special. More. As one he might have suffered himself. It began in fear, desire, and a shuddering curiosity. A somewhat complicated dream, unusually vivid, in which sounds and smells were exceptionally important, it left both Aschenbach, the dreamer, and Soby, the reader, in a highly agitated condition. But Aschenbach had merely dreamed it. Soby had been there in the flesh. Had been *where?* He referred his students to the scene in the book. Down the dark slopes of this dream, like so many howling beasts, fur-pelted men and women came in a mad rout toward a clearing in the forest given over to the rites of the *stranger God*. Some waved torches vomiting trails of sparks. Some beat on drums. All hooted with a drawn out *u*-sound that was both pleasing and disturbing. From the goings-on in the torchlight both the dreamer and the reader averted their eyes. Not that they didn't know. No, they knew only too well. Soby, after all, had actually been there personally. Or was it *im*-personally? One way or the other he bore the evidence in the flesh on his back. Sophia Demos had brought to Soby the disquieting knowledge Aschenbach merely dreamt of. A wisdom of the body. One that took precedence over the mind. Soby knew it well—if he but knew how to admit what he knew.

Two weeks later he was back in Rawley with vivid impressions of Ischia, Perugia, Florence, and of Venice, in particular of Venice, one place in Italy he had never been. He spoke of it often. He had always had an eye for macabre details. Rather than tiresomely explain that this Venice was a fiction, it seemed better to let it pass as a fact. Otherwise the impression, held by students and colleagues, that he had narrowly escaped death by plague on the Lido would have to be methodically contradicted, and this would take time. If certain of his particulars seemed a little dated, why not? So did Soby. With the war, and his deferment on the basis of his ten-twenty vision, he took up once more the researches he had abandoned. The Wisdom of the Body: both in fiction and in fact. Rawley seniors who had cut their teeth on Soby's contraband copies of *The Tropic of Cancer* were given *Death in Venice* as a purgative. There was, he archly suggested, more life and sex in it. What did he mean by that? One would have to wait till he finished his book.

After the war both his students and his colleagues asked Soby for the names of his friends in Venice, since he impressed them as knowing the place like the palm of his hand. No one thought of questioning where he would go on his sabbatical. If someone had, he might have preferred to go somewhere else. Impressions of the pestilence, vague but persistent, would have led him to prefer Aix-en-Provence, or Mallorca, healthier places, both, to carry on his researches. Since he had not been to Venice, however, a sense of guilt obliged him to go there, although he would be under no compunction to stay. When the winter fog set in he would go to Mallorca or the coast of Spain.

Soby's refusal to fly was predictable, based on his notion of a restful sea voyage, but he had overlooked the need to make his reservations in advance. Through the influence of a Rawley alumnus, passage was found on a liner that made many stops in the Mediterranean, the next to last being Venice. This proved to be a windfall since the boat sailed in early May, rather than June, and would put him in Venice ahead of the tourists and the summer heat. Striped canvas luggage monogrammed with his initials, and neatly packed with wash'n dry shirts and pajamas, was a surprise bon voyage gift from the faculty. Soby preferred his old gladstone, with its freighter labels, but he took the new one to avoid hurt feelings. He was driven to New York by an Ivy League youth who had spent the weekend with his date at Rawley, the car smelling of Chanel, the seat strewn with bobby pins. He had been twice to Europe and warned Soby to beware of French broads and Italian food. In that order. Venice he thought would suit Soby very well, since so little had changed since the twenties. Soby found assurance in the clear implication that this included himself.

two | The liner sailed at noon. Streamers of confetti stretched and snapped as the steamer backed into the river, under the buzz of helicopters taking photographs. On the Jersey side of the river an oil tanker, with a single stack, was being painted a bright lemon yellow by men who were seated on swings lowered from the sides. Due to the light, the long slanting shadows, and Soby's ten-twenty vision, what he saw was an abstraction suggestive of a lithe, sun-drenched body, the eyes masked, reclining on the golden sands of an island as yet untouched, as the posters had said, by a major cruise. Soby waited till they passed Miss Liberty, where uniformed girls stood in a line at the entrance, then he went below to the dining room where the steward led him to a table near a porthole. Two of the chairs were occupied. Bowing, Soby introduced himself.

Miss Winifred Throop, seated on Soby's left, a woman of generous proportions, held a napkin to her lips as she tilted her head, one eye dilated, exposing a face like that of Boswell's Johnson. A large amount of titian hair puffed through the top of her wide brimmed hat, without a crown, held in place by a veil and several long hairpins, capped with glassy bird's eyes. The head of a fur piece, flattened as if caught in a roller, dipped its nose in the piece of lace concealing her bust. In one hand she held the napkin, the other she dipped into coils of beads, gathered, like clothespins, in her ample lap. The smaller lady on her left was her companion and colleague, Miss Mathilde Kollwitz. Short and slight, with perhaps less hair on her head than Soby, Miss Kollwitz wore a sweater over a stylishly elevated profile. Her arms were crossed beneath it as if to lend support. Her alert, almost startled expression was perhaps due, Soby reflected, to years of respectful attention to Miss Throop's low voice. The breeze on the deck had dishevelled her hair. Miss Kollwitz wore no make-up, and brows seemed to be lacking above her eyes. On her plate, coiled like a serpent, was the skin of the apple she had just peeled and quartered. The pits of one quarter oozed at the corners of her mouth. These she added to the compost on her plate. There was no nonsense about Miss Kollwitz.

"Look here!" she said, with something like a bark, "what do you teach?"

No mention had been made of Soby's background. "May I ask why you think I teach?" he inquired.

Miss Kollwitz drew back as if to draw a fat worm from its hole. "You think," she said, in a voice that turned the heads at nearby tables, "—only clergymen are frocked?"

It set Soby back. Did she know what she had said? Miss Kollwitz's foreign extraction was less evident in her accent than in the emphasis she gave the familiar phrase.

"Mr. Soby—" Miss Throop said, the lids stretched taut over her eyes, "I must ask you to share, for the

crossing, the cross I have borne for thirty-one years."
She salted her soup.

"A cross? What is not a piece of the cross?" asked
Miss Kollwitz. From the basket of bread she gripped
a roll, bit into it.

"Might I ask what *you* teach?" inquired Soby.
Miss Kollwitz made a face like a tragic mask. Her
cheeks filled with wind, but she said nothing.

"Miss Kollwitz and I," Miss Throop intoned,
"mete and dole the law unto a savage race."

"I must say that describes it very accurately,"
Soby replied. Stimulated by such companions Soby
inquired for the wine list. To his suggestion that
Valpolicella went with their entree they agreed. Miss
Throop commented, just in passing, that the red wines
south of Naples had been among her favorites just be-
fore the war. Soby looked up to say, "Twenty years.
Has it been twenty years since I was in Paestum?"

"My dear young man," Miss Throop said, re-
leasing her beads to place the hand on his sleeve,
"not twenty, but forty. I'm afraid I mean the *first*
war."

For thirty-one years Miss Winifred Throop had
been the head mistress of the Country Day School in
Winnetka, until her retirement in June of the year before. She had postponed her trip until Miss Kollwitz,
who taught French and German, would be able to join

her on a trip to Greece. It was not the sort of venture one wanted to undertake alone. After a few weeks in Italy—she had a few friends in Florence—they would be joined by her niece who was making her first trip to Europe, a reward for the five long years she had spent in high school. An intelligent, attractive, but somewhat distracted child. Wasn't that true of so many of them? Soby suggested. Miss Throop stroked the foxhead inclined on her bust, the glassy eyes fastened on Soby. In her silence, the gliding lisp of her beads, Soby gathered the banality of his observation, and that the discussion began where he had left off. "I suppose I'm thinking more of the boys than the girls," Soby added. "The girls we get at Rawley are their superior."

"If that is true," Miss Throop replied, "it is because most of them come from Country Day." A fact Soby should have known, but of course he did not. It was the future of the girls he was concerned with, not their past. "You will be spared my niece, however, Mr. Soby, since she will be entering Oberlin. Her mother would not think of her wasting time in a school without boys."

"We find the Oberlin boy—" Soby retorted, "does rather poorly at Rawley. Currently the Ivy League is sorely pressed by the boys from the South."

"Look here!" Miss Kollwitz swept the deck with a wave of one knitting needle, to which was attached the beginning of a green sleeve. "It is boys she now gets away from. She has too many boys in Winnetka!"

"I wonder how it will prove to be in Greece," Miss Throop observed.

"I'm afraid an attractive American girl will not go unnoticed," Soby said with a smile, "especially when she is so attractively chaperoned."

Miss Kollwitz popped a quarter of the apple into her mouth. Miss Throop plucked from her sleeve not the short hair of the fur piece, but the long auburn strands in the crown of her hat.

"Young man—" she said, placing two fingers on the veined lids of her eyes, "I wish she had been here to hear you say that. She is not without breeding, but it would help her to distinguish the men from the boys."

They sat in steamer chairs, out of the wind, facing the rear deck crowded with tourists of the second class. Women by and large, in particular large, being of Italian extraction, with a few elderly men in pressed pants and new shoes, their caps puffed out with paper lining, at long last returning to their native land. Two groups of younger women were making chaperoned religious tours. Soby's experience as a chaperone led him to note a change in tribal behaviour—a Rawley girl first scanned the field for another female, checking her style and feathers, these young women scanned it for first things first, a man.

Soby, supported on both flanks, received a glance and a dismissal. At the fantail, hatless, leaning on the rail with his legs crossed, was a gentleman said to be active in the latest Italian movies. He wore a turtle neck sweater. Why was he slumming in second class?

"In first class, my dear," Miss Throop commented, "there are no children to stare at him. The poor dear may have felt deprived of oxygen."

On the deck Miss Throop's air of breeding made her speech a little hard to follow, so many of the vowels were blown away or lost in her nose. A good nose, Soby thought, or rather a beak (familiar to the readers of English novels), from which the features of her face suspended like a jacket with weighted pockets. Smudged particles of diesel soot darkened her eyes. She took the sun relaxed, partially deflated, her small fin-like hands crossed in her lap, her face that of a man dozing in a barber's chair. Not lost on Soby was the way she exposed her small feet, with the muscular ankles. The blanket spread over her legs she had drawn to her lap, as if tucking up a skirt.

To such frailties, and countless others, time had seasoned Miss Kollwitz, wrapped against the windy deck like a papoose. Her hands showed, little more, since the visor of a sunshade concealed her face, the underside of the brim used to file both straight and safety pins. A bag of tangled knitting wool occupied her lap. In the time alloted for the voyage she hoped to knit a sweater for Miss Throop's niece, knowing full well she would forget to bring one along. Travels in Mexico had convinced Miss Kollwitz that only wool was shelter from the sun, and she advised Soby to wear a double length of it around his waist. Half the troubles known to man came from diet, and the rest from intestinal chills. To make certain he heard this advice Soby had lowered his head from the deck wind, and put it toward her when she beckoned to him. To free the hand with which she had beckoned, she placed the needle with its knitting between her teeth like a flower, and with the wadded corner of a piece of tissue cleaned the soot from the wings of Soby's nose. The gesture was so natural, and so unexpected, there was little to be said. "There now," she said, satisfied with his appearance, and returned to her knitting. Miss Throop had taken it in through sealed eyes.

"You might as well resign yourself, young man," she said, "that you are under the care of Miss Kollwitz."

"Perhaps it's just what I need," Soby replied.

Miss Throop rocked her head but made no comment. From her bag of wool Miss Kollwitz fetched an orange, held it aloft. "You must eat it," she said, "for the grippe."

"The grippe?" Soby echoed, "I feel fine."

"It will please Miss Kollwitz if you catch it, my dear. She reports that we have several cases."

"You eat it." Miss Kollwitz placed it in Soby's hand.

"I shall save it," he replied, "until I have the symptoms."

"I'm so relieved to hear you say *shall,*" said Miss Throop.

On the deck there was a flurry as if someone had released cages of birds. One of the coveys of young ladies had swarmed in on the gentleman active in the movies. The chaperone, with a borrowed camera, searched for them in the wrong eyepiece. A spectator advised her not to take the picture against the sun. This required that the group manoeuvre so that Soby and the ladies were included. Miss Kollwitz, trailing a streamer of wool, took off. Miss Throop placed the sheets of the boat's newsletter over her face. With the help of a steward (the wine at lunch had made him drowsy) Soby made his way to the cabin he shared with Julio Lipari, who unbolted the door to let him in.

Neither large nor small, thin nor paunchy, somewhat rodent-faced as he squinted through his glasses, Mr. Lipari was on his way to an audience with the Pope. The letter of introduction, in a separate compartment of the wallet with the pictures of his grandchildren, he showed to Soby—not so much out of pride as the need for reassurance—that he, Julio world war, Miss Throop's light brown hair had turned white. As a younger woman she looked quite distinguished, would not hear of having it dyed. As an older woman, however, she had changed her mind. Since incidents with wigs were not uncommon due to the hazards of travel, Miss Kollwitz felt he should be warned. The sight of her without it could be quite a shock.

In this way, as he was sometimes briefed on the backgrounds of complicated students, Soby—between the peelings and quarterings of the apple he shared—learned something of both the leetul one and the fat one. That cloud of titian hair, her crowning glory, was more a part of the hat than her head, and explained her tendency to see in others more than met the eye; to comment a little wryly, as Soby had observed, on the nature of things. For the pectin, and its power over the grippe, Miss Kollwitz would slip a slice of the peel, as if taking snuff, under her upper lip preliminary to their walk on the deck. One of her shawls passed twice around her head and was looped beneath her chin. From this ambush the small scrubbed face was that of a prematurely aged child, or Greek orphan of the war.

Soby wore his tennis sneakers, for sure footing, a raincoat with his cap folded in the pocket, and one of his pipes with the smoking bowl inverted. The sea air, the exercise, led Miss Kollwitz to throw more windows of her mind open, most of them opening on the

Lipari, was to speak with the Pope. So the letter said. Hearing the words from Soby swelled his heart. He confessed, folding it away, that not every Cicero Italian was successful enough to *sweeeng eet*. There had been an influential clause in his will. The pilgrimage justified the generous mood that led Mr. Lipari to buy the box of cigars, Burns Panatellas, that he left open on the dresser, as well as the bottle of Italian brandy propped in the sink. At his age, what more was there a man should want? Brandy, cigars, and the blessings of the Pope? At one time he might have cast an eye at the black-eyed girls at his table, the one with the bust like a baby's bottom as he said. But no more. That was for Soby, not for him. Soby remarked that he, too, now found a good smoke, or a fine wine, as attractive as the more demanding pleasures of his youth. Mr. Lipari smiled somewhat enigmatically.

Soby was puzzled by the ease with which Mr. Lipari spoke of personal affairs, without touching on the area of privacy. Seated on the bunk—he did not find the chairs in the room to his liking—he rolled the panatellas on his puckered lips, now and then sipping the smoke like a good sherry. Could one speak of a disinterested curiosity? Mr. Lipari had it, noting the details of Soby's feet when he changed his socks, observing with interest the blood flecked lather as he shaved. Still, if he had it to live over, Mr. Lipari observed, he would rather be a man than a woman. Would Soby know why? They exchanged glances in the cabinet mirror. To do it and not to enjoy it—was that not a scheme of the devil? So much of your life spent in bed and flat on your back? For that alone he could not thank God enough and might increase the clause in his will when the time came. It was not like Soby, his lips frothy with lather, to say that this had not been his experience, that some women would thank God that they were women, not men.

"How many women you know?" Mr. Lipari asked, unimpressed. If that had been God's intention he would not have put woman on the bottom. On the top was a man's place, thank God for that. Wreathed in smoke, his legs dangling from the upper bunk, a man's position, Mr. Lipari gave Soby a professional, impersonal wink.

"How you like?" he asked, "the beeg fat one or the leetul one?"

The leetul one, Miss Kollwitz, her hair still wet from the shower, was always at the breakfast table before Soby arrived. Miss Throop, the beeg fat one, spent the morning in the cabin. All her professional life, Miss Kollwitz confided, Miss Throop had had the problem of getting started, which was where Miss Kollwitz had entered her life. She too, had the problem, but she had mastered it. A shower, followed by

deep breaths taken through the nose, exhale[d] the mouth, circulated the blood and opened dows of the mind. The metaphor came eas[ily] her shower-blue lips.

Familiar with the classics in three lan[guages] Miss Kollwitz had a flair for picturesque spee[ch] literary turn of phrase received a turn of he[r] "Look here," she said, "live and let hands off!" one of her own, however, to tap on Soby's sleeve her apple paring knife. At breakfast she threw the windows of her mind. While peeling the ap[ple] which she compared unfavorably with former app[les] she confessed that Miss Throop was subject to vani[ty] It was why she spent the morning alone in her roo[m] She had skillfully evaded all questions concernin[g] her age.

Soby countered that a woman who admitted she had been to Europe before the first war had that window in her mind ajar, to say the least.

Miss Kollwitz pointed out that it was merely an instance of her vanity. She fancied herself as something of a matriarch. She had made the remark purely and simply to hear it contradicted, but Soby's astonishment had been more than enough. It had said better than words that she was older than she looked. Before an incident occurred, as it was apt to, Miss Kollwitz felt obliged to warn him that what Soby saw on Miss Throop's head was not her own hair, but a wig. Following a tragedy, the loss of her fiance in the first

life and landscape of Miss Throop. A family of daughters. All but one of them scholarly and well bred. Her sister Evelyn, however, perhaps ten years her junior, had always been something of a problem, having the Brownell beauty rather than the Throopside brains. A woman given to manias, cults, fellowships for self-realization, and anything that had the slightest reference to love. To speak frankly, Miss Kollwitz found her unquestionably attractive, but somewhat simple-minded. Twice married she had lost one husband in the second war. This niece, Cynthia, was their child—he had been a commercial airlines pilot—and if the child's behaviour was unusual, Miss Kollwitz knew who to thank for it. During and after the war, one of the rooms in her mother's large rambling house served as asylum to young people who came to her and said that they were in love. Could he imagine the scandal? Soby could. Cynthia had been but a child at the time, but one did not have to be a student of Freud to guess this would have on her a permanent effect. As it had. Miss Kollwitz could vouch for that. Nothing willful, nor perverse, but such an easy-going way with men that a chaperone was necessary before she reached her teens. And how old was she now? Miss Kollwitz thought seventeen. She had already received the proposals of older men. This trip to Greece was not an award for getting out of high school—although she deserved one— but a barefaced scheme to clear the house of disturbing competition, since the mother was thinking of getting married again.

Would Soby please tell her what he thought the world was coming to?

Soby took a dim view of the world, but he reminded Miss Kollwitz that mothers and daughters had been in competition, some of it very serious, since the Greeks. Nor did he have to tell Miss Kollwitz, a keen observer of the younger generation, that girls today were maturing more rapidly. To parody the Rawley slogan, the Times change, and the girls with the Times. The amazing thing was that these rattled children, one day stomping their feet and shrieking like banshees at the sight of Elvis Presley, just a year or two later were young women pushing carts in the supermarkets, a child or two in the basket along with the food. As a matter of fact—Soby had paused to rap the bowl of his pipe on the rail—his own wife had been a young woman still in her teens. A Greek girl, as it happened, although she had not lived to set her eyes on Greece. Miss Kollwitz took the revelation with a blow of her nose.

It was odd, but not perhaps unusual, to find two people who were strangers sharing confidences that they were slow to share with old friends. Was it a sudden intimacy—or perhaps the contrary? One could be intimate because they were strangers, not in spite of it. Once off the boat they would not see each other again. Later, in the privacy of a shower, reflecting on

what he had said and why he had said it, Soby recalled that the most intimate relationship of his life
—that of passionate love—had been the most impersonal. Strangers could be intimate in a way that
friends could not. It seemed a curious knowing—
with unknowing at its base. Mr. Lipari, sipping his
cigar with alternate sips of brandy as he confided in
Soby what he would have withheld from his con-
fessor. Was it wisdom of the body, or the mind?
Soby made note of the fact in the pocket journal he
had bought for just such observations, filing it, after
some reflection, under the rubric *Love.*

three | Their waiter, Mario, a blond Italian
giant as tall as Soby and half again as wide, had the
face of those Renaissance men who stand holding
spears, sit astride equestrian statues, lob off heads
with clinical indifference, or gaze impassive at the
resurrection of Christ, or his descent from the Cross.
He said little or nothing, answered their remarks with
a nod of his head, an arch of his brows, or a clucking
sound made with pursed lips, blowing softly on the
finger that wagged the ladies quiet. The humor of a
good herdsman flecked his light blue eyes. For several meals the ladies and Soby protested at the
amount of food he served them, and a few moments later, more or less untouched, carried away.
"Look here!" Miss Kollwitz would bark, her cheeks
puffed with wind, but to no avail. Mario's conspira-
torial smile, the arch of his brows as he ladled the
sauce, implied that he knew the secret places of a
woman's heart. Knowing the ways of spaghetti he
spread napkins on the slopes of the ladies, concealing Miss Throop's fox head, and arranged one to
dangle like a white beard into Soby's lap. Out of
shame they began to eat. And eat. And eat.

Was it the tangy sea air? It proved habit forming.
Rising from chairs Mario managed to slide back as
he bowed, they would pause for mints, toothpicks,
and then take the lift to the deck. Antonio, who had
the short legs of a bear, but a head larger than
Mario's, would then wrap them like patients taking

the cure. If the ladies felt Antonio was somewhat free with their persons, the protestations had stopped. As he hoisted the legs, arranged the folds, he said Ahhhhh, oooops, tk, tk, tk, tk, Ahhhhhhhh, as a good mother would ease a child into its bath. They made no comment, with the exception of a few burps. Soby would fill and light his pipe, but it would soon go out. On the lips of Miss Throop the sugar syrup from the four lumps she dissolved in her espresso would form a lacquer; her head would loll in such a manner there was some danger to her wig. From her bag Miss Kollwitz would produce the sleeve of a sweater she had never finished, loop it around the head, the wig and the hat, transforming Boswell's Johnson into a contentedly dreaming hog.

Miss Kollwitz, her eyes merely slits, would count aloud, in German, the stitches on her needle only to find that she had dropped one just before lunch. The wool she unravelled, always several hours' work, she would pile in Soby's lap. He had been mystified by the cidery smell until he found that the parings of her mid-morning apple were kept loose in her knitting bag. The wool that she heaped, like green noodles, was to be the smart turtle, or bucket, neck sweater worn by the model on page seven of her knitting book. Miss Kollwitz had selected it since the model resembled Miss Cynthia, a tall, long-limbed child who had grown too fast. A pity, since it called for quantities of wool. Until the girl herself was on hand,

Miss Kollwitz used the arm of Soby, from the wrist to the shoulder, more to her liking than the pattern, or the short arms of the girls in second class. Disjointed, distracted, round-shouldered, with an almost horrifying indifference to posture, Miss Kollwitz still had to admit the child would be attractive once she grew up. Soby sat as if he had no more to do than hold up his arm for measurement, and offer his hands, the fingers spread, when the time came to rewind the wool. A light spray filmed his glasses, and by four o'clock, almost famished, he would slip four lumps of sugar into his tea.

Too much pasta and not enough pectin, in the opinion of Miss Kollwitz, explained why Miss Throop had succumbed to the grippe. She brought him this news at lunch, having been deprived of her usual breakfast. Miss Throop was like an ill-tempered child when she was ill. She could neither bear Miss Kollwitz in or out of her sight. Was there perhaps something Soby could do? If he was not afraid of infection he might just stop by at teatime, and chat a bit. Miss Throop's self-sufficiency was a pretense and a sham. Without people around her she simply lacked oxygen. Soby commented that this was one of the sadder effects of academic life, since the schoolroom supplied one with a captive audience.

With unpeeled fruit, wrapped in a napkin, Miss Kollwitz made her way to the lift, but she was not on deck when Soby appeared for his constitutional. Spray from a white-capped sea darkened the deck. There were signs urging the passengers to watch their step. Mr. Lipari, usually the first to take a seat in the lounge for the movie, was seated, the brandy bottle in his hands, on Soby's lower bunk. Was he perhaps ill? Mr. Lipari reminded him that never, no never, had he been ill. It was not sea-sickness he felt, but concern. The movement of the boat, not the sea, troubled him. He would feel better, for example, after he had received the Pope's blessings. What business did this boat have in rolling before that occurred? Soby assured him that it was nothing, shaved to show his confidence in the future, then asked if there was something Mr. Lipari would like him to do. Yes, there was. When he left would he leave the light on.

On its chain, Miss Kollwitz opened the cabin door. She wore a quilted gown, buttoned at the throat, and held the apple she was paring for Miss Throop. A towel, perhaps several towels, circled the head and shoulders of Miss Throop, suffering from a neuralgia brought on by a draft from the porthole. To that was added the grippe, lips chapped by the wind, and a sunburned nose. And how was the patient? Soby asked, stepping in. "All but suffocated," was the reply. The air in the room smelled strongly of mange liniment. A cream of some kind had been applied to the burn on her nose. Like a wax figure that the fever had melted Miss Throop sagged in a corner, something in the nature of a nightcap over her wig. A guidebook lay face down in her lap. She commented, in a hoarse voice, that the style was execrable, since the German mind used travel as a form of mental laxative, their minds sluggish with indigestible metaphysics.

How did Miss Kollwitz keep her peace? Soby interjected that he well understood the abuses Miss Throop had mentioned, but there were also such limpid writers as Thomas Mann. He had in mind particularly *Death in Venice*, which had considerable to do with his love of the city. It was Miss Kollwitz who regretted that the author of *Buddenbrooks*, in the last forty years, had done little but go down hill. His later works showed an old man's taste for sensuality. Aschenbach's morbid passion for a child was the dark side of the German mind, not the light. There had been little light, however, since Goethe had called for more of it.

Frog-like, Miss Throop exhaled a long hrrrrmmmmmph! From the purse at her side she flicked what she took to be a tissue, but it proved to be a letter, several snapshots spilling on the floor. Soby stooped to pick them up. "My niece!" Miss Throop croaked, extending her pudgy hand, then withdrawing it at a cry from Miss Kollwitz. Did she want to give Soby her disease? Her own hands sticky with apple, Soby held the snapshots, sepia tinted, with a scrawl on the backs.

"Do you find her attractive?" Miss Throop inquired. "She has already had half a dozen proposals."

"Pish posh!" pronounced Miss Kollwitz, but no more.

Soby turned so that he had advantage of the port-hole light. A girl, knee deep in the flowers of a garden, held a kitten cupped in her hands so that their noses lightly touched. Her hair appeared to be brown, her face no more than a patch of light. The arms, however, the long arms for which one of Soby's served as a sample fit like wings to her body, arched like the curved neck of a swan.

"One of these tall ones, eh?" he said, and drew back as if the child had moved closer. Was it the eyes? The mouth? Something glittered in the tuck at the corners. Did that explain the faun-like smile? Soby thought of the maidens on the porch of a cathedral, the Virgin's bemused smile at what she knew would come to pass.

"My dear," Miss Throop said, "a new penny for your thoughts."

"I see she likes cats."

"Cats?" Miss Kollwitz scowled, then plucked at her skirt as if for cat hairs. "Do not talk about cats."

"Not to Miss Kollwitz, my dear. We happen to have one travelling with us. The poor dear is in the hold. A zoo of poodles. I'm certain she thinks it is a hell for cats."

"A cat is a cat!" Miss Kollwitz cried. "One cannot

put milk in a bowl and go leave her."

Miss Throop put on a weary smile. "Her mother, my dear—" she glanced at the snapshots, "loves anything that will howl at night and have babies in her lap. Do you approve?" Soby made no comment. "If it had not been for the cat," Miss Throop continued, "we would not have had the pleasure of your acquaintance. Her care and feeding persuaded us to go second class."

In the pause Miss Kollwitz cleared one wing of her nose. To change the topic Soby shuffled the snapshots: he stopped to stare at one in color. An ivory-limbed girl ankle deep in blue-black water. Sunlight had sealed her eyes, but not her smiling lips.

"They *all* like that one," Miss Throop sounded resigned. "Would you like one? I'm well supplied with copies. Her mother seems to think we are a travelling marriage bureau." She groped for her purse.

Hoarsely Miss Kollwitz cried, "Look. She is only a child!"

"How often have I heard *that* expression!" Miss Throop's sigh was cut short by a sneeze. Her wig tipped forward on her lobbing head. Too late Miss Kollwitz, towel in hand, tried to shield Soby from the blast. As she moved between Soby and the door she opened it, flagged him into the passage. Soundlessly, her mouth opened and closed, the door shut with a snap.

Soby stood a moment swaying, inhaling the cooler

air, his face lit up with the froth at the porthole. A moment passed before he noticed the snapshots, moist in one hand. On the back of one—and why did he look?—was the name of Cynthia Pomeroy. A round, legible, as yet unshaped schoolgirlish hand. How well Soby knew it. How quickly it could change. He would have returned them all to the ladies if the gentleman active in the Italian movies, but suffering with the grippe, had not thumped him as he tilted past in the hall. They exchanged apologies, but it was Soby who sneezed as he turned and made off.

The light Soby switched off when he went to bed, Mr. Lipari, in just the tops of his pajamas, climbed from his berth sometime later to switch on. Was he perhaps reading? No, he lay facing the wall. Thanks to the light, the roll and pitch of the boat, the rock of the brandy bottle in the washbowl full of water, the whine of the ventilator nozzle in his ear, Soby did not sleep any too well.

A little after daylight he was up. A drizzling mist soaked the decks and screened off the sea. Soby sat alone at breakfast, sipping coffee, watching the water tip in the decanters, the flicking shadows of roaches not disturbed by the tip of the floor. A Mrs. Parlato, from Burbank, seeing him by himself did what she could to cheer him. A widow of four months she knew what it was to be alone. For a woman, she could assure him, it was worse. What did she know of business and such things as real estate? Mr. Parlato, God rest his soul, had been such a good provider Mrs. Parlato had nothing on her mind but stocks and bonds. Only a man knew his way among such things. Soby assured her that some men were as little at home in such a world as she was, in particular such a man as himself. Too old, he hastened to add, to learn.

With a selection of unpeeled fruit for Miss Kollwitz, and several extra lumps of sugar for Miss Throop, Soby begged Mrs. Parlato to excuse him and made his way to the ladies' cabin. The steward, with empty pots of tea and a plate of fruit peelings, was just leaving. The muffled voice of Miss Kollwitz warned him to stay away. Not even apple pectin, she advised him, would preserve a person from the blasts, of epidemic proportion, Miss Throop sprayed into the air. Did they have aspirin and cold pills? Miss Kollwitz would thank him to keep them. She was not one to stuff herself with drugs. Dimly Soby observed that her head was looped with the unfinished sleeves of sweaters, open at the front for the horn-like blasts of her nose. To his suggestion that he stop by later she gave no encouragement. The wigless head of Miss Throop, snug in a lavender nightcap, seemed unrelated to the body, like a beached seal, strewn with wadded pieces of Kleenex like paper flowers. A movement of the boat closed the door in his face.

The fruit bulging in his pockets Soby went to the

bar, where he took his own aspirin, then made his way to his cabin where he found the door locked. Mr. Lipari liked it that way while he slept. Soby got it open, stepped in, then turned to see Mr. Lipari, not asleep in his bunk, but sitting erect in the chair he did not like. He wore a life jacket, which he had on backwards, his head bulging, squid-like, at the top, some sort of monster that had just arrived from space. His light green cap stuffed with paper lining topped it off.

"A drill?" Soby asked, thinking he had missed the warning bells. No, there was no drill. Mr. Lipari merely believed in being prepared. The Lord helped those who helped themselves. The pockets of his coat were stuffed with what he felt obliged to take along. Soby pretended nothing could be more normal than to sit in a cabin wrapped up in a lifejacket. For all of his clothes, however, Mr. Lipari looked cold. His small hands, one with a dead cigar, were partially withdrawn into the sleeves of his coat. His eyes followed Soby with the mute appeal of a leashed pet.

Soby had meant to lie down—he hadn't slept too well, and felt he might be catching something—but he slipped on a sweater and a raincoat, went to the deck. Ropes had been stretched to help the passengers keep their feet. Mrs. Parlato, with the three of her charges who were not seasick or down with the grippe, swayed on the ropes, now and then uttering the cries of birds. The purser, a stocky, well preserved man who did handstands on the diving board, twice kept Mrs. Parlato on her rather large feet. In his glance there was a growing interest in stocks and bonds. Soby stood at the rail, spray stinging his face, relieved that he could leave to others the care of widows, and the dance that made the world go round. Wet through, reasonably certain that he would be confined to his bed by dinner, he asked the steward to see that the ladies got the unpeeled fruit, and the envelope of snapshots. He found the cabin blue with the smoke of his cigar but Mr. Lipari was gone. An empty brandy bottle in the basket under the bowl. Soby peeled off his wet clothes and went to bed. Was he so tired, or did the roll of the boat rock him to sleep? When he awoke his throat was dry, the light burned in the ceiling, and Mr. Lipari, a frog-faced spaceman, sat humped in the lifejacket. The green cap shadowed his face.

"Much more?" he said, seeing Soby's eyes open.

"Storm?" Soby said, and shrugged. Mr. Lipari shook his head as if it hurt him. No, no, not just storm. How long?

"At sea?" Two more days to Lisbon. Then perhaps four more days to Naples. But that would not be so rough. The Mediterranean would be smooth. Mr. Lipari did not comment. After sometime he said,

"Liss-pon? Where is at?" He turned to steady the new bottle of brandy rocking in the bowl.

"There's a map in the lounge," Soby replied. A

large map with flags on it. If he looked at the flags he could see where they were.

"Where we are I do not want to know!" Mr. Lipari cried. He spoke with some force. His head emerged from the collar of the jacket, his hands from the sleeves. It occurred to Soby that he had not seen Mr. Lipari at lunch or dinner.

"You'd feel better if you'd eat a bite," he said. "You can eat it here. I'll speak to the steward."

"Eat, eat, eat!" Mr. Lipari chanted. "Why you eat? You eat for feeshes?" Fish-like, his mouth a puckered disc, Mr. Lipari returned his gaze. A piece of the cigar wrapper lined the inside of his lip like brown paper. "Eat for feeshes, eh? You feed feeshes, eh?" Soby was slow to grasp his meaning. Perhaps the life jacket suggested that to Mr. Lipari something new had been added. If he was less Mr. Lipari, on his way to the Pope, he was more of a force. His gaze was that of something outside the porthole, not this side of it. "Eat, eat, eat, eat, eat, EAT!" he chanted, as if the notion had possessed him. His small hands gripped the chair arms like claws, as if about to pounce. "Beeg feeshes feed leetul feeshes, yes?"

Without comment Soby got into his clothes. He did not shave, Mr. Lipari's bottle floating in the bowl. Unblinking, with the glaze of fish too long out of water, Mr. Lipari stared like a man who had lost the powers of speech. What he felt, what he feared, he could not express. Was it the color of the lifebelt that made Soby think of a fuseless firecracker—one that had been lit but not gone off? That would come later, when someone stopped to pick it up. Perspiring slightly, but not from a fever, Soby dressed himself for dinner and stepped into the passage before he remembered he was meant to be sick. He felt better, however. He stopped at the bar for a drink. Mrs. Parlato and five of her girls were seated on the stools, having bloody Marys, listening to music said to be coming from Portugal. The purser had lent them his portable, all-wave radio. Mrs. Parlato asked Soby to explain where they now were, since she could not read maps, and Soby explained that they were now, if the flags could be trusted, in the neighborhood of the Azores, unhappily invisible because of the storm.

At dinner a quartet of waiters sang authentic Neopolitan airs to a small, but appreciative, audience. At the special request of Mrs. Parlato, the gentleman active in the Italian movies accepted her invitation to dine with her girls. They wore evening gowns, two with price tags visible, it seemed to Soby, at a greater distance than their charms. Alone, with a bottle of wine that Mario insisted on pouring, Soby ate animella brasata, which proved to be sweetbreads, boneless duck with cherries, coleslaw, beetroots, overripe camembert, and a Genoa tart with whipped cream, stewed fruit, followed by a pot of cafe espresso. A piece of the duck, wrapped in a napkin, he put in his pocket for Miss Throop's cat, pausing in the lounge for a brandy and a cigar. In spite of the roll, or because of it, Mrs. Parlato and her girls insisted on dancing with the purser, the gentleman associated with the movies, and members of the orchestra. Through the doors hung with Japanese lanterns and crepe paper Soby observed them. Such tunes as *How Deep Is the Ocean*, and *On the Street Where You Live*, were played. Soby applauded when the purser, spurred on by his partner, tried to jitter-bug. On the chance that the ladies might be awake, he stopped by to deliver the slice of duck. He found the door ajar on its hook. Through it he saw that Miss Kollwitz's bunk was empty, but that Miss Throop, propped in a corner, appeared to be playing solitaire in a cloud of cigarette smoke.

"May I deliver a small parcel?" Soby said, smiling.

Miss Throop flagged the smoke from her face to stare at him. Her wig, with its pins, sat a little slantwise on her head. Smoke from the cigarette in her mouth creased one puffed eye.

"My dear Soby," she said, "do come in. It will keep me from cheating." Her thumb flicked the edges of the stack of cards. The fan of cards in her hand she used to dust the ashes from her front, the slope more precipitous than usual.

"Isn't this a quick recovery?" Soby inquired. He had put his head into the ceiling of menthol flavored smoke.

"Not recovered, my dear, just bored." Miss Throop turned up a card and looked the situation over. "Just let me cheat once more," she said, "do you mind?" She slipped the card under the pack, dealt herself one more.

"And Miss Kollwitz?" Soby inquired.

"Soaking in the tub, my dear. She insists that all poisons leave the body through the pores."

"I'll just put this right here," Soby said, wagging the parcel. "Boneless duck for the cat."

"Do sit a moment—" She glanced up from the cards to see what there was to sit on, but there was nothing. A water bag of flesh-colored rubber occupied the bed, like some limbless monster. The arms and seat of the chair were strewn with objects Soby carefully ignored. He sat himself on a bag, a steamer locker, with labels stating its destination as Florence.

"You go directly to Florence?" Soby asked.

"Directly? My dear Soby, does anything go directly in Italy?" Soby smiled to indicate how well he knew that, although he did not. "We go first to Rome," Miss Throop continued, "where we shall be joined by my niece. She flies from New York on June 3."

"I'm afraid I'm against it," Soby said. "If one gets somewhere so fast, where has one arrived? The longer it takes, the farther one has travelled. Don't you think?"

"Does that go for love too?" Miss Throop did not lift her eyes from the cards. The tip of the thumb she flicked on her tongue was of the same pink color.

"I've not given that much thought, I'm afraid," said Soby. "It would seem to exclude love at first sight."

"I'm afraid it's not for Cynthia if it does," Miss Throop observed. Was it the ribbon of smoke, or did a nervous tic flick the lid of one eye, winking at him?

The warmth of his neck and face reminded Soby that he must be blushing. Miss Throop made no comment. Her pudgy fingers skillfully shuffled the cards. From the coverlet one of her small, blue-veined feet, the sole pink, thrust into the light. "Stewart and I were in Rapallo when the word came. He was in Philosophy. I can't remember that it helped him. We held hands for seven days. I never saw him again."

"I'm afraid no philosophy," Soby said, "is adequate to every situation."

"May I quote you?" Miss Throop said, and placed a card on the board with a snap. Powder flaking from her jowls sprinkled the collar of her robe. What had he said to agitate her?

"I'd rather you didn't," he said, "unless you are making a collection of bloopers. To be perfectly frank—"

Miss Throop put her small hand with the palm toward him, and let it wag. "Not that," she said, "if you don't mind. To be imperfectly frank is horrifying enough. Miss Kollwitz should never let me out of her sight. She seldom does. Boneless duck? Do you mind if I eat it?" She did not trouble to check if Soby did or not. She peeled the napkin like a banana to where the meat was exposed, bit off a chunk.

"If I had known—" Soby said.

"You wouldn't have brought it. I know you!" she said. "You're worse than Stewart. Sensible, respectable, invulnerable. . . ." She broke off to take a large bite of the duck. Swallowing she added, "You know what we are? Fossils, my dear. You know about fossils? Evelyn says there are two types. The extinct and the non-extinct. Cynthia says she hasn't quite made up her mind about me."

Soby made no comment. The neck of a bottle, no more, uncorked, thrust up from the pile of wadded tissue in the waste basket. It had not occurred to him that Miss Throop's tongue might be lubricated by more than frankness. There was a pause in her eating. She lifted one of her plates to clean her gums.

"Did you get the snapshots all right?" said Soby. As he arose from the trunk he put his head through the ceiling of smoke. The blurred face of Miss

Throop appeared to be submerged.

"My dear, there was no rush. Would you like one? There will be more waiting for me in Florence. Her mother keeps me posted since the child grows so fast."

Edging toward the door Soby said, "An unusual child. I can see you have a problem."

"Can you, my dear? In what way? Do you feel there has been a falling off in fossils? I can't imagine what sort of problem she would have with Stewart."

Was it a smile that stretched the skin on Soby's face? At his back, down the drafty hall, he could hear the strains of dance music. Nearer by, the wheezy toot of a horn of merriment.

"I doubt if fossils will appeal to her," Soby smiled as he backed into the corridor.

"Her mother may be mad," Miss Throop said, apropos of nothing, "but I've never called her stupid."

Soby adjusted the hook to hold the door.

"I won't tell her you were here," Miss Throop continued, "since she would know that I've shocked you. She would never get on with that sweater until she knew why."

Soby made his way, slowly, toward the sounds of revelry and the bar. The sight of Mrs. Parlato, wearing a conical hat, blowing on a tube of paper that tickled the face of the purser, led him to change his mind. A shrouded figure, turbanned with towels, and the assured stride of Miss Kollwitz, went before him leaving damp tracks on the passage floor. He manoeuvred through the lavatory to the opposite corridor.

He found the cabin door locked, as usual, and the ceiling light on. Mr. Lipari, the image of a bear secure in the hug of a life jacket, sat propped in the corner of his bunk, but his eyes were closed. He had held off disaster, but not sleep. He had surrendered the lover, the man of experience in the affairs of beeg and leetul women, for the Ur-mensch widely experienced in fear. But had he gained, or lost, in the exchange? Was a man still small if possessed by a giant terror? Soby would have given it more thought if he had not, while brushing his teeth, noticed a slightly scratchy sensation at the back of his nose. Getting out of his clothes he twice sneezed. In bed he felt cold, he got himself up to add his raincoat to the covers, pour himself some brandy from the bottle in the sink. In its glow he lay quiet, a phosphorescent light flashed like a beam at the porthole, and Mr. Lipari cried Ahhhhhhh, twice, as he received the blessing of the Pope.

four | During the night the fog horn, during the day the apple-scented voice of Miss Kollwitz, her hot water bottle now on his chest, now in the small of his back. The white jacket of the steward, coming and going, and the tomb-like silence of the boat when they docked at Lisbon, through the porthole the hills of Portugal green as artificial grass. These impressions and a few others—the gassy fizz of nine bottles of mineral water—were Soby's memories of Lisbon and the west coast of Spain.

Not so Mr. Lipari. Not once he had set foot on land. The feel of it had restored him. A Spanish barber in Lisbon had given him a new face. Did the hair wave become him? Soby assured him that it did. In an expansive mood, a cigar in his mouth, the life jacket like the pelt of a trophy, confidence and good fellowship glowed in Mr. Lipari's new face. He had made it. How? By the skin of the Pope's teeth. What he wanted to confess, however, was his admiration for a man like Soby. Admiration? How he lived without the blessings of God. To do that in the middle of the ocean Mr. Lipari could not fathom.

Why did they not get off the boat at Gibraltar and celebrate? For a better look at it Mr. Lipari went to the deck. Soby saw it through the porthole, small clouds at the summit like puffs of cannon smoke. Unexpectedly green were the cloud-shadowed mountains of Africa. Invisibly anchored to this rock Soby felt the weight of history and advertising, Greeks who built their fires on the coasts of Europe before insurance claims.

Miss Kollwitz, in a green beret, wearing crepe-soled shoes that announced her approach, came to the door to order him, in no uncertain terms, to the deck. Did he know where they were? At the rim of Ulysses' world. The same sun that shone on the Greeks was there to shine on him. Out of Africa came the wind that had filled their sails. In her charge—one of her unfinished sleeves circled his neck, then dipped into his armpits—he made his way to the deck, into the blaze of light. Mrs. Parlato's girls, shrieking like gulls, leaned over the rail like a bargain counter to try on sandals, tie on scarves, screw rings to their ears. A hole in the deck proved to be a swimming pool. Ringed with fire, glistening with oil, the purser poised on the diving board, waiting for their attention. Miss Throop, her auburn wig flaming in the topless hat, beckoned to him, smiling with the powder-caked face of a clown. Something like a duster worn by ladies who went motoring in the first open cars circled her throat, stirring in the breeze out of Africa. She wanted to thank him for the loan of the book, *his* book, lying open in her lap.

"My dear Soby!" she cried, patting his sleeve, "I've been reading your author. Enchanting! Do you plan to pursue your studies in Venice or just beautiful boys?"

Miss Kollwitz was there to spare Soby a reply. His

steamer chair facing the deck, she turned to face the sun, the sea of the Greeks, and the healing wind off the continent of Africa. A lozenge in his mouth, sun cream on his nose and lips, Soby peered into the face of Mrs. Parlato, her head wrapped in a kerchief stamped with an intimate view of a harem. Had he been ill? He could well use a woman to look after him. For him, she had bought this lighter but it had no fuel. Not one to beat about the bush was Mrs. Parlato, leaning toward him to shade the match from the breeze, giving him a close look at the veiled beauties in the harem scene.

Barcelona? The head of Miss Kollwitz, in the shroud of her babushka, turned from the porthole in the dining room to wag at them. Her eyes were not too good. Could one see the spire of the cathedral? Soby could not. Very little of the city was visible. "Look here!" she cried, "One must see it!" taking an orange from the basket as she left the table. They would share the expenses of a cab. One must see the Gaudi building. Miss Kollwitz had stumbled on the illustrations in her guide. They were delayed by Miss Throop, unable to decide what to wear, in such changeable weather. She appeared veiled, a silk scarf fastened her hat to her head, then coiled about her throat, the hat brim curled to form a tunnel through which she gazed. Did the light reveal a touch of carmine on her lips and cheeks? The hand she rested on Soby's sleeve was gloved in black lace, with open fingers. The nails were polished like mother-of-pearl. Miss Kollwitz made an adjustment of the scarf over her elevated bust.

Impressed with Soby's facility with the language —he had haggled convincingly with the driver—the ladies were unaware that he did not know the value of the peso. He sat between them, translating the asides tossed to him by the driver. Miss Throop was amazed to find the city so much like Paris. Fruit arranged in a mosaic on a fruit stall caught Miss Kollwitz's eye. Miss Throop observed she had spent a weekend at a nudist camp in the Tirol, but old men leaping naked over bushes had not been for her. Miss Kollwitz sealed her eyes and ears against the thought.

Soby's view of the city was obstructed by the hat of Miss Throop as she leaned forward to question Miss Kollwitz concerning the sensuality of Goethe. One might as well—Miss Kollwitz sprayed Soby with the scent of orange—accuse the spring of being erotic as accuse Wolfgang Goethe of sensuality. A piece of nature, he was, not a mere man. A few affairs that might otherwise be tiresome were the source of his sublime poetry. This could not be said of such a figure as Aschenbach. His passion was not merely literary, but fin de siecle. Nothing could be farther from the ardors of Goethe, an unspoiled child of nature, than the morbid fantasies of this Aschen-bach.

Miss Throop's pince nez popped from her nose with a snap. Pillowed on her bust, she slapped the knees of Miss Kollwitz with her purse. Aschenbach, whatever his crimes, did not use love as a rubber exerciser to develop the muscles of his verse. The child of Nature, Goethe, fed on maidens like a Cretan Minotaur. While he was writing this sublime verse he kept a plump hausfrau in his Weimar ken-nel. In a voice that brought the cab to a jolting stop, Miss Kollwitz cried, "Look here!"

Soby reassured the driver that the lady had merely been pointing out the sights. There were many, but Soby glimpsed few. White-faced, Miss Kollwitz sat as if stoned. If Soby had not forcefully intervened she would have got out and walked. Was life, or death, in Venice the cause of it? Groping for tissue, Miss Throop revealed she had the volume right there in her purse. Lifting the veil to blow her nose she ex-posed the flushed face, flashing eyes, of one who has knowingly dealt a lethal blow. Goethe a kennel keeper, a madchen Minotaur.

"Gaudi, Gaudi!" the driver barked, wagging his finger at a structure that resembled a nightmare, stone that appeared to have been squeezed from a pastry tube. Soby blinked as if he peered through rippled glass. The ladies were neither interested nor amused.

They passed without seeing the Cathedral, crossed a square burning with light like a bullring, stopped, at the request of Miss Kollwitz, to buy fruit. Without dining, or refreshments, or the brandy for which Spain was famous, in the heat of the siesta they drove back to the boat. The driver who had understood Soby so well seemed to have misunderstood him. He shouted. His eyelids heavy, Soby paid. The ladies begged to be excused.

Filmed with sweat, a little dizzy from the incline of the gangplank, Soby ate the peanuts in the bowl on the bar, drank a bottle of the mineral water. Without taking off his coat or his shoes, he sprawled in his bunk. A moment later Mr. Lipari called to him from the door. He needed help. Hugged in his arms were half a dozen bottles of Fundador. One he had opened, as he had walked along. The time was short. He had but thirty-six hours to drink it. One could bring it on, but not take it off the boat. In his excitement he had walked all the way on the cuffs of his new trousers, his arms being too full to hoist his pants. Perspiration darkened the crown of his green cap. At this moment, clutching the brandy he had bought for eighty cents a bottle, his nostrils full of Spanish tobacco, the wave still in his hair, a gleam in his eye, the gods should have called Mr. Lipari away, as they had called Aschenbach. Never before had Soby gazed on such perfect felicity. Hoarse-voiced, not a little frog-like, swaying as if he held in his arms a baby, Mr. Lipari sang of his return to Sorrento, a place he had never been, but where now, with the blessings of the Pope, he one day hoped to go.

To make up, in Miss Kollwitz's opinion, for the inconveniences they had suffered on the Atlantic, the Mediterranean spread itself like a basking pond. A few cirrus-like ripples, such as one saw in the sky, or on the surface of the bouillon Miss Kollwitz cooled for Soby, disturbed its calm but nothing more. Three small boys used the swimming pool to fill their water guns. Otherwise it sat empty, being too small, and the water so far below the deck Mrs. Parlato's mermaids might as well have stayed in the hold. Sun bathing, however, was another matter, the gentlemen featuring the parboiled face and chest, the ladies, by and large, especially the large, featuring the parboiled rear.

Most of the ladies, however, in spite of the heavenly weather, spent their time in preparation for the Bal Masque, or in explaining that such affairs were not for them. Prizes would be given, Miss Kollwitz pointed out, in such a manner that all of the revelers would get one, the classification being as varied as the passenger list. Those who had not thought to bring a masquerade costume were free to look over the assortment, a large collection of salvage dating from the twenties, in the storeroom next to the barber shop.

A small room, smelling of sachet and mothballs, both the door and the passage were usually blocked by clusters of ladies with the parts, but not the whole, of a costume in their hands. A Mrs. Ordway, travelling alone, was accused of hoarding a costume, of gold and silver sequins, into which it was obvious she could not get. A pair of lovers—the phrase was Mrs. Parlato's—obviously more attractive with their clothes on, had been persuaded, she reported, to go as Adam and Eve. Her comment was that the exposure would be small. Hourly, on religious grounds, one of her charges would refuse—an hour later she would be persuaded—to go as a nun, or Joan of Arc.

Miss Kollwitz and Soby, sunning on the deck, were greatly amused. What a Bal Masque life was, in Miss Kollwitz's opinion, when people had such an urge first to take their clothes off, then to put other peoples' on. What did they want? To reveal or conceal themselves? Soby observed that such childish goings-on revealed a deep disturbance in the psyche, having to do with who one was, and what one would secretly like to be. Were they not all masqueraders privately? Was not one part of the soul, so to speak, always hidden behind a Bal Masque? If Miss Kollwitz would excuse the reference, this sort of thing would have amused Gustave Aschenbach, the elegant and distinguished gentleman deranged by an absurd passion. Had he not allowed a barber to redo his face like the simple Mr. Lipari? Like a woman of the streets he had rouged his cheeks, painted his lips. His thinning hair had been darkened up and waved. One might say that poor Aschenbach's problem was that it had been brought into the open—he was obliged to actually transform himself. It was no longer enough merely to pretend he was somebody else. The crux of the problem seemed to be that even sensible people, like themselves, were not too sure about such things privately. What had Marvell said?

> *The Mind, that Ocean where each kind*
> *Does streight its own resemblance find;*

Very pretty, but the ocean had its depths. And contained, needless to say, many strange fish. Was not the problem aggravated by the illusion that one could choose, say, at random? That the body, so to speak, had so little to do with it? An ugly duckling might well think he was a swan, or a dachshund a mastiff but. . . .

"Look!" Miss Kollwitz cried, and held up her knitting like a curtain between them. Had Soby said something disturbing? Or had she merely dropped a stitch? Both perhaps, since she was silent as she pulled out the wool she had knitted that morning. She regretted, she confided, that at this critical time of her life, a climacteric, so to speak, Miss Throop had stumbled on such a morbid little book as *Death in Venice*. Had Soby noticed the new look to her face? She spent a good deal of the morning toying with it.

She was increasingly vain of her small hands and feet. There was something grotesque in a woman of her age thinking what she was thinking. One could be grateful for such things as the Bal Masque! Miss Throop planned to participate? Soby asked. Did he know why she was not with them on the deck? She sat in the cabin with scissors in her hands, pins in her mouth. Miss Kollwitz blushed to say it but she was making a costume out of Italian travel folders, the pictures pinned to the satin slip of her Liberty print. Who did she think she was? None other than *Miss Italy!* To make certain this was not mistaken she would wear a sign. Miss Kollwitz thanked the Lord that at least her face would be masked. What disturbed her was that a woman of the greatest probity and personal prudence should give in to this impulse to make a fool of herself.

Soby would have commented if Mr. Lipari, shaved, perfumed and powdered by the ship's barber, had not appeared before them with the message that the First Mate desired to speak to Signor Soby. On what business? Mr. Lipari was sworn to secrecy. A song on his lips, with a touch of brandy, he escorted Soby to the purser's cabin, where the door was softly closed. Soby was offered, and accepted, a filter-tip cigarette. The success of the Bal Masque, confided the purser, was not, unhappily, in the hands of the ladies, but as in life, in the hands of a few men. The most important detail in The Arabian Nights, the motif of the Bal, was the figure that led the weary caravan. It must be a camel. That was where Mr. Lipari and Signor Soby came in. It called for a tall, broad-shouldered man to serve as the hump, and carry the head, as well as a shorter, but indispensable, man at the rear. They would be led by a veiled young lady in a suitable harem outfit, and there was never a question, since he was the judge, as to who got the prize. Without a camel, alas, something was missing from the Arabian Night.

Soby opened his mouth, but the purser put a finger to his lips to hush him. There were spies everywhere. Under no circumstances must the word leak out. The costume was ready. The stewards would come to their cabin when the time was at hand. Once the Bal Masque was under way, of course, they could take it off. No small consolation for their efforts would be the bottle of Italian brandy, given as first prize, plus the illustrated volume of *The Beauties of Italy*.

"You front, me rear!" Mr. Lipari croaked, and took up the position he thought appropriate, wagging his tail. Soby said nothing. A habit of long standing. Year after year, without exception, due to his scale and genial nature, he had ornamented the college stage in productions that were said to be hilarious. Never had he been a camel. That would be something new. "Molto bene!" the purser said, sealing the agreement with a handclasp, and Mr. Lipari offered them both one of his Spanish cigars.

five | Both halves of the camel slept most of the afternoon, conserving their strength. Miss Kollwitz stirred Soby up, as the day cooled, to look at the craggy coast of Sardinia, barren as clinkers with something about it like the gates of hell. They avoided speaking of the Bal Masque and Miss Throop. Miss Kollwitz spoke instead of Winifred, the cat, and how in three days she had not eaten. No wonder, since for two weeks she had been living in a zoo. Seven years old—which made her *their* age—she showed the strain in much the same manner. A bald spot had returned to the top of her head. A nervous symptom. It had first appeared when they had acquired a vacuum cleaner. What concerned Miss Kollwitz, however, was the news that on some of the Greek islands cats were eaten. A wartime measure, but what if it had lingered on?

Soby reassured her, then took the trouble to say, since in the morning they would dock in Naples, that his trip owed a good deal to having shared it with such companions, and he looked forward to the chance that their paths might cross again. Miss Kollwitz certainly hoped so. Had he seen the number of their bags? Did he think they had any business sailing alone to Greece? Miss Kollwitz would not have given it a thought, having travelled to the Orient and elsewhere, if Miss Throop had not shown this aberration. How long would it last? To an Italian a woman was a woman—never mind what age. Had Soby noticed how they ogled her feet? Soby reassured her that Miss Throop, once she had had her little fling, would settle down, and once in Florence their hands would be full of her attractive niece. Would that be better or worse? Miss Kollwitz was not sure. Three women and a cat showing nervous symptoms could use the counsel and the strong arm of a man like Soby, an arm she needed to measure the girl's unfinished sweater sleeve. Interruptions, distractions, and aberrations had left her with one sleeve yet to be finished, the green wool already knubby and somewhat faded from the sun. Look here, would Soby have one? A pullover? Those with buttons gave her nothing but trouble. If he would give her his address she would send it to him. Sailing to Greece she would have time on her hands and what long arm did she know as well as Soby's? It would be brown, with patches on the elbows if he so desired.

Sparkling wine, with the crackle of champagne, perhaps explained the animation at the Captain's dinner, the cries that went up with the pop of every cork. Three young men with beards, known to be third class, with the permission of the Captain and the purser, were the guests of Mrs. Parlato and her hostages. If somewhat beatnik in appearance, they were the very soul of wit. Plates of food sat cold while the girls giggled and shrieked. Soby sat alone, since the ladies had been asked to sit at the Captain's table, Miss Kollwitz in a severely simple gown of black lace, with a clerical collar. Through the smoking tapers of the candelabra she resembled a sallow choir boy.

The chair reserved for Miss Throop sat unoccupied. Prematurely hurled by Mrs. Parlato, a puff ball fell in Soby's cream velouti, serving notice of the carefree time to come. Out of Soby's sight, but not earshot, a party given by Mrs. Commager and her daughter featured gentlemen and ladies in formal attire, down slumming from first class. Ribbons in her red hair, her arms freckled, Mrs. Commager was usually mistaken for her daughter, a black-haired divorcee with wing-like shoulder blades. Over the display of cold buffet Soby could see no more than their comical hats, the streamers of confetti they tossed in the air. One of the singing waiters, a natural clown, passing a table where a cork had popped, threw up his hands, which were fortunately empty, spun on his heel, and fell as if mortally wounded. They cheered as his comrades carried him from the room. Soby, too, joined in the singing of *He's a Jolly Good Fellow,* following the Captain's speech and welcome to sunny Italy.

Having had most of the sparkling wine to himself he would have preferred to sit there, pleasantly dizzy, but the first mate left the Captain's table to speak to him. Was it the time to tell him that the rear of the camel lay drunk in his bunk? He thought not. That would be apparent soon enough. Soby went along with him—a breath of air from the deck helped to clear his head—to the cabin where, seated on Soby's bunk, Mr. Lipari sat smiling in his camel pants. "You front, me rear!" he barked, and rose to wag the tail. Several stewards, their arms full of camel parts, reconstructed Soby according to plan. Except for the head and neck, which he would hold on a pole, the beast consisted of lengths of burlap, yards of it rolled and pinned to Soby's long legs. Through a slit in the neck he would be able to see the camel girl chosen to lead them. Mr. Lipari would keep his eyes on Soby's feet. With one of his hands he would wag the frazzled rope tail.

It took some doing, partly due to Mr. Lipari's enthusiasm, followed by his insistence, camel or no camel, to sit down. In one piece, they were led down the passage to the room off the ballroom, where Miss Fatima, the camel girl, took them in hand. Through the slit Soby saw only that Miss Fatima had been well chosen. She carried a stick in case Mr. Lipari should lag behind. The caravan, largely consisting of ladies in a wide assortment of disguises, and exposures, formed a serpentine line at the camel's rear. One in particular caught Soby's eye. Made entirely of travel folders pinned to a yellow satin slip, something more than amplitude, or the titian hair, gave Soby the shock of recognition, the assurance that he gazed on the figure of Miss Throop. The way the volumes were poised. The costume allowed just a glimpse, no more, of the yellow kid pumps, the blue veined foot, the ankle as trim and sinewed as a prize hog. On her hip, dangling a fan, rested one of her small fin-like hands. A trumpet sounded by Mr. Ghandara, dressed in the flowing robes of a desert Arab, signalled their entrance to the Bal Masque. Miss Fatima swayed her hips to the tune of *Hindustan.* Turbanned like bedouins, the orchestra sat under a full desert moon. The voice of Luigi, the bass viol thumper, could be heard above the disordered syncopation.

In Hin-doo-stannnn
Where we stopped to rest our weary caravannn

The dance salon had been transformed into an Oasis, shadowed with palm trees, the air scented with the perfume of Turkish cigarettes. Their instructions called for once around the floor, passing before the eyes of the guests and the judges, before the weary caravan stopped to rest on the purple sands. The music, perhaps, syncopated versions of numbers dating from Mr. Lipari's young manhood, started him jigging with rhythmical wags of the camel's rear. Soby could hear the approval of the crowd. Spurred on, Mr. Lipari whipped his rope tail, made assorted camel noises, and raised his leg suggestively as they passed one of the pots supporting a tree. As the music ended, he dropped into a seat at one of the tables. It stopped the show, as well as the caravan. Neither Miss

Fatima, nor the Arab escort, could persuade him to move. Since the caravan had to continue the front of the camel was disengaged, leaving Mr. Lipari among the spectators. The awarding of the prizes seemed an afterthought.

Nothing compared with the divided camel, the front half, led by Miss Fatima, appearing before the judges to receive the prize: brandy for the camel, Chanel Five for Miss Fatima. Covered with sweat, his hair stringy with burlap, Soby was allowed to retire with his bottle. A hat packed with melting crushed ice was placed on his head. There it sat, dripping like sherbet on his face and neck. Streamers of confetti obscured the floor but Soby saw Mr. Lipari, his tail wagging, go by in the arms of Miss Fatima. Gentlemen from the first class, dressed as waiters, created what might have been a disturbance if ladies from the tourist class had not also been on hand.

No doubt about it, the place was jumping, as Mrs. Parlato stopped to tell him. With her fingers she removed bits of confetti and burlap from his hair. If his knee had been exposed, she would certainly have sat on it. As a moustached Bedouin drew her away she patted his cheek. Miss Kollwitz, happily, Soby did not see after the warning about the fire hazard, but Miss Throop, her hair flaming, was not so easily concealed. As she waltzed, coils of confetti joined her to her partner, an Arab with his robes tucked up to reveal his British walking shorts. Soby had been part of nothing like it since Humphrey Bogart in Casablanca.

It seemed perhaps even better, or rather worse, until the music stopped. Cold. Nor did it, after two or three beats, start up. Not a sound, just the whisper of the falling confetti, the wheeze of winded dancers who stood, or inclined, in their partners' sweaty embrace. A joke? If so it went on too long. Without music a crowded dance floor is a curious spectacle. *What* are they doing, *were* they doing, *did* they plan to do? Shadowy nightmare figures in a smoky bacchic frieze. In Soby's early years at Rawley the suffragette wife of one of the older, less active, professors, asked if she would like to dance, blandly replied, "What if the music should stop?" He had thought it an example of her Bloomsbury wit. In the odorous silence before anything happened Soby swore that he heard, like a trilling in his nerves, that long drawn out *u*-sound, both wild and sweet, seductive and terrifying, that had haunted the dream of Aschenbach. From where did it come? From the dancers on the floor? An exhalation, a humming in the nerves that became audible, like a pulse beat, or that secret piping that only dogs are supposed to hear. But Soby heard it. All too plain it trilled in his ears. No need for nightmare figures, clad in goatskins, hooting as they came streaming down the mountain, their eyes rolling, the torches they waved vomiting sparks. No need for jungle slopes, nor cave-like men, nor pelted women who shrieked with their breasts in their hands, nor boys who went off in a pack after the she-goats. No need for dreams, nor sleep haunting nightmares, nor drugs taken at bedtime: no, all that was needed was a little hep music and a Bal Masque. One might step from one wild scene into the other, remarking little change in the behaviour, both under the spell of the stranger God, so to speak, and the grape.

A sound like a tray of glasses sliding, then crashing, led the dancers to move back and Soby to rise. Over their heads he saw the orchestra, dappled with moonlight, their turbanned heads faceless since they had turned in their chairs to look to the rear. The pianist? He sat on his stool, staring at the drummer through the music rack. Soby's view of the drummer was obscured by the white back of Mrs. Commager's daughter, her shoulder blades contorted as she danced for him, *her* dance. Her head was drawn back as if a lover's hand gripped her by the hair. With a fling of her leg she kicked the cymbal at his side. But she was not merely dancing, she was advancing: he sat transfixed, mesmerized, his sightless gaze on the rack from which she had swept the music with a wave of her leg. What next? What did the law of the sea recommend? What were the legal, not to mention the moral issues, involved? She had him, from his paralyzed hands she took the sticks, hurled them into the air, and as they fell on the floor, scattering the dancers, she sprawled in his lap.

One of the ladies nearest the bandstand collapsed.

A low, but audible moan, more animal than human, cat-like, was interrupted by a crash of several toppling music stands. From the hall, from the deck where the mind breathed healthier air, members of the crew, several of them, forcefully carrying out simple orders, took the creature bodily and went off. She made no sound. Was that worse than if she had screamed? A movement of the dancers, as if the ship had rolled, made room for their departure. Soby saw the grim faces of the stewards, but no more. In the swathing of burlap his body was chilled with sweat. Some voice—was it Miss Italy—cried PLAY! PLAY! at the orchestra, and play they did, like members of those bands who keep the music going while the ship is sinking, the drummer with his hands, since he had no sticks, a mask-like grimace on his sweaty face. With a clenched fist he banged his cymbal, like a gong. How did it end? As if a ghostly figure moved among the dancers, tapping on their shoulders, they left the floor to glide between the tables out of the salon. Mrs. Parlato, maskless, was seen rounding up her nuns, and Joans of Arc. Unattached males, bareheaded and turbanned, strewn with spaghetti-length strands of confetti, sat at separate tables dozing under collapsing palms. In Soby's drink the bubbles no longer rose. He listened to the dying music, his eyes on the lights in the exit signs. Stealthily, under a waning moon, the sheiks in the orchestra took their leave across the purple sands. Ice melting in silver pails was the only sound. Soby was still there, half man half camel, with his empty brandy bottle and other prizes, when shirtless members of the crew appeared to clean the place up. No one asked him to leave. He did it quietly, on his own.

In the cabin, the door standing open, the portholes glowed with the green light of dawn. The light was not on, nor was Mr. Lipari in his upper bunk. He lay on the floor, his head on the pillow he had pulled from Soby's bunk, his arms hugging the basket into which he had whooped his baba au rhum. Still coiled around one arm was his camel's tail. Soby left him there, moon-kissed, his face lit up with the light of Hindustan, where his weary caravan had stopped to rest.

Through the porthole, as if he gazed through a gun barrel, Soby saw the shell-pitted port of Naples, a rain fine as mist veiling the city like smoke. On the pier, using their hands like deaf mutes, several men haggled over Mr. Lipari and his luggage. He crouched on his locker, his new green cap the color of the puddle into which it had fallen, placed screw-wise on his head by some hand other than his own. In his hand, gripped like a purse strap, the camel's tail. On the gangplank, concealed by an umbrella, Soby recognized the figure of Miss Throop, her plastic rain cape puffed like a deflating balloon. Miss Kollwitz, in a dark green slicker, her head in a coil of wool, carried a box in the shape of a house, with a shingled roof. Stencilled on the roof was the message

MISS WINIFRED THROOP

WINNETKA, ILL. USA

like the names of chewing tobaccos on the roofs of mid-west barns. She was followed by a porter with their luggage, Mrs. Parlato with her girls, their white blob faces streaming with tears or rain. That was all of Naples, and Mr. Lipari, and except for a note delivered by the steward, tipped into the book she had borrowed, that was all of Miss Kollwitz and Miss Throop. The note expressed the hope that their paths might cross in Venice, from where, on the tenth of June, they sailed for Greece. It would give them the greatest pleasure to spend a few hours together in the city that he loved, and knew, so well. They could always be reached through American Express.

six | In the peace of the morning Soby observed the orderly evacuation of the flooded city. That was his impression. There seemed little to contradict it. Beneath him flooded the Grand Canal, its waters moiled by a boat collecting the last survivors. They stood tranquil and resigned on the floating piers, or erect in the funereal gondolas. No shouts or cries. The end had come with a predictable serenity. And why not? The miraculous had been a commonplace in Venice since Bellini had painted the *Miracle of the Cross*, the citizens as sober and self-assured in the flesh as on the canvas. Had they not transformed— without divine intervention—a disaster to the city's eternal advantage? A spectacular, still enjoying an unbroken run. The view toward the sea was from the wings of a stage preceding the last, heralded performance. Soby loitered, gaping, as if waiting to be paged.

Had anything of importance changed since Aschenbach crossed the scenic bay to the Lido? The snorting vaporetto shortened the trip, but made no alteration in the destination. The properties were the same. Perhaps even the characters. Professor Parsifal Soby, currently in quest of he knew-not-what.

Did he perhaps look it? A young man with the smell of fish on his hands stopped to point over the roofs, draw a map on the sky, beam, bow, and then leave Soby to shift for himself. As if led by a seeing-eye dog Soby strode off. But not far. Within a few strides he came to the heart of the matter. A small bridge, hardly more than a culvert, rose to a door bricked up like a tomb. Soby paused as if the occupant had spoken his name. On the surface of what appeared to be water, garbage floated like creamed spinach, a broken gondola oar thrust from beneath it like a jagged bone. No louder than bubbles rising on champagne he caught the sound of nibbling. Who was being eaten? Fish or fisherman? The penetrating odor was to be expected—did he detect a whiff of disinfectant? If the voice of Aschenbach had spoken, he would have replied. Those who thought, as he once had himself, that life was just a series of unrelated gestures, had simply not arrived at that point where the pattern could be read on a pond of spinach.

The voice he heard was real enough, but it was not that of Aschenbach. A small boy, spying Soby from the sunlight, pronounced him to be lost and in need of a guide. Which he happened to be. In Venice such things arrange themselves. "O-kay, o-kay!" he cried, gripped Soby's hand, and led him off. The tour concluded where Soby, dipping a hand in his pocket, heard at his back a sound like flailing. Rushing water or wings? Through a pillared arcade he saw pigeons swirling like schools of fish. Clusters of figures, dwarfed by the scale, served as points around which the birds wheeled, a subterranean grotto with a sunken cathedral at the far end. A woman crowned with a hat of live pigeons disappeared beneath the corn she tossed into the air. Single birds cruised about like windblown hats, others rose in a cloud, or hovered as if tethered, or swarmed like a froth of feathers on the sea-like floor.

"Bella! Bella!" cried the guide, and added Soby's coins to a pocket weighted with tourist loot. One arm aloft to defend himself, Soby entered the square.

Another Bal Masque?

Before him went a frocked priest, herding a crowd of attentive boys. The stride that flipped the tails of his cassock exposed feet veined like marble, the toenails black. The rope coiled at his waist swung a knot like a bell clapper. Music, some of it alive, blended with the stream that swept him toward the sea. On a clock tower two pelted bronzed figures hammered a bell. Ahead the sea, a blue wedge of it, showed between the winged lion, looted from the east, and the St. George garbed like a Roman senator. The yellow sail of a boat, like a prop moved in from the wings for the next performance, screened off the isle of San Giorgio. In this motley cast, numbering thousands, his way was blocked by the flagging arm of a woman. Did the banner she waved look familiar to Soby? It did. The brown sleeve of an eventual sweater—without the patch on the elbow—unfurled, then settled on the green beret of Miss Kollwitz.

"Look here! How are you?" Without waiting to hear she led him away, clutching the sleeve of his jacket. In the sea of tables, however, she had lost sight of the one she had left. "You see them?" she said. "He has a beard." He *who?* A long brown arm, bent at the elbow in that fashion peculiar to women, waved what appeared to be an orange popsicle on a stick. A peeling strip of bandaid hung loose from a vaccination scar. "There! There!" Miss Kollwitz cried, pointing. The titian wig of Miss Throop served as a beacon. At her side, proffering a chair, was a man Soby took to be the headwaiter. He wore elegant black. A white smile on his bearded face. Seated, her back to Soby, the brown hair pinned up so her shoulders would be cooler, the girl had pushed back her chair to look for something on the ground. Her knees were spread. She gripped the stick of the popsicle. Soby noted the vaccination scar, the peeling arm, the vertebrae along the spine like knuckles, the white line left by a halter, the green line left by a chain presumed to be gold.

"My dear Soby!" Miss Throop cried, fanning her face with a menu, "may I present Signor Condotti-Pignata." The bearded gentleman bowed, Soby bowed. They stood smiling, divided by Miss Throop's flaming wig. "He speaks no English, my dear, but I must say he has done very well without it." Did Miss Throop's good eye flicker, or was it her characteristic tic? Signor Condotti-Pignata's face, what little of it showed, had the whiteness of his large, boldly staring eyes. "I know how you feel—" said Miss Throop. "Isn't it Giorgione? One of those men with a glove, with a hat, with something. Signor Pignata is an artist himself."

In appreciation of their attention, Signor Pignata bowed. Was it a corset that gave way, or did he sigh? Several centuries of nature imitating art had resulted in Signor Pignata's quattrocento profile, the pugilist's nose, the well bred, assured mouth. Handsome, aromatically virile, totally opaque. The Renaissance giants who passed their time courting like peacocks, or sitting for their portraits, perhaps explained—it seemed to Soby—the enigmatic smile of Mona Lisa. She was too old to giggle, too wise to laugh out loud. The situation called for, and received, the smile. On Soby, Signor Pignata settled the gaze of a hard pressed member of the Donner party, obliged to share with a stranger the last toothsome damsel. And where was she? Still crouched beneath the cluttered top of the table. A gap in her sundress exposed the creamy small of her back.

"Cynthia!" Miss Throop called, rattling a spoon in her cup. "If you'll come out from beneath the table I'll present you to Professor Soby."

A moment passed. Did Signor Pignata feel less threatened? Did he sense in Soby a lack of appetite? Toward him he extended a lighter for the cigarette he was absently holding. Was it his hand, or the fuel, that gave off a scent? Anything simple with a complicated purpose won from Soby a grudging admiration: such things as lighters, hairpins, and lovers of the sort of Signor Condotti-Pignata. With shapely fingers he stroked the wings of his pugilist's nose.

From beneath the table the voice said, "Suppose you *all* just relax. I got to *fix* something." The head of Miss Kollwitz dipped below the table. "Go away!" the voice cried. It reappeared.

"Won't you two sit down?" Miss Throop turned to Soby. "It may be for some time."

There was one chair. Soby bowed, deferring to Signor Pignata. With the hiss of an adder, Signor Pignata summoned a waiter. Several chairs appeared. Soby was pressed to one of them.

"My dear—" Miss Throop said, "I must say it's not entirely her fault. It's something new to her and the Italians. The zipper keeps slipping."

Signor Pignata remained standing until the girl's head, then her shoulders, appeared before them. Was it her color? Crouching beneath the table had brought the blood to her face. She blew at loose strands of brown hair, then drew them away with brown fingers, the movement that of parting a veil. On the long stem of her neck the head tipped, the shoulder lifted, and her eyes dreamily gazed at Soby. Was she sizing him up?

"Now *what?*" she said. Had Soby been staring? Her wide mouth narrowed to a small one.

"Braces, my dear Soby." Miss Throop made a face as if she tasted metal. "I'm afraid it's made her frightfully self-conscious."

"I'd rather be *self*-conscious than *un*-conscious!" At the corners of her mouth gold glinted where the lips parted. Soby avoided her eyes. He glanced skyward to see the pigeons wheeling.

"We can't have you hiding under the table everytime we take a step outside, my child. We'll take it back. I warned them we might be back."

"Nothing should open in the front!" pronounced Miss Kollwitz.

A sound, a small bark, as from a stuffed animal, stepped on. Did it come from the girl?

"Everything is a laughing matter," said Miss Kollwitz. "Everything."

"It's certainly not the thing for Greece, I'm afraid," said Miss Throop. "My dear Soby, do you think so?"

Was Soby at pains to know what he thought? His teeth were clamped on his pipe stem, there was a fixed arch to his brows. As if an expert in such matters, his gaze was fastened on the *thing* in question, the zipper joining the two cups of the strapless gown. Where the flesh was strong, the zipper tended to be weak. Anything else? Yes, the odd effects produced by a tremor in the lids of Soby's eyes. When he blinked, a display of northern lights flashed on the lids. Was that customary? The tremor appeared to be related to the beating of his pulse. Too much espresso? From the zipper fastener dangled a charm of golden slippers.

"As a cautionary measure—" he said, "might I suggest a clothespin?"

"My dear Soby," Miss Throop observed, "are *you* punning?"

From the sky, where his gaze had shifted, Soby lowered his eyes by stages. St. George in his toga, the mast of a schooner, a tourist steamer with the rail crowded, to the brown hair, parted, the too-wide forehead, the slight "prickly-heat" just below the hairline, the gaze that of a patient who has just been asked to say AHHHHH. Having passed his life among children who ripened before his eyes into women, Soby was not a stranger to the Occult. She sat as in a seance, hands in lap, as if stooping had left her exhausted, the wide eyes at *their* disposal, but not the smiling mouth. At the corners the lips were parted, gold flecked, but sealed at the front. Did that mean her bite of the apple was still in her mouth? Her head, as if her thought had shifted, tilted to one side to let a coil of hair slip from her shoulder into her glass of diluted Coca Cola. Miss Kollwitz leaned forward to curl a finger around it, fish it out.

"Bottle coke sets a wave," said the girl, "you know that?"

The eyes of Miss Throop closed as if the lids were heavy. "Dear Soby," she said, "fortunately for us all our host does not speak the language—if that is what it is."

"Cee-Pee takes in more than you think," replied

the girl. Did Soby hear it correctly? Cee-Pee? She slurred the phrase since her teeth were clamped on several bobby pins. The eyes of Miss Throop remained closed, but those of Signor Condotti-Pignata opened wide. "Ex-coosay?" he said, puckering his lips. The girl stretched her arm toward him, resting a quieting hand on his sleeve. Signor Pignata drew back his head, arched his shaggy brows. He gazed intently at the arm, the hand, as if a falcon perched there, hooded. The hand he raised slowly to his lips, his eyes gazing along the supple arm to her face. Amusing? Soby was not amused. Anywhere else in the world he would have mercifully raised his eyes or closed them, but the gesture came as natural to the girl as to Signor Pignata. The long brown arm joined them like a strip of veil, or floating drapery.

"God knows what he thinks it means," exhaled Miss Throop, "but I'm certain it's something special."

"It means she is a laughing stock!" Miss Kollwitz puffed her cheeks, showing her windburn, and slipped her hands into her armpits. But who was laughing? Not Soby. Nor those who sat as if charmed at the nearby tables. He raised his eyes to see the orchestra leader rapping on his stand with his violin bow. He beamed at Soby, at the ladies, at the loving pair. A handkerchief flowered from the unbuttoned collar of his shirt. Smiling, he inquired if the bella Signorina did not have a request. Yes, she had one. "*Ciaou, Ciaou, Bambino!*" she called, her head framed in the curve of her arm. The vocalist's enthusiasm made conversation inadvisable. Now that the blood had left her face one side seemed to be darker than the other. As did one arm. The driver's side of the car. Miss Kollwitz used the pause, while the arm was idle, to apply a fresh bandaid to her vaccination scar. The rabies shot she had not had. Miss Kollwitz cautioned her to beware of rusty nails. Signor Pignata, his fingers laced, one pressed to the wing of his fleshy nose, watched the girl as he might a washing cat. His expression was that of a man who shared his compartment with strangers. And Soby? His expression was harder to define. Was he at ease? Not noticeably. When the music stopped he loudly applauded.

"Ex-coosay." It was Signor Pignata. The hairy wrist in which his watch was embedded he extended so Miss Throop could observe it. But first she needed her glasses. Miss Kollwitz found them under the shawl that concealed her bust.

"Good heavens!" she said, and stirred preliminary to rising. She gathered the beads coiled in her lap. "My dear Soby, the child has been posing all morning. We just stepped out for a breath of air."

"Posing?" Soby repeated the word to make sure he had heard it. Miss Kollwitz, fishing for her bag, put her head above the rim of the table.

"Look here! Must we tell him?"

Miss Throop leaned heavily on Soby's arm as she arose. Did he feel her weight or the pressure of her hand? Her glasses popped from her nose and zipped beneath her shawl. "He's doing this portrait, my dear," she said. "He wants to finish it, of course, before we sail on the tenth."

Ash falling from Soby's pipe Miss Kollwitz brushed from his front with a napkin. Signor Pignata had stepped behind the girl to draw back her chair. As she arose, in sections, and hung out straight as if on a hanger, he disappeared behind her. They waited for him to reappear. Long in the waist, but short in the leg, Signor Pignata seemed to lose height by rising.

"A portrait?" Soby said, to say something.

"I'd hardly call it a likeness, my dear, although I'm sure it's flattering. He calls it Primavera—after Botticelli."

"Pish Posh!" Miss Kollwitz wheeled to leave but her knitting needles caught on the arm of a chair.

"Primavera!" As he pronounced the word Signor Pignata formed a circle with his thumb and forefinger, as if sampling a sauce. The sound from his lips turned the heads at the nearby tables. They stood silent while the girl fished an ice cube from her coke, slipped it into her mouth. As they stared her eyes closed with a grimace of pain. Miss Kollwitz stepped forward to slap a hand on her back. Did that help? The lower lip was held fast by the upper. The paroxysm passed. Calmly she said, "You just can't chew ice wearing braces."

"I'm relying on your grasp of the teen-age mind," Miss Throop observed. They waited while the girl picked up her compact, her purse, two packages from beneath her chair, the charm bracelet on her arm dangling dice, bells, and miniature gondolas. Miss Kollwitz stepped forward to check the zipper as she arose. A whirring flight of pigeons drew the girl's eyes upward, the lower lip still impressed with her teethmarks. At her glance the bronze men on the clock tower hammered their bell.

"My dear Soby—" Miss Throop said, "Signor Pignata has adopted us, although I fear he has his motives."

"Who don't," said the girl. Soby saw no more than the whiteness of her scalp where the hair was parted.

"Who *doesn't*." Miss Throop's correction was detached as a reflex. "My dear—" she continued, "where can we reach you? You must come and have dinner with us. We are at the Danieli." Through her chubby hand the beads sifted, the lid flicked on one eye.

"I'm temporarily on the Zattere," Soby replied. "The Locanda Lucchi. When do you sail?"

"This coming Friday, my dear. I'm afraid Signor Pignata is pressed for time."

Hearing his name, Signor Pignata bowed. He came up smiling, his gaze in the light over the Piazza. No question he was handsome. His jaw gave the point to his beard. A somewhat flattened nose, the nostrils hairy, in profile he resembled a bearded doge. Did a woman detect a masculine smell? Soby's fancy toyed with those tales of inhibited spinsters and Italian males, lovers not prone to certain refinements or distinctions. Such as? That between the spinster, al dente, and the green adolescent child. Like a tuning fork, Signor Pignata plucked his nose.

Unleashed from the chair arm, Miss Kollwitz made off. In a moment she was back to warn them of purse snatchers, point out the religious procession entering the church. From the sky, unobserved, pigeon droppings fell on Miss Throop's wig. From the Mole, over a sea of heads, Soby pointed out the residence of Petrarch, and observed that Henry James had passed a season in a house nearby. For a time he had considered taking up residence. Perhaps he had been disturbed by the air of unreality. That too had troubled Aschenbach, a man not unlike James in elegance and appearance, but in other respects, fortunately for Venice, his opposite. It was from here, where they were standing, that he had taken his hooded gondola to the Lido.

"Aschen-*who?*" It was the girl who interrupted, her lips pursed as if whistling.

"Never mind!" the warning came from Miss Kollwitz.

"A fiction, my dear," Miss Throop put in. "I'm afraid Mr. Soby is succumbing to Venice." Turning to Soby she said, "I'm sure the author would be pleased to hear you speak of him as a real person."

Soby apologized. The slip was quite unintentional. Here in Venice it was hard—was it not—to distinguish in such matters? The real and the unreal? The fiction from the fact. Was not Henry James—with all due respects—obliged to be something of a fiction, and was not Aschenbach obliged to be something of a fact? Here in Venice, that is? He would not risk the statement anywhere else. He was aware—with the sun in her face, the gold at the corners of the girl's wide mouth—of a perceptible tremor in her parted lips. Was she about to giggle? Or bark at him like a stuffed dog? How well he knew the symptoms! One of Adam's ribs peering from the leafy jungle of Eden, applejuice at the corners of her smiling mouth. It could be charming, it could be touching, it could be hell on wheels to her senior adviser, a man whose researches touched on the fall of man, so to speak.

"But if I'm not mistaken," Soby said, "Miss Cynthia will find it is recommended reading." He smiled at Miss Kollwitz, to ease the blow.

"For seniors. It is not for freshwomen!" Miss Kollwitz cried.

"I must say, I'm not so sure it's just what she needs," Miss Throop observed.

"Nobody's told me what it *is* yet," said the girl.

"Perhaps Professor Soby will lend you his copy."

"No, no!" Miss Kollwitz stepped between them.

Calmly, Signor Pignata put up a finger as if to test the breeze off the sea.

"Ex-coosay," he said, and settled the matter. Soby gripped the hairy fingers he was offered, remained to stare as Signor Pignata led the ladies away. The brown head of the girl appeared to be carried by Miss Kollwitz, on a pole. On the Bridge of Sighs reflections off the water dappled her arms, the lighter side of her face. A flower amid the alien corn, the stalk supple, the limbs faintly disordered, Soby stared as if he might see what he had unaccountably overlooked. The color of her eyes. To match her plastic purse there were red bows on her high heeled pumps. Putting one hand to his face Soby noted something stronger than the scent of his tobacco. Eau de cologne. Expensive. Signor Pignata, in small things also, was a man of taste.

With the siesta over a second day seemed to have begun. Soby loitered, he peered in windows, returned the gaze of what proved to be rabbits, peeled like bananas, hung by the ears with their popping eyes intact. No guide took him in hand. He discerned, in the stream of traffic, a current that appeared to be going somewhere. He went along with it. It brought him back to the arching Accademia bridge. From the rail, the sun at his back, he gazed at the spectacle in the harbor; below him the reflections of the windows were like the stripes in awnings. A gondola of tourists recognized him as one of their kind. The ladies waved, exposing the stain under their sunburned arms. A voice—Soby thought he heard Cee-Pee before he recognized it as So-Pee—hailed him from the shadow side of the Accademia. Adrianno, Signor Lucchi's son. He wore a lettered T shirt, the tails once used to clean paint brushes. An urgent message? No, a signorina. At a lope Soby went along with him. Had the lady been waiting? Yes, yes, Adrianno advised him, for some time. The lady, in fact, had paid him to go search. Where the light shimmered on the umbrellas and the water lapped, the tide rising, Soby pulled up to catch his breath and wipe the sweat from his face. The signorina—Adrianno pointed—sat on the platform over the water, under a tilted umbrella. A wreath of smoke circled her head. A scarf painted boldly with Venetian scenes concealed her face. Soby did not recognize her until he approached and she cried— "My dear Soby!" and rose to greet him, spilling the strands of beads gathered in her lap. They swung freely beneath the cornice of her bust.

"I'm sorry," he said, "I had no idea—"

Her chubby hand gripped his sleeve. "My dear, I've been here forever. I hardly know where to begin —" The saucer beneath her empty glass of brandy was lined with cigarette butts. Soby signalled to Adrianno, peering from the door, to bring two more.

"Will you please sit down," she said. He sat down, feeling the dampness of the chair slats through his trousers. The light behind her, he saw only the shredded wisps of her wig, glinting like copper shavings. "My dear Soby—" she repeated, but no more.

"Signor Pignata?" he suggested.

He waited while she struck a match, lit her cigarette. The flare made him apprehensive of her wig. A little wearily, her head wagged as if he had been guessing wrongly for some time. No, no. No, it was not Signor *Condotti*-Pignata. He stood corrected. No, if that was a subject, it was still not a problem.

"Miss Cynthia—" Soby said, rapping his pipe on the rail, "is not exactly what I expected."

A hiccup jerked the head of Miss Throop. "My dear Soby," she said, after a pause, "it is not what I expected either."

Holding a match to his pipe Soby smiled. If there was one thing in the world that he knew, he knew about *that*. The child who stepped from Ivanhoe, in May, to Mr. Eliot's Prufrock in September.

"I know—" he said, fanning the smoke, "but I must say it must have been a happy surprise."

In what way did Soby gather the remark was inept? Was she silent to let him say what she had too often heard?

"My dear Soby," she said, "a bastard child is certainly a surprise, but not particularly happy."

If there had been some inflection in her voice, there

might have been more in Soby's. "This Pignata—?" he said, but he didn't believe it. Miss Throop had put a hand on his sleeve as if to detain him, but he had not moved.

"No, no—" she said, "not poor Pignata."

Not Pignata? What was it she saw in Soby's staring face? She laughed: on her broad shoulders the shawl fidgeted like a flynet. She patted his sleeve to calm him down. "My dear Soby—" she said, "no lynching. I'm afraid the evidence is circumstantial. All we have at the moment is the child's word."

"You have her word?" From the bowl of his pipe ashes dropped into Soby's brandy.

"We have the child's word, my dear, that she spent three days in Paris, three days and four nights, with a gentleman not yet identified. She met him on the plane. She describes him as the image of Gérard Philipe."

"Three days in Paris—" Soby paused to wet his lips.

"Three days, my dear, and *four* nights."

"—is a little circumstantial," said Soby, "if you are thinking in terms of a—of a child."

"It was her suggestion, my dear, not mine. I asked her, naturally, what in the world happened. I won't know till the fourteenth of the month, she replied."

"The fourteenth?" Soby echoed.

"Her next period. What she so elegantly describes as the curse."

To screen off the thought, Soby lidded his eyes. His mouth, till then hanging open, he closed. How many interviews with Professor Soby had hinged on the prospect of a missed period? How many had proved to be premature?

"Isn't it possible that *nothing* happened?"

"Nothing? My dear, I wish she could hear you say that. She has her mother's uninhibited humor."

"I mean nothing—calamitous," said Soby.

"On the fourteenth, we shall be in Greece, my dear. Corfu, I think. Shall I wire you?" Miss Throop's tone had changed to banter, as if the problem now lay with Soby. From her bag she took a puff, slapped the powder on her nose. The ferry from Giudecca, the cabin dim as if it were lit by gaslight, rocked on a wake of creamy foam as it thumped against the pier. As the motor idled Soby said—

"And Signor Condotti-Pignata?"

"In the street, my dear. In Florence. He ran toward us crying Primavera, Primavera! You know how they are. My first thought was that it must be *him*. But no. No, she had never seen him before. He led us like children to the Uffizi and showed us the Botticelli. I fear the likeness is more toward his Venus. We are his captives. Could he be of any moment if he's paid so well?" Did Soby look puzzled? "On our way here, my dear, we stopped overnight at the Villa Condotti near Ravenna. If the child *must* do something, I must say she could do worse."

She finished off the brandy in her glass, rocked it noisily on her saucer. Was she perhaps a bit tight? Was the story a piece of ridiculous fiction? Her eyes looked bloodshot in the flare of a match. Like a toy cannon she puffed the smoke into his face. "My dear Soby—" she said, plainly reading his mind, "I am working on the principle that a bird in the hand is worth two in the bush."

"Bird in the hand?" he said, as if he saw it, perched on her chubby fingers. She flicked the ash into her purse.

"I know her mother, my dear. She would be dee-lighted with an heir named Condotti-Pignata." Soby made no comment. He watched a barge cough past, the man a midget at the huge tiller. Was it now Soby's worry? Miss Throop placed a reassuring hand on his sleeve. "My dear Soby—" she said, rising, "it will not be the first eight months' child in that family." On her feet she added, "Nor will it be the last!" and took his arm.

"Are you so sure?" Soby replied. "Some of these young ladies will surprise you."

"Surprise? My dear Soby, do you think I am not surprised?" Soby made no comment. He turned to lead off, but she drew him back. "Would *you* like a surprise?" she asked. It was not for him to choose. Holding his arm she confided, "She said to me, give it away or sell it, Aunt Winnie, but for godsakes don't save it!"

Soby's hand went up as to ward off a blow, or test the wind.

"That's her mother." Miss Throop's voice was without inflection, as if they looked at snapshots. "She has done both. One can't say she doesn't follow her own advice."

A toot like that of a carnival horn signalled the approaching vaporetto. Soby walked her toward the pier, water lapping the marble steps that seemed to emerge from a submerged ballroom. A make-believe ballroom. Was that not the nature of the place? Was it not what made such ridiculous confessions possible? On the lagoon, approaching from Giudecca, ten or twelve men stood upright, the light in their faces, as if they had risen at a sign from the sea, the prow of the gondola going before them like an uplifted sword. Souls being ferried? That was how they looked. But were they arriving or departing? Was the real world where Soby stood, or the opposite shore? They came from below the vaporetto landing since the incoming tide had washed them westward. Down the lagoon, a spectre in the twilight, lights glowed faintly on the deck of a steamer. Figures moved on the gangplank. A white jacketed waiter leaned on the rail.

"One of Miss Kollwitz's pennies for your thoughts, my dear?"

"Would that be your boat—" he said, "for Greece?"

On the stack the winged lion of Venice, burnished

like gold, seemed about to leap. Miss Throop strained to see it, but said nothing. "Things will look different from Greece," Soby said, "you wait and see."

"My dear—" she said, stroking his arm, "I'm sure they would if you were along."

Before Soby could reply the pier rocked with the thump of the vaporetto. The boarding plank, thanks to the low tide, sloped sharply downward as the door to a cellar. Miss Throop swayed a moment, poised on her small veined feet, then toppled into the arms of several laughing young men. Soby saw their teeth white in the shadow of the cab. Did she call? The racing snort of the motor covered the loud guffawing of the young men, the smoke of the exhaust concealed what Soby preferred not to see. Coming toward him down the quay, her braids flying, Signor Lucchi's chambermaid Dorinna held before her, flapping, what Soby recognized as Miss Throop's forgotten purse.

His Roman head through the door, his cropped pelt snug as a helmet, Adrianno rapped his knuckles on the marble washstand. "On the phone a signorina," he said. "You are here?"

Yes, Soby was there. In his pajamas he made his way to the hall phone. "Look here!" said the voice. "I wake you up?" No, no. Up for some time. "Look here! She has gone!"

"Gone? *Where?*" Soby spoke so loud he heard the echo on the stairs. "With Signor Pignata?"

"No! No!" Through the window. Or was it a door. A French door to the balcony. From there she had gone to the roof. And on the roof she now was.

There was no light in the hall but Soby placed a hand over his eyes. Miss Kollwitz had her own problems. Not Miss Cynthia but Winifred, the cat.

"You say she is on the roof?"

She is, or at least she was. But here in the room, in her house, mind you, was another cat. Inside. Nothing would budge her out.

"It's probably a tom cat," Soby suggested. There were lots of cats in Venice. Just a friendly visit.

There was no comment. He heard her intake of breath.

"I'll be right over. We'll think of something."

"It has never happened before. A cat in her house."

"I'll be over—" Soby repeated, but the phone was still at his ear when he heard the voice imitating a cat. A mating call. "You think you are a cat too!" Miss Kollwitz cried, and hung up.

Signor Lucchi would not let him leave without an espresso, two spoonsful of sugar giving it the consistency of fountain syrup. He called to Soby's attention the beauty of the day. Signor Lucchi, himself, tossed off the glass of wine that had collected under the spigot, sniffing the fingers with which he had given his lips a twist. Soby was cautioned to watch his wallet while loitering in the Piazza, and not buy luggage or perfume without Signor Lucchi's advice.

A light spray salted his face as he sat up front on the vaporetto. From the basin he thought he detected a perceptible tip in the Campanile. The pigeons were idle. Two policemen, in tourist regalia, stood where they gave scale to the empty Piazza, fingering the hilts of their swords with white gloved hands. A photographer dozed in the shade of his hooded camera. The Hotel Danieli, facing the harbor, would have pleased such a traveller as Aschenbach, but seemed a bit on the elegant side for Soby's taste. He stopped at the desk to check the room, ask the clerk to announce his arrival, then, in a cage no larger than a phone booth, constructed of a fret of open grill-work, he rose toward heaven like the figures in Venetian paintings, his eyes upraised.

seven | Miss Kollwitz met him at the door. She wore the green dressing gown with the looped belt ends she was inclined to step on, a wool scarf to reduce the draft on the back of her neck. In an adjoining room Miss Throop was having her breakfast in bed. Soby caught a glimpse of the tray in her lap, on her head the blue nightcap with the ribbon drawstrings. On a table near the balcony, the doors thrown open, sat the Cape Cod house of Winifred Throop, currently occupied by a freeloader of unknown name. A saucer of milk, untouched, sat before the open dutch door. From a safe distance Miss Kollwitz stooped to peer within it, pssssting gently, her hand up both to beckon Soby closer, and keep him away. Soby adjusted his eyes to the light on the balcony. The girl's head seemed in scale with the dome of the church across the harbor, her baby blue quilted robe shimmered with light like the sky. The idea of such a child in "trouble" made Soby smile. Had she thought up the story to dramatize herself? She was feeding pieces of her breakfast roll to a spotted cat.

"Look here!" Miss Kollwitz cried. "It is not kind. It is cruel," and went toward the door with one arm waving. Without troubling to check the disturbance, the cat went off. On the balcony Miss Kollwitz flagged both arms as if attacked by pigeons. "Go home!" she cried, "go home!" The girl was not upset. What was left of the roll she put into her own mouth. "It is not kind!" Miss Kollwitz said. "Today you are here. Tomorrow you are gone. But the cat he comes back forever. Who is here then? I tell you. Someone who does not like cats!" The finger of Miss Kollwitz wagged as if it were bitten, and might snap off. In her robe, tassels dragging, the scarf fluffed up at the back of her neck, she looked like a monk. "Do not believe me!" she barked. "You ask Professor Soby. Is it kind or cruel!"

"I'm afraid she's right," Soby said. The girl spread her fingers, licked the tips. "The cat comes to expect it. The disappointment is worse than the momentary pleasure." The girl made no comment. She continued to break off pieces of the roll and toss them over the railing. "Pigeons I do not mind about," Miss Kollwitz said emphatically. "Only cats."

Feeling the point might not be clear Soby said, "It's a question of involvement. If we're not going to be responsible, we shouldn't get involved."

"There!" cried Miss Kollwitz with satisfaction. "You hear that?" She folded her arms.

"I heard it," said the girl, simply. "It's baloney."

For a moment Miss Kollwitz said nothing. It took time for her to grasp what she had heard. "It is *what?*" she said, holding her gown at the throat as if it might open.

"Ba-low-ney," said the girl. "I said that it was ba-low-ney!"

The last of the roll she threw into the air, brushed her hands so that all of the crumbs were falling, then turned and left the balcony. Soby blinked, as if in passing she feinted a blow. Her destination was the bathroom, where, in a moment, they heard the shower drumming in the tub, then the ring of metal as the curtain slid along the bar.

"My dear," Miss Throop said, "we can smell your soap. Would you mind closing the door?"

It closed with a bang, and Soby said, "Now about this tenant problem," as if nothing had happened, and stooped to peer into the cat house. Flint-like, without luster, two eyes returned his gaze. One appeared to be lidded, flawed with streaks of rust. As if stroked by an invisible hand one ear lay flat, the tip hairless; white hairs blended with the grey on the bridge of the nose.

"Boy or girl?" Soby queried, with professional detachment.

From the bedroom Miss Throop called, "A baritone, if I am not mistaken. He serenaded us most of the night."

"How did he come in?" Soby asked. Miss Kollwitz beckoned him to come out on the balcony. She turned him to face the roof of the building adjoining, a slope of red tile with several mansard dormers, full of flowers, potted in cans. A cat sunned in each window. There was also a cat on the peak of the roof. A rather ordinary cat, if any cat is ordinary, her head cocked to one side as if she listened to the music of the spheres.

"That was her illness," said Miss Kollwitz, "an abscess," and tipped her own head to one side to explain the symptom. "To see you right, that is how she must look at you," Miss Kollwitz explained. From the peak of the roof the world seemed to look agreeable to Winifred Throop. "Winnie, winnie, winnie!" Miss Kollwitz chanted, but to no effect. Miss Throop, whose cat it was, called from the bedroom to say that her name was really Sitwell, but people called her Winnie due to the name painted on the roof. One could not fight something like that. She was Sitwell at home, *Winnie* when she travelled. Whatever she was called, Soby said, smiling, she showed her breeding in insisting on a bird's-eye view of Venice. Miss Kollwitz was not amused. What if she refused to return to her house? What if she took up with these vagrant Venetian cats?

"What a way to go!" Miss Throop intoned, in a voice that was not at all like her, sucking the coffee from a cube of sugar she held to her lips.

"Do not say that!" Miss Kollwitz said. Then to Soby, "It is the girl who says it. Whenever she knows not what to say, she says 'what a way to go.'"

"It would make a good travel slogan," added Miss Throop.

The humor of it was lost on Miss Kollwitz. She faced the bay, the island of San Giorgio floating in the morning mist, like a gift from the sea. Hugging herself, she slipped the tips of her fingers into the tight fold of her armpits. In the bathroom the sound of the shower had stopped. The sun at his back, Soby's long shadow crossed the room to shade the cat house, the occupant half in and half out of the dutch door, lapping the milk. One ear lay flat, like the damaged wing of a grey moth. Something odd about his jowls proved to be, on reflection, the absence of whiskers, the surface like a cactus without its thorns. A patch of fur had been plucked from his underside.

"Look!" Miss Kollwitz flagged him back.

"Show Mr. Soby the portrait," Miss Throop called, but Soby's gaze had already settled on the easel, the canvas turned to catch the light. There were no more than three or four dabs of color, suggesting the intended color pattern, the eyes more green than grey, flecks of gold in the corners of the charcoal mouth. Soby stared without comment. Was it the likeness he found so astonishing?

"Look here," Miss Kollwitz said, her hand on Soby's sleeve, "a penny for your thoughts."

"That won't do any more, my dear," Miss Throop replied. "You must make him a better offer."

"What is there about something—something unfinished?" Soby said.

"Isn't it ourselves?" Miss Throop held a napkin to her lips, the face of a man veiled with a purdah. "I told him if he'd stop right there her mother would certainly buy it. It's Evelyn. Or so she would like to think. I'm curious what the child sees in it herself."

The *child*, as if paged, stepped from the bathroom wrapped in a towel, another like a turban about her head. She left a row of wet tracks as she silently crossed and left the room.

"He seems to be very skillful," Soby said, the eyes of the sketch holding him as if the child peered at him over a veil. Grey-green. Was that their color? Or Signor Pignata's Primavera?

"We call him our baby sitter," Miss Throop observed. "Wouldn't it be the time all of the shops close?"

"He's going to have to work fast, I'm afraid," replied Soby, "if he hopes to finish by Thursday."

"Thursday?"

"You sail for Greece," Soby volunteered.

"My dear, didn't I tell you? We all do. He presents to me his passage. It is a boat. He is free to sail on it if he pays his fare."

In a terry cloth robe printed with the wisecracks usually found on aprons and beach towels, her feet in clogs, the girl came back through the room to the sun on the balcony. A new robe, Soby had the impression that in the last ten days she had outgrown it.

"Look here!" Miss Kollwitz said, "A good thing he does not read!" and pointed at the slogans criss-cross on the shoulders. *Slow down, curves ahead*, etc. In the small of her back, moving to where it rested like a hand on her hip, were the words *What a Way to Go*. She stood stroking the cat, his or her back arched, a thin rat-like tail up like a cane, milk from the saucer like drops of paint on its nose. Was there something unusual about the reach of his tongue? The girl had scooped him up in her arms, his face close to her own, between licks of his tongue peering into his mouth.

"Down, down!" cried Miss Kollwitz. "You get lice, you get fleas!" She moved as if to take him, then took a step backward.

"You know what? He's got no teeth!" She put a finger into his mouth and he gummed it.

"Look—look!" Miss Kollwitz hissed the words at them. Her arms were spread-eagled to hold them back, as if she thought they might leap. On the balcony rail, the light burning like a gas flame around her, Winifred Throop walked to where a chair seat spared her the leap down. There, however, half up, half down, she looked up to see the figure of Soby, a non-familiar object, distinctly not a cat. "Go, go!" Miss Kollwitz hissed, plucking at his sleeve. "You must go. Come back later." Soby edged away as silently as possible.

"No teeth?" Miss Throop pushed up in the bed to see what explained the silence. Soby had reached the door. Miss Kollwitz still crouched as if she meant to leap. A sound came from the bedroom where the silver on the tray rattled. "No teeth!" Miss Throop exclaimed. "Wouldn't that be her luck!"

Soby departed, easing the door shut on the girl's

bark-like exclamation, the flight of Winifred Throop from the rail on the balcony. In the street, a moment later, he glanced up to see the figure of Miss Kollwitz chanting Winnie, winnie, winnie, as if leading a call to prayer. One arm hugging the toothless lover, the girl waved with the other, bent, Soby saw distinctly, the wrong way.

Was he lost? He stood in a narrow, pie-shaped clearing with his own kind. Like whales sliced open to reveal their take of tourists, gondolas lay prow to hull in a pattern that revealed not an inch of water. Each had its gondolier, its full quota of occupants. A young man with a megaphone beckoned toward Soby, and reached for his arm. Soby fled; sometime later he came into the Piazza just below the clock tower, just as the Mori on the roof hammered the bell. The great square shimmered with light, pigeons, and the white caps of sailors, all seemingly in pairs, from the fleet of toy destroyers in the bay. Unfurled in the breeze was the flag of the United States. Soby reminded himself to count, at the first chance, the number of the stars.

Signor Lucchi, his lips moist with the drip from the spigot, stopped him at the bar to give him a message. Adrianno, who knew the language, had written it.

You expect diner?

Miss Droop

Soby would call her later, and check the message to avoid a misunderstanding, but after a lunch of bean soup, cheese and wine he went to his room for a short nap. He woke up staring at the ceiling, the whistle of a passing steamer in his ears. It was perhaps only natural he believed himself somewhere at sea. Water reflections played on the ceiling; through the balcony screen he watched the movement of the wall, ornamented with portholes, from left to right. Which boat was moving? He raised on his elbow as Adrianno, putting his head in the door as he rapped, advised him that it was now ten minutes to six. Signorina Droop expect you dinner, he said, and showed the whites of his eyes.

At ten minutes to seven, not freshly shaved, but dressed in a different suit than the one he had slept in, Soby called from the lobby to inquire if he had kept the ladies waiting. No, no. They preferred to dine European style. The evening was cooler, the celebrated view from the Danieli roof was better once the sun had set. Why didn't he just give them five minutes, then meet them on the roof? Soby spent four minutes considering the list of celebrated guests who had dined where he was about to, as well as being featured in the pages of Life magazine. In the fretwork cage, with several elderly ladies who hoped that Soby might be somebody, he rose to where Signor Pignata, elegant and funereal in his tailored black suit, stepped forward to take his hand with a bow. The ladies were reassured, but distracted, thinking Signor Pignata might be the head waiter. Soby checked the impulse to comment that the sky was molto Giorgione, since the parallel might be inaccurate. They remained in the hall facing the elevator. It did not seem to trouble Signor Pignata to stand, saying nothing, as if they were both in the cage. Who would guess, from Signor Pignata's gaze, that he stared at the dial indicating the stops? Such a head, and piercing gaze, might be found among the men who gathered, for purposes of composition, at the base of an altar painting. It brought them the ladies, Miss Throop in the frock she had worn on the boat, a scarf looped around her throat, the crown of her hat aflame with the glow of her auburn wig. Miss Kollwitz wore a gown trimmed with sequins, a scarf to cover her shoulders, the dolphin earrings that were inclined to drop off into her lap. Soby gave no more than a glance to Miss Cynthia. Having chaperoned countless junior dances the sight of a girl in what resembled a nightgown, the puff of sleeve just off the shoulders, was not something to disturb him or make his eyes bug. They followed the ladies to a table fronting the view.

"Look here!" Miss Kollwitz exclaimed, and brought them to attention. A gondola tour, hung with lanterns, glowed on the water like electric eels. On the Lido flickered the lights of cars. A fatal habit of irrelevant comparison led Soby to compare it to the mouth of a river in time of flood. Streets and fields under the mirror of water. Chickens and dogs on the roof.

"One cannot believe it!" said Miss Kollwitz.

Miss Throop plucked the sleeve of the girl. "I am struck by Miss Cynthia's silence," she said. "She usually has something diverting to say. Winnetka ice cream is richer. The water is wetter in Lake Michigan."

"Life magazine ruined it for me," replied the girl. There was no comment. Soby found it hard to reflect on what he had heard. Signor Pignata drew out the chairs where the ladies would be seated, reserving for himself the seat with his back to the view.

"May I see the wine list?" Soby inquired, gazed at it several moments with absorption, then lifted his eyes to those he felt staring at his face. Green as a cat's. At the corners of her mouth a gold-flecked smile. "I take it everything is under control?" he said, smiling, aware of what he had said only as he heard it.

"Control? I wouldn't say *that*," said the girl, and glanced down her front, a small stone on a chain about her neck lying in the groove between her breasts.

"I meant the cat," Soby explained.

"It would seem to be cats, my dear," Miss Throop replied. "That sound we just heard, if I'm not mistaken—"

But she had not been mistaken. Very plainly stated

they heard it again. Their balcony was at the front, Soby recalled, just two flights down. Spreading her napkin across her ample lap Miss Throop commented, as if in passing, "I wouldn't say control either. I'm still searching for just the right word."

Did the situation whet Signor Pignata's appetite?

Relieved of the need to speak or to listen, he devoted himself to eating. Lobster cocktail *al catsup,* a platter of antipasto, with eggs, herrings, anchovies, celery and olives, a salad of greens he mixed himself, first removing bits of a snail shell, a veloute Solferino, spaghetti with butter, roast young capon, zucchini and buttered string beans, sliced tomatoes and a serving of beet roots, where he paused to see at what point in the course the rest of them stood. Miss Kollwitz had leaped from veloute to a cold buffet of boneless duck with cherries, in appearance like food made of wax to decorate a restaurant window. She ate the cherries, folded the slice of duck in her napkin for the cat.

Miss Throop, who felt she had done nothing but sit and eat since they left the States, confined herself to a fruit cup, consomme, and a slice of lean sirloin of beef. From a jar of Nescafe she spooned the powdered coffee she took without cream but several lumps of sugar, letting the lumps dissolve like mints in her mouth. Miss Cynthia did no more than toy with the food on her plate. Signor Pignata had taken her to where they served hot dogs and malted milks. Although half starved, having skipped both lunch and breakfast, Soby overestimated his range, bogging down midway in the plate of spaghetti with mushroom sauce. For old times sake he had ordered two bottles of Lacrima Cristi, one of which supplied himself and the ladies, the other he placed at the disposal of Signor Pignata. The first glass he took straight, but diluted those that followed with bottled water. Absorbed with his food, he was not diverted by sharing his table with strangers. Ex-coosay, he said, reaching. A hand cupped to his mouth he sucked air through his teeth. They sat in a crescent facing the view that his head partially obstructed. When the girl spoke he studied her mouth, as if reading her lips. With the fruit, Soby joined him with selections from a tray of cheeses. Miss Kollwitz peeled her pear with her own knife.

"And how did today's sitting go?" he asked, to brighten things up. To see the girl he had to peer between several tapered candles. They had burned so that the flames were level with her eyes. The effect— a flame-like iris—was enhanced by the way she stared without blinking, as if the smoking points of light had her hypnotized. Miss Throop tapped her spoon on the rim of her glass—

"It's to you, my dear, that Professor Soby is speaking."

In the candlelight she appeared to have no more face nor expression than the portrait suggested. It led Soby to smile.

"What's so funny?" she said, putting a tongue to her lips.

"I was thinking," Soby said, "how much you flatter the portrait."

Miss Throop stirred, but made no comment.

"That isn't *all* you were thinking," said the girl.

"By that token, my dear—" Miss Throop exhaled a sigh, "you will know civilized people." She tipped forward to accept a light from Signor Pignata. With a cough she exhaled the smoke.

"You see!" Miss Kollwitz barked. "Filter or no filter!"

"Miss Cynthia has a point, though—" said Soby. "I think she knew it before I did."

"Knew what, my dear?"

"—what I happened to be thinking," replied Soby. "It led me to smile, I'm afraid, without really knowing why."

There was no comment. Miss Throop eyed him warily. Veiled by the smoke the girl's eyes reflected the flame of the candle.

"What struck me," Soby persisted, "was how much she appeared to resemble the portrait."

"Is that so unusual?" Miss Throop fanned the air.

"I mean at this moment. I mean—" Soby formed a shape with his hands between the candles. "I'm afraid I express it very badly."

"Perhaps we should ask Miss Cynthia, my dear, since she knows so well what you are thinking."

"He means he likes it *better!*"

"Better?"

"Than *me!*" Her head thrust forward and the flame of her eyes dilated. "That's why he likes it the way it is. *Un*finished!"

Miss Throop coughed up another cloud of smoke. It screened them off, each from the other, and from out of one wing of it Miss Throop said, "Why are you shouting? I hardly blame him. Portraits certainly have much less rude manners!"

"Ex-coosay?" Signor Pignata put his head up. They ignored him.

"If Miss Cynthia will bear with me," said Soby, "I was struck by a sort of fancy. That the portrait, Miss Primavera, not Miss Pomeroy, had joined us for the evening. Like the artist, I meant it to be flattering. Isn't the artist's purpose to present us with something new? Something more life-like, if possible, than life itself? Nature might well imitate art, but art has more to do than imitate nature. Wouldn't Miss Cynthia agree that the artist's purpose is to transform? Isn't he—like the lover—something of an alchemist? One who takes the ordinary stuff of life and makes it, presto, somehow more life-like. Perhaps more beautiful—as difficult as that might sometimes be." There Soby paused to smile. The face between the candles did not return it.

"You think that was *all* you were thinking?" she inquired.

"My child," Miss Throop's sigh fluttered the candles, "whether that is all or not, it is enough for this evening. It has been a long day. I fear it is likely to be a long night."

A long night? As Miss Kollwitz arose she put a finger to her puckered lips, blew on it softly. A wail, a low, undulating moan came in with the cooling breeze. It seemed hard to localize.

"Look here! That is her!" Miss Kollwitz headed for the railing.

"That is *not* her, that is *him*," replied the girl. "Poor old Aschenbach."

Soby stood up as if summoned. "Poor old who—?"

"Aunt Winnie calls him Ash-en-bock."

"My dear Soby," Miss Throop said, rising, "the parallel is not exact, but they do have much in common."

Signor Pignata hissed for and signed the bill as they stood waiting for Miss Kollwitz. She leaned over the balcony rail, mewing softly, the droop of one bloomer exposed like a turned down boot top. Perhaps she sounded like a cat. The volume of the wailing increased. Two of the waiters, with napkins, leaned over the railing to snap them like towels. Cheeks puffed, Miss Kollwitz turned to object but she was seized by a fit of sneezing. They waited in the foyer for a plate of food scraps to be prepared. The cage of the lift accommodated five people but not if one was Miss Throop, another with a plate of food scraps. Soby deferred to Signor Pignata. Signor Pignata deferred to Soby. Like Alphonse and Gaston they stood bowing, deferring, until a signal from a lower floor closed the doors of the lift, and carried the ladies away. Through the open bars of the cage Miss Throop called good night, Miss Kollwitz advice, Miss Cynthia tipped to them the mocking curve of her smile.

Her smile? Or did Signor Pignata think it was his? He turned to Soby, he shouted words Soby did not understand. With the animation so highly esteemed since the rise of the Italian movies, he shook the bars, pushed on the button, shouted down the lift well a last judgment—but when it rose from the pit the ladies were not inside. It was still occupied, however, by Miss Throop's scent, suggestive of Airwick, two wads of tissue, a mirror that reflected one half of Signor Pignata's bearded face. Did it seem a long ride? Soby detected a change in the climate. Signor Pignata's eau de cologne seemed almost pleasant: a human scent. The back of his head did not arouse in Soby an impulse to club it. What did he feel? A troubling sense of male predicament. Signor Pignata was a bird in his own gilded cage.

As they stepped from the lift Signor Pignata wheeled to bow, muttered the word ex-coosay, then crossed the lobby toward the bar, along the bar to the gentlemen's room. In the lobby mirror Soby observed the smile on his own face. He seemed to hear the girl's voice exclaim, "Poor Pignata!" with the same feeling as she had sighed, "Poor Aschenbach!" Poor Pignata, indeed. Had his infatuation led him to transform the object to suit his illusions? There were, of course, less brutal ways of putting it. In these matters Every-man, like Aschenbach, was his own Pygmalion. The boy, Tadziu, became a marble faun, and the girl from Winnetka a gold-leafed Primavera. Was that wisdom or nonsense? Of the body or of the mind? It seemed to Soby nonsense—nonsense, that is, to see a child from Winnetka as Signor Pignata saw her. Not that he didn't have talent. Oh, no, he had talent, but he was not familiar with the type.

With the type? What type?

Well, the somewhat elusive, still evolving, inde-terminate type. Professor Soby knew it well? Yes, Professor Soby knew it well. On the last vaporetto of the evening he sat at the front, where the spray would douse him, toying with the idea that if *he* were a painter—what would he choose to paint? His subject being the still evolving, indeterminate thing it was? Wisdom of the body would settle the matter, perhaps —but whose?

eight | He slept till the hoarse-voiced Dorinna put her head in his door, then pounded on it. She announced she had come to make his bed. That he was in it seemed of no great matter. Below he heard the baying voice of Adrianno. Soby rolled out of bed and shooed her out of the room, then stepped out on the balcony. Had it rained? The sky dripped light like a sketch with the colors still wet. The ferry from Giudecca floated in a creamy lather. Adrianno sat at a sidewalk table typing the weekly menu. Beside him, pigeons feeding from the arm she extended, Soby saw the small head with its thinning hair, the clutched bag of fruit.

"Look here! I get you up?"

Soby smiled, waving the arm she now knew so much more about than he did, and when the voice of Adrianno had lowered an octave he said he'd be right down.

"Look here," she said, "I must get back," as if she had forgotten why she had come. Soby calmed her. The shoulder under his hand seemed a little thinner than he remembered. With the feeding of the pigeons and the cats, there was no time for the feeding of herself.

"And how are the cats?" he inquired, accepting a slice of the pear she was peeling. Would he care to know? Winifred had howled half the night with the others. There were now several. But no mistaking her more cultivated voice. One never knew, however, who would turn up in the house. The cat Aschenbach had no white spots that glowed in the dark, and his eyes were clouded. One could only tell if he was in the house by the weight of it. At Miss Kollwitz he growled. Only Miss Cynthia could handle him.

Soby reassured her, between spoons of cold egg, that all would be well once they were on the boat. Wasn't that tomorrow? It could be seen beyond the vaporetto landing. A very beautiful cruiser. He almost regretted not sailing himself. With a crook of her finger Miss Kollwitz removed the pulp of seeds and pits from her lips. "Look! Look! You must!"

Soby smiled. "My dear Miss Kollwitz—" he began, but she wagged her fruit paring knife beneath his nose. No, no. Look here. It was for this that she had come. But wait. Did he think it had just crossed her mind? Did he know she had thought of it before they had left the boat? It was her doing—if he would believe it—that they had come to Venice several days early, since she had wanted him to grasp the problem for himself. There she paused. From the bag she took grapes, snipped off a cluster, passed it to him. "Good for you!" she said, and popped several in her mouth.

"The problem?" She let him wait till she had skillfully removed the compost. Did he think there was not one? Having so little interest in the subject himself, it was only natural he failed to notice how the child, Miss Cynthia, attracted the men like flies. In

Florence they had trailed her like dogs in the street. The fair complexion. In her youth Miss Kollwitz had suffered from it. If she had agreed to the present arrangement it had been purely a matter of desperation. It was one man or dozens. Signor Condotti-Pignata had proved to be a gentleman. A big watchdog, he had kept the other dogs off. But now, since the previous morning, he was prepared to sail to Greece with them. For what purpose? To finish the portrait? Did he think Miss Kollwitz a woman of no experience?

Soby had put up his hand, the palm toward her. Wasn't a man, a *gentleman,* precisely what was needed? Hadn't Signor Pignata really solved their problem?

A gentleman he might be on terra firma, she cried, but on the high seas he would be first an Italian! One thing she knew. These Mediterranean types. If the truth were known—Miss Kollwitz paused before making it public: the truth was something she was hardly prepared to discuss. Hint at it she might, but no more. Had he not perhaps noticed a change in Miss Throop? The devil-may-care attitude. The strong scents she wore. Was it lost on him the way she now painted her lips, her face? The appalling truth was it was not Miss Cynthia who weighed on the mind of Miss Kollwitz. She could do—and she probably would—as she pleased. No, the great weight on her mind was Miss Throop. The climacteric? When delayed it appeared to be worse. If she spoke to him in this manner it was both because he was a man of experience, as well as being responsible, in his fashion, for what had occurred.

Did Soby look stunned? She leaned forward to fleck a bit of soot from his cheek. She had warned him, had she not, not to tempt her with that book on Venice, dealing, as it did, with obviously morbid states of mind? He had smiled. How well she remembered that smile! Well now let him admit to what he had done. Winifred Throop, distinguished educator and woman of no small repute, painting her face like a clown and unnecessarily exposing her bust. The exposure of her ankles was not new, merely increased. She had always been vain about her small feet. The final blow—and would it were final—had been when Miss Kollwitz discovered she openly *encouraged* Signor Pignata and did nothing whatsoever to *discourage* her own niece. With unmistakable deliberation she suggested that the light and air of Greece might help Signor Pignata's portrait, as it had helped so many artists in the past. Miss Kollwitz paused to lick the froth at the corners of her mouth.

"My dear—" Soby said, "I think you forget—"

She probed his sleeve with the blade of her knife. Forget? Leaning toward him, her breath pear-scented, "What I do not forget!" she cried, "is who is Italian! For an Italian nobody is too old!" The prospect hovered between them, palpable, fluttering its wings. Soby was the first to turn away from it, lidding his eyes.

"Look here!" she cried, popping from the chair, and drew from her bag a rolled muff of green wool. It looked familiar. Part of a sleeve, the sleeve part of a sweater. "Stand up!" she said, plucking at him, and he did as he was told. "The arm," she said, "hold it out," and raised her own to indicate in what manner. It extended like a bar-rail just above the level of her eyes. Taking a cloth rule from her bag she measured it from wrist to armpit.

"I think her arm not so long," Soby suggested.

"*Her* arm?" She looked at him. "It is for you." He made no comment. None. "It is," she observed, "if there is enough wool." His arm remained in the air until she drew it down to examine a hole. Another pipe burn. "I will mend it on the boat!" she said, "where there is time!" Into the bag she stuffed what she had removed, including fruit and paring knife. "I must go," she said, and left.

"Wait!" Soby called, but she waved him to stand where he was. He would disturb the pigeons that formed her escort, a hovering cloud. From the church of the Gesuati, from the shuttered windows, as if released from invisible cages, they spilled their shadows on the hatless balding head. As she passed the stones of Venice seemed to come alive. Signor Lucchi, holding the cat that sometimes sipped from his wine glass, called to him that he was wanted on the telephone. "So many signorinas!" he said, as Soby passed, and sighed.

"Can you speak a little louder?" Soby asked. He could hear nothing but his own winded breathing.

"I'd rather not, if you don't mind," Miss Throop replied.

A moment passed. "My colleague is there?"

Soby's head shook. "No, she just left. She is now on the vaporetto."

"She came to tell you I have lost my mind, my dear, but I shall not trouble you to look for it."

"She seems a little bewildered," Soby said, "by recent events. I tried to assure her that Signor Pignata—"

"You did?" she interrupted. "My dear, on what basis?"

Was that her humor? Soby could not tell without the tic that gave one eye its winks.

"I'm afraid she has cooked up a scheme that perhaps even I should join you."

"You overestimate her, my dear. You owe it to your latest admirer, Miss Pomeroy."

"I can't believe that," Soby replied, in a way that made it clear he didn't.

"My dear, it is her scheme, but we are *all* happy to take credit for it."

"If I'm not mistaken," Soby said, "Miss Cynthia

and I do not see eye to eye—" Oddly enough, he saw her eyes very clearly as he said so. The grey-green eyes of the portrait.

"Men can be very entertaining—eye to eye or not."

"It seems very short notice," Soby replied. "I very much doubt there's a place on the boat, for one thing."

Miss Throop made no comment. "What I called to say, my dear, is that we would like you for tea. Purely mercenary. Aschenbach seems determined to take over the house."

"May I ask why—" Soby paused.

"Why Aschenbach? My dear, you should hear him. It's heartbreaking. Not a tooth in his head but he roars like a lion."

"I hardly think of Aschenbach in those terms," Soby replied.

"Terms? My dear Soby, who is thinking in terms? As Miss Cynthia would say, *What a way to go!*"

Did she hang up? "Hello, hello," Soby called, jangling the hook, but there was no reply. The buzzer flicked. The operator questioned him in Italian. Signor Lucchi sensed something of the crisis since he pulled the lever on his espresso machine, lighting the dark corner of the bar with a cloud of steam. He exchanged with Soby the look of a man who knew the ways of women. Although there was nothing in the glass beneath the spigot he tossed it off. Soby had an espresso on the chance she might call back.

Signor Lucchi suggested, it being such a fine day, he take a vaporetto sojourn to Torcello, or perhaps to Murano, where the ladies still made lace. In a few weeks the season would be at its height. He led Soby to the door to show him where a pontoon bridge constructed by the army would join for one night the island of Giudecca with the Zattere. Half the people in Venice would flow over it. The lagoon would be crowded with boats like a lake. Music everywhere. Fireworks would light up the night. A festive night, with people strolling about the streets until early morning. Anything might happen. On occasion it actually did. Soby inquired as to when it was, hoping it would not fall, as he said, during the short time he expected to be in Greece. He was leaving? No, no, he would keep his room, leaving a few things in it, since he would only be gone for a week or ten days. His friends, the American ladies, had prevailed upon him to join them on a tour that would take them to Athens, and the isles of Greece.

"To the ladies!" Signor Lucchi exclaimed, not to any signora in particular, no, but to the species in general, as one might say to the isles of Greece. The occasion, for so it was, called for a snifter of spirits from that bottle in which a mermaid swam among the sea-like grasses as the spirits were poured. A blur of tears filmed Soby's eyes: he smacked his lips. He left word, if anyone should call, that he was taking care of a few matters incidental to his departure, the following day, for Greece. Dorinna, hoarsely bawling his name, ran after him as though he was a thief, waving an umbrella that Signor Lucchi, sniffing rain, insisted he carry. Gripping her braids as if to hold her head on, she turned and fled.

nine | The agent was surprised to learn from Soby that one of their steamers was at the pier. Was Soby certain? He commented he had seen it with his own eyes. The *Hephaistos?* The young woman seemed surprised but not alarmed since the cruise boats had a flexible schedule. Soby may not have understood her perfectly since she spoke only Italian and German— it was unusual, she said, to have an American on the tour. As a rule it was subscribed well in advance, but there were usually vacancies at the last moment. A Signor Condotti-Pignata reserved one of them. A Wilhelm Grote from Freiburg had cancelled, leaving Herr Perkheimer in a large cabin. It adjoined the cabin occupied by Miss Kollwitz, Miss Throop and Miss Pomeroy, his countrymen, or was it women?

Soby was shown the location on the boat plan. The boat seemed smaller, on the plan, than the impression he had of it on the water, but that, one might say, was understandable. On the wall above her desk was an aerial view showing the *Hephaistos* entering the harbor, but it might have been an island in the lagoon. He paid his fare, which he thought a bargain, learned that the cruise would last eight days, and received brochures describing the sights and shore tours. Corfu, Piraeus, Athens, Mycenae, and Rhodes were pictured. And when did they sail? Tomorrow at 8 p.m. The boat could be boarded any time after four o'clock. With his ticket—a surprise for the ladies—he entered the Piazza just as the Moris on the roof of the clocktower were ringing the bell, and several thousand tourists had tipped their faces to the sky.

Soby put in the time buying a few postcards, a pocket guide to Greece, a book of phrases for tourists, and, while sunning in the Piazza, wrote the cards to his colleagues, back in Rawley, informing them that he was about to take a brief junket to Greece. He used the word junket to play down the impression he was using school funds for extra-curricular pleasures, played up the impression the Mediterranean lay at his feet. As it did. Corfu, the port of Athens, Mykonos, Rhodes—without the pressure of the ladies he would have missed it. They were doing him more of a favor than he was doing them. As Miss Pomeroy put it, who wanted to read about Death in Venice? Who indeed? All of that would wait. Aschenbach himself, if offered the chance, would have done the same. To impress the ladies with his practical know-how he exchanged a traveller's check for Greek drachma, buying a separate purse in which to keep the bills and coins.

A little in advance of the tea hour he strolled along the Mole toward the Danieli; on the Bridge of Sighs he thought he heard someone call his name. Out of habit he looked around for the hoarse voiced Dorinna, her braids swinging, or Adrianno with his smooth Roman head. He recognized no one. Nevertheless the word "Soa-py, Soapy!" was reasonably clear. A stranger touched him on the shoulder to turn him around, pointing skyward, where a figure on the balcony waved at him. Soby recognized the disturbing bend in the long supple arm. He waved the umbrella—then cocked his head to hear what she was saying. Would he bring her a gelato? A what? She leaned over the rail to point at a pedlar, with a white cart, who sold ice cream on a stick. Soby bought two, chocolate covered, holding them at a distance as he rose in the lift, in case they dripped. Miss Cynthia met him at the door. On the balcony he had seen nothing but her hair, her supple waving arm. Her shoulders bare, a sequinned bodice, not much larger than a swimming bra, fit her snugly as a coat of mail. From the high waist a skirt of black material, in loose folds, hung to the floor, transparent against the strong light on the balcony. A patch of it in his eyes, Soby stood and blinked.

"It's going to melt if you just stand there," she said, and reached for the sticks of ice cream. "Two—?" she said, "Who wants one?" She turned with a movement that showed some practice, holding high in the air the stick of ice cream. Signor Pignata, a pale green smock over his shirt and vest, his elegant black, sat holding a drink in which the ice had melted. His head tipped, he gazed across the room as if listening to music. Miss Throop was seated on a sofa at his back.

"My dear Soby," she said, "I warn you. The child will not confine herself to popsicles."

"Who wants one," said the girl, "before it melts? Cee-Pee you want one?" Hearing the words Cee-Pee, Signor Condotti-Pignata gave a nod of recognition, but withheld his attention. His gaze, that of a man who did not quite follow the discussion, remained on what he saw across the room. The portrait? It had been moved to catch the light. "I guess you have to eat it," the girl said, and returned the stick to Soby. With it, the girl going before him, they walked to stand just to the left of Miss Throop, turning to face the portrait. What had happened? It took a moment to puzzle it out. Strips of gold leaf laid on flat, then scored to give a crinkled effect, hung like a medallion from the girl's tapered neck. Snippets of leaf indicated the corners of her smile. Soby recognized the eyes, even the face, but the drawing seemed so mannered she resembled a blonde Nefertite, with actual gems for her eyes, gold ornaments dangling from invisible ears. And the mouth? It had been put in, then smudged out. Enough of the expression remained so that Soby thought it no wonder: the smile of expectancy, of awakening, had been carried too far. With such a smile the open eyes should have been closed. The impression was that of a girl who offered her lips with her eyes wide open.

"We are of two minds," Miss Throop said, stirring, "it's not exactly our idea of Primavera, is it yours?"

"I'm not *supposed* to be Primavera," said the girl.

"I see," replied Miss Throop, "then who?" She exchanged a glance with Soby.

From the bedroom adjoining, Miss Kollwitz cried, "A woman of the streets, that's who!" She came to the door holding several skirt hangers, about her neck the wool scarves she did not want to forget.

"Mathilde is packing," said Miss Throop, "to make sure we get off."

"If *that's* a woman of the streets," said the girl, wagging her ice cream stick at it, "they're *some* streets!" She tipped her head as if eating grapes to catch the drip from the ice cream. Miss Kollwitz ran forward to make sure she didn't drop it on her dress.

"You get it dirty you cannot exchange it!"

"Who says I *want* to exchange it," cried the girl.

"You'll never wear it at Oberlin, my dear," Miss Throop sighed.

The girl would have replied but she found better uses for her tongue.

"How does the artist like it?" Soby inquired. His shoulders shrugged as if he understood the question. Where he had run his hand through his hair it was flecked with bits of gold. A pad of paper, interleaved with goldleaf, weighted down one pocket of his smock. He took a short swallow from the liquid in his glass, made a wry face.

"They never know when to stop," Miss Throop said, sighing. "It's a little strong for Evelyn as it now stands."

"Mother would love it," said the girl flatly. "She'd think it looked like her."

Up over her head, sealing off her ears, Miss Kollwitz looped the scarf she was wearing. Eyes and lips also sealed against evil she went off. As if he sympathized with that judgment, Signor Pignata, gripping his glass, crossed the room to take a stick of charcoal from the easel, insert a dripping ice cream stick into the girl's open mouth. "Voila!" he said, threw the charcoal on the floor, and walked down the hall as if to leave them. At the bathroom, however, he stopped. The door closed with a snap behind him. There was no sound but the rasping stroke of the girl's long tongue.

"Temper, temper!" she said, as if scolding a child, her attention still on the ice cream.

"The mouth has been giving him trouble," said Miss Throop, "and little wonder. It's so often open."

From the adjoining room Miss Kollwitz cried, "Not one but two grown up children."

"Anything in common is not to be sneezed at," Miss Throop replied. A dull plop, like a blob of falling ice cream, led Soby to look at the girl.

"Oh Mr. So-by!" she said. "You dropped it." The blob had fallen not from her stick, but from Soby's. It occupied several square inches of the marble floor. The stick he held, dripping with chocolate, was like something new in tongue depressors for children.

"I'm saving the sticks," she said, took it from him,

inserted it to the hilt into her mouth, then drew it out
clean to show him the maker's name stamped on the
wood.

"Are you saving the ice cream too?" Miss Throop
turned her head from the mess on the floor.

"Let me—" Soby said, but before he stooped Miss
Kollwitz was there with several paper napkins. She
worked the soft center on to the saucer left by Signor
Pignata.

"I saw it coming," she said, matter of factly, and
carried it across the room to the table with the cat
house. "Look here!" she said, scratching on the half
door, and peered inside.

"Heavens!" said Miss Throop. "I'm afraid I for-
got about him. Poor Aschenbach."

"He's not so dumb," said the girl. "He knows
when he's got it pretty soft."

"What did I say?" cried Miss Kollwitz. "Now you
spoil him. Now he likes it. Now he thinks we belong
to him. That is how he thinks!" Her cheeks puffed,
she dipped her finger into the blob of soft cream,
wagged it like bait in the dutch door. He did not
come.

"Man does not live by bread alone," Miss Throop
intoned. She started to rise, but changed her mind,
felt around on the floor for her glass.

"Are you sure he is there?" Soby inquired. It was
not an approach that interested Miss Kollwitz.

"Winifred is next door," volunteered the girl,

"she likes to watch the caged birds."

"They hate water!" Miss Kollwitz added. "It is no place for cats."

Miss Throop had found the glass under the hem of her robe. She used the spoon to fish out a fruit peel, slip it into her mouth. "Mathilde saw a little drama last night, my dear, from which she has not recovered. A pussy cat and a flower pot. The cat was large, the pot was small. The only dirt in Venice— so it seemed—was in the pot. I must say, he or she thought of everything possible."

"He is not there!" Miss Kollwitz cried.

"Isn't that what we've been waiting for?" Miss Throop replied. With the saucer of ice cream Miss Kollwitz went out on the balcony. All of this time Soby had been standing. He continued to stand. The voice of Miss Kollwitz seemed to be calling all cats to prayer.

"Perhaps Professor Soby would like some tea." Miss Throop turned to look for the girl, but she had left the room. Through the open door Soby observed the shadows cast by a goddess undressing. "Where are you?" cried Miss Throop. "Would you order this poor man some tea?"

"Don't bother," said Soby. He glanced at his watch and gave the stem a twist without observing the time. An automatic, it required no winding.

In the bedroom the girl's voice said, "Uno tay, per fa-vor, con dulce, molto grazia."

"Since he is coming," called Miss Throop, "let him bring me one more of the same."

"Uno wees-key, y uno coca cola, per favor," the girl said.

A smile on her lips, Miss Throop heard the order with lidded eyes. Raising the glass in which the fruit pulp floated, she eyed it with affection, pouch dilating. "Mathilde does not like the floating garbage," she said, "she would have preferred to stay in Florence."

Hearing her name, Miss Kollwitz came in to take the glass Miss Throop was holding. Over its lip-smeared rim she gave Soby a pop-eyed stare.

Did Soby know what Miss Kollwitz just loved about Florence? Miss Throop plucked at his sleeve to draw him closer. In a shouted whisper she confided that Miss Kollwitz loved Leonardo, the first great quiz kid. He gave up love for just loads of information. What *didn't* he know? Was it any wonder Mona Lisa smiled?

Miss Kollwitz put a hand to her mouth. Her eyes wide.

Did Soby know what Miss Throop just loved about Florence? The smell of roasting human flesh in the summer air. Savonarola's lovely pogroms. Setting a style trend that had recently enjoyed such a revival. There were paintings in the Uffizi showing the lords and ladies at these festive occasions. For the love of God. Venice was merely carnal, exposing flesh with another purpose. Little more than books had burnt in the Piazza. Apoplectic, her cheeks puffed like a chipmunk, Miss Kollwitz looped her shawl over her head, sealing off her ears. Still gripping the glass with the smeared rim she entered the bedroom.

Did Soby know what Miss Cynthia *loved* about Florence? Miss Throop's gaze, the lids heavy, moved from Soby toward the portrait—but a film seemed to screen off what she hoped to see. Her head nodded, as if the sofa communicated a pleasant lulling vibration. She paused to recall what she had meant to say. A rap on the door was answered by the girl. "Momentito," she said, then appeared in a sunsuit stamped with nautical designs, buttoning up the back as she walked down the hall. The rattan seat of the chair had left a waffle imprint on her thighs. "Molto grazia," she said, at the end of the hall, then appeared with the tray of tea and pastry, a Coca Cola bottle, two glasses, and a jigger of amber fluid. Soby made a place on the chair to set it down.

The girl poured the jigger of whiskey over the cubes, then turned and said, "Here's your cough syrup, Aunt Winnie."

Held erect by her corset, the small hands like tiny furless pets in her lap, the head of Miss Throop tipped as if to see the portrait more clearly through the tight, faintly transparent lids of her eyes. Through an oversight, no more, the pupils had not been drilled. Her parted lips still smiled at what she saw, or had meant to say. "She's plastered," said the girl, matter of factly, and turned to offer the drink to Soby. He dunked the cubes with a tap of his finger. The girl poured her Coca Cola over the ice cubes in the tall glass. The bubbling fizz blended with the sound of rain drumming on a plastic curtain, a man's voice singing *Ciaou, ciaou, Bam-bi-noooooo*, but not very well. Did it come from the balcony? No, Signor Pignata in the shower down the hall.

In the adjoining room, Miss Kollwitz sneezed, blew her nose. "Look here," she said. "Ask him if he goes with us?"

"You going to Greece with us, Mr. Soby?" The girl took a pastry from the tray and popped it in her mouth. A fraction later she removed the candied cherry, more or less intact.

"I'm thinking I might," Soby replied, taking a sip of the drink, blinking at the light on the balcony where two cats, black against the wall of light, lapped the last of the ice cream from the saucer.

"It may be cruel," she said, "but at least he knows what it's like."

To simplify matters, their clothes were packed, and as there was also the need to retire early, they had a light meal of sandwiches and fruit brought to the room. A warm night—Soby referred to it as balmy—

they sat between the doors that opened on the view, although the draft of air came from the hallway at their back, rather than off the sea. The smoke from Soby's pipe partially screened off the view. He had stood up to point out, while there was light, the single stack of the steamer that would take them to Greece, just a few yards down the Zattere from his pensione.

What explained Soby's expansive mood? Signor Pignata was not there with his match pack and nimble fingers, nor, in the customary sense, was Miss Throop as animated as usual. Was she plastered? She did not bounce back, or seem inclined, after a short catnap, to further cynical comments. On a small cork board, using miniature cards, she played a game of solitaire that lent itself to cheating. "Aunt Winnie cheats at it," said the girl, making a play. "Not unless necessary," Miss Throop replied. Miss Kollwitz continued her knitting on the sleeve she had measured for Soby, inches shorter due to several stitches dropped while agitated. The unravelled wool lay heaped in her lap. Miss Cynthia put down scraps of food for several cats. They could be heard, if not seen, dropping from the roof to the balcony rail, and from there to the floor. The toothless Aschenbach was among them, since the girl supplied him with crusts taken from her own mouth. No comment came from Miss Kollwitz, or Miss Throop.

Had travel, in so short a time, altered them? In the flare of the match he held to his pipe Soby cautiously glanced at their faces. He saw no clues. They seemed to be attentive to Soby's voice. If one liked to dine in the footsteps of others, he was saying, and who didn't, there was nothing like Venice, where one could still sit, on benches made famous by celebrated bottoms, and use the silver they had once carried to their lips. Chateaubriand and Byron, D'Annunzio and Barrès, had all suffered from the diving pigeons, and gawked at the tourists in the Square. Henry James had been a familiar at Florian's. With a little effort, Soby added, one could sense these ghosts in the stones of Venice, just as one could sniff, on the summer air, the faint whiff of memories less pleasant, the antiseptic odor of the pestilence. Not that he meant to be morbid. No, it was simply that, as James would have insisted, one could not sense the past without danger —like Aschenbach, one could not come to Venice without a risk.

Miss Kollwitz did not speak, but the clicking of her needles stopped. Her head tipped to sniff the night air. Speaking of James, Miss Throop observed, which so many did rather than read his books—she was amused to hear his name coupled with that of poor Aschenbach. Was that by accident or intent? Had Soby come to feel—here in Venice—that an imaginary author was the same as a real one? Had he inquired at the bookstalls for his books? They sounded dull—not so interesting as Aschenbach himself.

Quite unintentional, Soby replied, but perhaps not without its meaning. How did one put it? That nature imitated art? A ticklish subject, what was fiction and what was fact. Miss Cynthia, more than likely, was more familiar with it than they were—were the people she knew as real as those she had met in books? Excluding, of course, the present company. Not that he meant to be impertinent. Just the disturbing nature of what one called reality. Where, so to speak, did one draw the line? Not having personally known Henry James, Soby's James, like Aschenbach, was a fiction, having derived from the assortment of books he had read. How say one was real, one was not? For the purposes of history, perhaps—but in time what was history? A fiction that prevailed over the facts. What man wanted to see was what he saw. top. 137 If poor Aschenbach—as they had come to call him— had not brought the beauty he sought for to Venice, he would never have found it in the child Tadziu. To the others he was merely a thin somewhat unhealthy child. To Aschenbach a sublime marble faun. Under his gaze the marble became flesh and blood. A mere glance from the eyes was enough to freeze his blood. That was perhaps an exceptional instance, but take poor Aschenbach himself. The dreamer of the dream was a dream himself. Oddly enough, Soby found him more convincing—with his painted lips and bloodshot eyes, the strong scent of the barber about him, made into a fool by his absurd passion—

135

than the actual compact figure of Henry James. And James. He would have bowed to it with a smile. What else had he spent his life trying to prove? That the virus of suggestion, injected into the blood of the artist, resulted in creatures more durable than themselves.

His pipe cold, Soby sucked on it wetly as he struck a match, like a flare, then concealed himself behind the cloud of smoke.

"Are you listening, my dear?" Miss Throop did not raise her eyes from her cards. "He was never like this on the boat."

"He sounds like a real cool cat," said the girl.

Miss Kollwitz raised her arms, clutching the knitting, as if lifting clothes from a tub, then let them fall.

"Mr. Soby, my dear, or Aschenbach?"

"Who's Tad-zi-ooo?" the girl countered.

"A fiction, thank goodness!" supplied Miss Kollwitz. "Do you understand he talks about fictions?"

"Sure," said the girl, "if they weren't fiction somebody would have picked him up."

Her voice came to them from below the table level, where she stroked one of the cats. Miss Kollwitz, a knitting needle between her teeth like a dagger, held the sleeve before her face like a veil. "Eins, zwei, drei vier funf—" she muttered, counting the stitches.

"Are *you* listening, my dear?" Miss Throop turned to Soby.

"I think she has a point there," Soby said, "but I wonder if it holds in Venice. The line is not so clear between fiction and fact. It is harder to know, so to speak, whom to pick up." The Piazza was a stage— he went on—indeed, from the vaporetto, the scene was like a tremendous opera, with people pouring onto it from the wings. Take the costumes. Were they not all crazy enough? People of every description wearing everything imaginable, or nothing; the music of several bands; thousands of pigeons swirling in the air: a festive ball to which one could go, masked or unmasked, since it hardly mattered. *Who* was one? Wasn't that a common sentiment? A source of both pleasure and disquiet? Was it an accident that led Aschenbach to come here? Where else could it have happened? Where else could a man of culture and distinction, chameleon like, change his nature? Dye his hair, paint his face and lips, sleuth around the streets with a leering smile like some distracted male Ophelia, a demented lover, trailing a fragile teen-age boy.

One could not talk and smoke a pipe. Soby groped in his pocket for another match.

Was it not strange, he continued, that only lovers could compete with artists? Transform the object, that is, according to taste? Thus the beloved became a fiction, possibly a work of art, an image of the heart's desire. But to possess the beloved, the lover must become something of a fiction himself. Witness poor

Aschenbach. The man, not the cat. He transformed the child, Tadziu, into an immortal marble faun, but in so doing he was also obliged to transform himself. Not merely his lips and his eyes, his cheeks and his dyed hair, but that innermost man he believed himself to be. Another man, an Ur-mensch, asserted his rights. This knowledge made itself apparent to him in his dreams. A buried life, much of it horrifying, but he recognized its wisdom. From whence did it come? One might suggest it was less of the mind, than the spinal cord. That living root that connected the brain of man with his primeval tail: the slimy ooze from which he emerged with his eyes. The eyes. Did they know about the eyes? Fabulous. Not their color, no, nor their beauty, but something of their *nature*. It defied comprehension. The mind itself could not cope with it. It was commonplace to admire the eye of a camera, but the eye of a simpleton put it to shame. If they would forgive him the pun, he would put it this way—the eyes have it. What did he mean? It was customary to speak of the mind's eye, but more accurate to speak of the eye's mind. For it had one. Yes, wonder of wonders, it had a small brain of its own. A tiny bud of the brain was attached to the back of it. At that point, not in the brain, the visible world was made visible, the facts became a fiction congenial to man. Fiat lux! It was the eye that gave the command. A wisdom of the eye, so to speak, preceded that of the mind. Just to that extent certain tastes were determined long before the notion of choice existed; the mind merely ratified a choice already made. Free will? Did any smitten lover ever feel he was free to choose? He was chosen. His delight and despair lay in that knowledge. What else did one mean by love at first sight, or a fatal rendezvous? There were many ways of putting it. One might say that it was in the cards. No doubt that the brain was there in the head—that curious bone bubble where impressions were sorted and exaggerated—but the mind was in the eye, the ear, the touch, what were sensibly described as the senses. It was knowledge of this sort that led men to speak of the head and the heart. Was it not common to speak of things that took *guts?* The brain was in the head if one was lucky—but what one called the mind was in the body, and the wisdom of the body counselled the brain what to feel and think. It was the source of fiction, as well as what were known as facts. Few would deny that of the lover, whose knowledge derived from all of his senses, but this was also true, in Soby's opinion, of the artist's imagination, in the artist the wisdom of the body became art. The personal was elevated to the impersonal. This sensation was available to the lover, but being no artist he disowned it, believing it a flaw, rather than a virtue, in his love. To that extent he lacked, one might say, the wisdom of the heart.

Had he finished? On his eye's mind Soby detected

a film of floating spots. In his chest the unwise thumping of his heart.

"Do you agree with that, my child?" Miss Throop
did not lift her roving eye from the cards, her thumb
flicked the deck.

"Play the jack on the queen," said the girl, leaning over to do it for her. The sound from Miss Kollwitz was that of tearing a long row of perforations.
Had she dropped a stitch? She stopped pulling the
yarn at about the point where she had started.

"Which fiction do you prefer, my dear, Primavera
in Venice or Lolita in Winnetka?"

"You mean *me?*"

"I don't believe Mathilde is faced with the choice,"
Miss Throop observed, using the thrust to cheat.

"What are they reading at Rawley, my dear, *Pey-
ton Place?*"

"I don't know," said Soby. "I don't know but what
she might not be herself."

"Heaven forbid!" barked Miss Kollwitz. No
more.

"You can just re-*laxxxx,*" said the girl. "Who
knows what *that* is? Miss Korngold says *nobody*
knows who *that* is, and a good thing."

"Miss Korngold is applied psychology," observed
Miss Throop.

In the flare of his match Soby saw the eyes of the
cat the girl had lifted to her lap. One crimped like
tinfoil, the other flawed like petrified wood. "As-

chenbach—" she said, stroking his pleated ear, "you a real cool cat, or you a square?"

"You'd better read the book, my dear," Miss Throop said, "I don't think Mr. Soby knows what a square is."

"Oh yes I do," replied Soby. Their eyes on him he smiled and said, "I'm a square."

The girl did not deny it. Miss Throop flicked the tip of her thumb on her tongue before dealing a card. "From the way he howls," she said, "I would say he was more than a panty-raider. I am given to understand that panty-raiders are not cool cats."

"Play the ten on the jack," said the girl, which she did, then the seven on the eight, then shifted one file of cards to another, till the display had been reduced to four. "There," she said, "you win."

"Did anybody see me cheat?" Miss Throop inquired. She put her tapered fingers to the bruised bridge of her nose.

"Look here!" cried Miss Kollwitz, "you do not know?"

"I know, my dear, but is it necessary that I admit it?" She gathered up the cards and arranged them into a neat crisp pile. Her left eye peered at him from the ambush of her twisted lashes. "Cynthia goes to Oberlin this fall," she said, "providing she survives the summer's reading."

"Don't you worry about me, Aunt Winnie," said the girl. "Just you worry about yourself."

ten | Had they managed it alone? With Adrianno's assistance, they were gathered in the guest wing of the lobby, surrounded by their luggage. The five pieces they would leave with Soby were labelled with large tags. And Signor Pignata? He would meet them on the pier, at the time of sailing. He had supplies to buy, and clothes more suitable to life on deck. Miss Cynthia? Adrianno held two pieces of luggage while he stared at her, the stupefied expression of Dorinna a mask on his face. Cynthia had so plagued them, since they arrived, for a ride on one of the motoscafi, that Miss Throop had decided to kill two birds with one stone. They had taken the ride direct to Soby's door. It was spray that Soby saw gleaming on Miss Throop's auburn hair.

Everything had gone well? It depended on one's point of view. Miss Cynthia had skillfully managed to soil the one dress she had left unpacked, in order to persuade them to buy the one she had on. How did he like it? Soby assumed a disinterested professional air. She stepped forward and showed him the front, then the rear. A three piece ensemble, of knitted jersey, it did conceal her knees, a former problem. Other problems, however, had been revealed.

"Bella, bella!" Adrianno commented, although he hadn't been asked. Soby pronounced it sensible and attractive, squinting from side to side, as well as up and down. Were they wrong in thinking it fit her a bit too snugly? One had a problem with jersey, since it would certainly stretch. The child was tired, and with reason, of having all of her new clothes too large to start with, since her mother realized that within a few months they would be too small. But Soby was reassuring. No, he thought their choice was just about right. Her grey-green eyes, in the shade of her hat, a soft velour felt with a dust of spray on it, might have been touched with flecks of gold to go with her smile. Was there something odd about it? As gold leaf might have been added to the lips of an archaic nymph, her lips were no longer sealed on the golden smile.

"She has her mother to thank for the teeth, my dear, but Signor Pignata for the smile. How do you like it?"

"Gioconda!" The comment came from Adrianno, his Roman head nodding, forming a circle like his father with thumb and forefinger, his eyes fastened on the face with its faintly perceptible smile. "La bella Gioconda!"

"Does he paint?" Miss Throop had turned to Soby. Opening her napkin she added, very matter-of-factly, "Thank him, my dear, but say that she simply doesn't have the time."

Quite by accident—Miss Kollwitz paused to take a pear from the bowl, sniff the stem for ripeness—quite by accident she had discovered that Miss Throop had left both money and instructions for the care and feeding of Aschenbach. One thousand lire. Did she think that insured a cat's life? With Soby, when they returned from Greece, Miss Kollwitz would leave their address so that he might advise them of the condition of Aschenbach. So long as he survived they would see to it that he was supplied with milk and fish. One must finish what one was foolish enough to start. Soby assured her he would keep an eye on the situation while he was in Venice, although the cream and the mush might not always end up in the cat. Miss Kollwitz stopped him with a wave of her fruit knife. That could not be helped. One could not be the hand of God. What happened to the cream and the mush after the boy Mario acquired them, like so many other things, was in the hands of God. There she would let it lie. More than that was asking too much. A quarter slice of pear silenced Miss Kollwitz while she waved her knife at the flies. They droned like bees above the peel coiled on her plate. Following the soup, a minestrone alla Genova, with two slightly watered glasses of Soave, something like animation had led Miss Kollwitz to put aside the sleeve of Soby's sweater and lecture them. Twice she had said Passen sie auf—forgetting this was not her seminar in Winnetka. Was it the promise of Greece? No, it was simply that Venice did not suit her. Dante's Florence, if not Savonarola's, was more to her taste. One knew where one stood. Here in Venice one did not. There was too much water. Except in flower pots, there was no earth. In a street cafe she had watched a poor kitten scratch hopelessly in a very small pot, in which there was neither room to crouch, or to stand. What she had not tried! Miss Kollwitz had known precisely how she felt. It was no place for creatures who needed contact with the good earth.

How did one explain, Soby inquired, the great number of cats in Venice?

Could it be that a certain number were females? Miss Throop observed. She fanned herself with a menu that stirred the hair framing her face. It was not the remark itself, but the tone that seemed a little uncalled for. The packing, perhaps, and the lack of her customary nap after lunch. Openly Miss Kollwitz dipped her sticky fingers into her glass of wine and water, dried them on her napkin. Not only with Soby, but with Miss Cynthia, she exchanged the glance of a woman who no longer concealed her problems. "Look here!" she cried, taking charge of the cat house, "it's time."

A gondolier, a friend of Signor Lucchi's, who doubled as a waiter on the busy weekends, sang operatic airs as he paddled the luggage, the girl, and Soby the three blocks to the pier. The ladies walked, waving at them from the promenade. A gondola is a gondola. Soby and the girl sat side by side. Those seated along the water smiled unmistakable smiles. Soby wore no eye patch, nor pith helmet, the hand gripping his pipe was not tattooed, but the impression he conveyed was that older men must make the best lovers. Miss Throop, pausing to catch her wind on the bridge over the Rio Trovaso, waved the tasselled ends of the shawl coiled around her arms. Miss Kollwitz went her way alone with the cat. Five or ten minutes it lasted, no more, to where they put into the slip for motoscafi, and the gondolier began to unload their bags. Did it seem a little quiet? No one marched up or down the gangplank. A single dark-faced sailor eyed them from the deck. The soldier who guarded the gangplank came over to watch the gondolier.

"To where?" he inquired.

"To Greece."

Not to Cairo? What a pity!

Why was it a pity not to Cairo?

Why? Because this boat went there. What a pity without the *bella fanciulla!* The gondolier understood the language, Soby the implications.

This boat did not sail in an hour for Greece?

The guard sighed and wagged his head sadly. No, neither in an hour, or a day, or a week. It never sailed for Greece, but for Alexandria.

His gaze blank, Soby stood amidst the luggage, his eyes on the medallion on the stack of the steamer. The word on the prow of the boat was Greek, but not the word *Hephaistos.* Farther down the promenade, across a small bridge with a gate, several freighters appeared to be loading. In the gap between the freighters the white top of a stack was visible. Several tattered banners, or flags, twisted on a slack rope.

"Look here!" Miss Kollwitz plucked at his sleeve. "It is not this one for Greece. He says so!"

Who says so? Like an awning, his shadow darkened Miss Kollwitz and Soby. He stood holding the cat house like a lunch box under one arm. The face Soby peered up to seemed without eyes. Slits, no more, under sun bleached, bushy brows. Wide as a slice of melon, however, was the smiling mouth. He wore lederhosen, the color of soiled harness, hair like copper wire on his enormous hams. Behind him, orderly, were ten or twelve small cuttings from the same vine.

He says so? The young giant pumped a head that had no neck. Seamless, no more than a ripple where the blonde mane lapped his collar, the back humped with a rucksack and a bedroll, a belt dangling pots, knives and hardware, like ornaments. On the sleeve of his shirt he wore an insignia, a bird with the letter V as a crotch to perch on.

"Nein!" Lifting a huge hand, he let it fall on Soby's shoulder. Beneath it Miss Kollwitz peered upward as at a ceiling beam. With his free hand the giant pointed down the pier toward the freighters. Speech—Soby took it for such—rumbled in his chest but seemed to clog in his throat. Sounds emerged from his mouth as if for the first time.

Soby thanked him, then turned to grapple with the pile of luggage. The big fellow nudged him to one side, scooped up the bigger pieces. Two of the young men at his back grabbed up what remained. Off they went without Soby, but not without Miss Kollwitz. She went up front, a trainer with an act of trained bears. Soby, the girl, and Miss Throop tagged along. They were checked at the gate for their tickets, then allowed to assemble on the pier facing a boat, a river steamer, of the sort Soby had often taken up the Thames from London, flat-bottomed, or so it looked, with the lower portholes just a yard above the water. This was the luxury steamer for Greece? So it seemed. It had arrived at noon, and the cabins were now being cleaned. Bits of rubbish tossed from the portholes floated on the sea. The ladies—Soby remained standing, as if to voice a protest—sat on the luggage the giant and his crew had neatly piled near the gangplank. They would accept no money. It was no more than one should expect from the *Wandervogel,* wanderjahre jugend who were on their way to Greece. Boys and girls. About three dozen blonde heads in all. They gathered, seated on their bedrolls, where the sun continued to tan them while they sang.

The big fellow who had carried Soby's luggage plucked a guitar—a ukelele in his hands—with his head tilted to one side as if to empty water from one ear, or listen to his own small voice. The larger voice, an organ loft contralto, came from the blonde head at his side, a pitch pipe gleaming at the dip in her peasant blouse. She wore her braids pinned up, a honey-blonde halo, rope soled sandals were on her large dirty feet. Was she young? Not only her voice had a matronly amplitude. On the frizzled knee of the giant beside her she slapped her hand like a metronome. A dirty tan gave her the look of an Indian with peeling war paint.

Finished, they received an orderly, uniform applause. The touch of monotony—if that was the word—was more in their faces than their voices. Damen und Herren, the Damen peeling fruit or the foil from bars of chocolate, the Herren draped with cameras and binoculars, were seated on their luggage, patiently waiting to board the boat. A palpable sense of togetherness joined them one to the other, like hens roosting in a henhouse. Some of the Herren wore knickers, Damen und Herren wore a uniformly homogeneous expression. A toot on the pitch pipe brought their attention back to the singers. They sang —allowing for certain problems—*Home on the Range*. It was Soby who applauded.

One of their number, a blonde child with looped braids, a purse dangling from a strap about her shoulder, stepped forward to accept contributions from the Damen und Herren. A sign too small for Soby to read hung from her neck. She would have passed them by, since they sat apart, if Miss Kollwitz had not beckoned her over. She accepted the offering with the smiling assurance that it was well spent. From where was she? And where were they bound?

To Greece, of course. To see it as the Greeks saw it, on foot. In her honeyed smile did Soby detect a glint of judgment? Could *he* sing or dance? Did he plan to *walk?* Did he think Greece could be seen through a porthole? She accepted his coins as partial payment on his guilt. Uniform with her companions she wore the expression that went with the legend on her sign—

Wir sind

WANDERVOGEL

Wir singen die welt zu Sehen

Translating, Soby said, "We are Wandervogel. We warble to wander."

"Do you suppose—" Miss Throop inquired, "if we gave them more money they would *stop* warbling?"

"Don't think it wouldn't cost you plenty!" said the girl. She sat, cross-legged, on the roof of the cathouse.

One should be grateful, Miss Kollwitz replied, that the world still contained jugend who used their legs for more than ornamental purposes. Who were still—as so many were not—young and innocent in heart. She was silenced by a new wave of song. Russian, perhaps? The cords showed in the neck of the guitarist: all but inaudible, however, seemed his voice. Soby heard little but the vacuum sweeper in the porthole at his back.

Before they had finished, however, Miss Kollwitz popped up to cry, "Here, here!" as if her name had been called. She put up her arm to wave, but it was too short. She gripped one of Soby's. "It's him!" she cried, and pointed down the pier to where they had entered. Signor Pignata? One hand to his eyes, Soby pushed up to see a crowd of workers homebound from Giudecca. Signor Pignata was not among them. A gentleman, however, groomed in a manner so that he might be taken for him at a distance, emerged carrying a cane and a gladstone bag covered with steamer labels. He wore a low crowned panama straw with a wide limp brim. A little portly, his shoulders back, he walked with a measured constitutional stride. Seeing his knickers, Miss Kollwitz clapped a hand to her mouth, sat down.

"In Florence—" said Miss Throop, matter of factly, "we signalled every male over six feet. She was certain it was you."

It was not Signor Pignata, by some forty or fifty pounds, and almost as many years. A reading glass gleamed like a coin on his vest. Binoculars sat in the curve of his hip. At his side, wearing one of those outfits designed to give boys the assurance of men, the trench coat belted and smartly tailored, his chest criss-crossed with an arsenal of cameras and gadgets, strode a hatless figure about the size of a ten year old boy. Not those of a boy, however, were the wide gargoyle smile, the hawk-like beak. He carried a tripod, a small leather bag, and what appeared to be a short-barreled gun, in a case. Were they travelling companions? At the pier gate, stopped for their tickets, the older man stepped through alone. To the ladies and Soby he tipped his hat, squinting with a scholarly, near-sighted gaze. A nosegay ornamented the slit in his lapel. Had Soby seen him somewhere? Even the back view seemed familiar, the jacket belted, one pocket weighted with a guidebook. He walked as if assured that the boat had waited, they all had waited, for his arrival. At the gangplank he wheeled as if he felt Soby's eyes on the back of his head. The wide brim of the hat shadowed his face. It was the girl, however, Miss Cynthia, who tipped her head in acknowledgement of his gaze. Slantwise, Soby caught the flicker of gold at the corner of her lips.

"Look here! You know him?" Miss Kollwitz barked.

"You don't have to *know* people to *like* them!"

They were distracted by the shouting at the gate. In German, then French, then in Italian, like an argument in a polyglot nursery, the creature in the trench coat shouted at the officials. It was a shrill, but not a boyish voice. The suggestion of a stutter was due to the butt of a cigarette, like a spout, that seemed attached to his lower lip. It flicked as he talked. He used expressive Italian gestures. They let him in, Soby felt, to shut him up. It seemed unlikely anyone so small could do much harm. How big was he? His eyes seemed on the level of Soby's *seated* gaze. As he passed, however, it was those about him who appeared to be distorted, the others who lacked a proper harmony with their parts. He seemed to be a small scale model for something big. The Wandervogel had stopped singing and sat mute, as if for their portrait. Had his victory at the gate put him in a state of glee? The straps of his arsenal creaked like harness as he walked.

At the gangplank a line had formed, orderly, even as Soby got to his feet. On the deck a shirtless member of the crew, looking like a raw fowl with the head roasted, shouted directions in what might have been Greek, French or Italian. The boat seemed to tilt as the deck was occupied. Soby advised the ladies to go on ahead while he watched the luggage, and waited for Signor Pignata. It seemed unlikely there was room on the boat for the crowd on the pier. Miss Kollwitz was persuaded, providing she and Miss Cynthia could carry the cat house between them. With Soby she left her reticule and paper bag of fresh fruit. The movement on the gangplank proved to be slow. One of the ship's officers, in a jacket, a seaman's cap like a soiled bandage on his head, entertained himself examining all cameras and binoculars. Through the glasses he sometimes gazed at Soby, sometimes at the sights of Venice. A young Greek, a finger's breadth between his curly hair and his bushy eyebrows, held him—plastered, as the girl would say

—upright and in one place with one hand like a crutch at his armpit. No perceptible expression disturbed his somewhat pitted marble face.

Signor Pignata arrived by sea, in a motoscafi. With him were porters to handle his luggage, new bags, painting supplies, a green and white deck umbrella. He wore his usual black, a knubby raw silk fabric, but as a concession to travel a pair of dark glasses, a high crowned straw hat, and a pair of shoes with red rubber soles. He arrived, but if Soby had not been on the pier he would have departed. Was this the boat for Greece? Soby assured him it was. Surrounded by his porters, his luggage, he sat under the awning of the motoscafi. Would he remain or depart? It seemed in the hands of the Gods. Their earthly representative, Miss Kollwitz, coming to the rail to speak to Soby, settled the matter by crying out "Look here!" With his porters, his luggage, and his rubber soled shoes he was soon on the gangplank, Soby at his heels. The steward with the pitted face led them through the lounge, still being vacuumed, down a passage smelling of disinfectant, to a cabin where the door stood ajar on its hook. Steam from a shower filmed the mirror and the closed portholes. As the door pushed open a cloud of it formed about Soby's head. Herr Adrien Perkheimer, who shared their cabin, greeted them with nothing on but a towel, his face screened with wet tassels of his taffy-colored hair. He greeted them with his gargoyle smile, a courtly dripping bow.

"Mon corps mis a nu!" he said, in the lilting voice of a Wiener Sanger Knaben, lapping the towel over one arm like the cape of a bullfighter. His small moist hand he offered to Soby, then to Signor Pignata. "One littul moment!" he said, showing his back, and crossed the room to open one of the portholes, leaving tracks on the floor like those in a nursery, shining like ice. Soby, the porters, and Signor Pignata stood in the doorway, silent, till he beckoned them to enter.

eleven | An outside cabin, the berth above the portholes appeared to be designed for Herr Perkheimer, being six inches shorter than usual at the foot end. This permitted the bunk to be lowered, like a table-top, when not in use, making it possible for the occupants to stand up all at one time. Once part of a double cabin, or suite, a sliding panel that would not quite close separated the adjoining compartment, occupied by Miss Cynthia, Miss Kollwitz, and Miss Throop. A light burned, casting shadows as the ladies moved around. Due to a rise in the floor, and a dip in the ceiling, Soby could stand erect only at the door or between two beams just above the washbowl. These beams were polished with the sweep of hats and oily hair. A wire cage protected the small bulb screwed in the ceiling. The advantage of this arrangement—due to the persuasion of Signor Pignata —was that the panel might be opened during the daytime, giving the ladies the benefit of air from the portholes, and during the morning and evening the superior lavatory facilities. Miss Throop had identified a puzzling ornamental object as a bidet—one without plumbing connections. A perfect place for the cat house of Winifred Throop.

For hangers—there was only one hook, the wardrobe being part of the ladies' compartment—Signor Pignata went in search of the steward. Did that please Herr Perkheimer? Soby detected a change in his style. Seated on a pile of luggage, since there was no chair,

Soby listened to Perkheimer's polyglot prattle. Did it mean he was at ease, or ill at ease? He seemed anxious to hold Soby's attention. As if he feared he might leave, he manoeuvred so that he blocked the door. Was he proud of his figure? He had the arms and chest of a well-developed, hairless early-teenage boy. The sight of so much luggage—he meant that of Signor Pignata—made him smile. Herr Perkheimer travelled light. Such clothes as he thought he might need, he wore. His socks and shorts were drying in the shower. His trench coat was so made that it served as a sleeping bag and a rucksack. Both he demonstrated. His arms drawn up into the sleeves, the flap zippered, he beamed like an award-winning boy scout. The wide smile showed the red lining of his lip, like the gill of a fish. A piece of cigarette paper adhered like a bandage to the spout. The wingtip ears, shell-pink against the light, enhanced his resemblance to a waxwork gargoyle. Tassels of wet corn-silk hair veiled his eyes. The head was small, in harmony with the body. Was it the features, or expression, that seemed large? A facial tic, or a mannerism, arched one brow, popping the eye like a monocle. With it, as with a camera, the dilating pupil zoomed in for closeups. White as if frost-bitten was the cartilege tip of his nose. In what way did he impress upon Soby that if he, Perkheimer, was an oddball, Herr Doktor Soby, as he called him, was something of a very unusual square. Birds of a feather? So Herr Perk-

heimer skillfully implied. Otherwise why did he go
on and on?

Did he, Herr Doktor Soby, know about Austria?
A clucking sound in his throat followed every statement. It was said of Germany, he continued, that the
situation was serious but not hopeless, of Austria, it
was hopeless but not serious. He, Perkheimer, was an
Austrian—but *echt Deutsch*. Who else would have
been made, that is, as he was, to go with the new
miniature cameras? Was that not serious? Was that
not a triumph of Deutsche technik? As the cameras
got smaller and smaller, so would the cameramen of
the future. Enter Herr Perkheimer, first of the new
mini-men.

What was Soby to make of that? Was it his own
long leg, or the short one of Perkheimer that was being pulled? Like a parrot he tilted on his perch,
fastened him with one eye.

That explained, he went on, what might appear to
be an excess of photographic equipment. He carried
five, each loaded with a different country. Did Soby
get his meaning? Yes, yes, he nodded, each with a different *country*. Another triumph. No longer was there
loss of film and shots. They came with the camera.
Small cameras would suffice for small countries.
Switzerland, Monaco, Albania—and recently Israel.
The Jews were a problem. Would they consent to be a
mini-country? Or would national pride insist on
larger cameras? A touchy subject. One he well under-

stood being three-sevenths Jew.

There he paused to slip on the T shirt that was still damp, to hasten the drying. Was he waiting on Soby? Did he perhaps feel Soby was perhaps two-sevenths Jewish? A flick of apprehension disturbed the popped eye.

Mon vieux—he said, as if testing, eyeing the port-hole—did he, mon vieux, know that the echt Deutsche cameras came loaded with pictures of Greece? To take the shot one merely exposed the film to the Grecian light. Sepia and in color. Sepia featured broken columns and mutilated statues. Color, the more severe and bloody mutilations, seen against the wine dark Grecian sea. Another milestone in Deutsche photography.

Unhappily it had led to the widespread impression that Greece was a fiction, exported from Weimar. To correct this impression Herr Perkheimer had been engaged. Did Soby guess it? He, Perkheimer, like Schliemann before him, hoped to ascertain if Greece was a fact or a fiction. Put more bluntly, he, Adrien Perkheimer, sought to rediscover Greece. The island that lay buried under half a century's fall of photographic ash. That explained his presence on the *Hephaistos,* and that explained his mission. That also explained his "cannon," the object that resembled a sawed off shotgun. It was no gun at all, but a tele-photo lens fixed to a walnut gunstock. With it, he, Perkheimer, hoped to photograph the Greece that had never been seen. The last triumph, needless to say, of German technik.

A wild, extravagant humor? A plain or fancy nuttiness? There was no hint of sarcasm in the small bold voice. When he mentioned Schliemann, pronounced the word *triumph*, he had the marble gaze of Wandervogel with the legend *Deutschland uber alles* stamped on their brows. Ceremoniously he bowed, his small heels together, straightened to slip the tails of his shirt into his pants, light a cigarette, leave the door on its hook as he stepped into the hall. The voice of Miss Kollwitz stopped him in his tracks. Through the crack in the panel Soby saw Miss Cynthia stroking a cat with a face like cactus, one ear flattened, both eyes like pieces of petrified wood.

"No, no!" cried Miss Kollwitz.

"O My God!" sighed Miss Throop.

"Poor Aschenbach," said the girl, "What a way to go!"

The dining salon, a low ceilinged room of the sort usually converted to Epworth League socials, was divided down the center by screens to distinguish between the second and third class accommodations. All the tables appeared to be occupied. On the third class side a group of Wandervogel were seated on the floor, singing. Soby, the ladies, Signor Pignata and Herr Perkheimer stood at the entrance, having answered the second call. Was there some mistake? A slight miscount, it seemed, due to the number of last minute additions to the passengers who slept on the deck, but nevertheless had to eat. A question, therefore, of first come, first served. Herr Perkheimer found a folding chair for Miss Throop. The cocktails Miss Throop had taken in her cabin—following the discovery of Aschenbach, the stowaway—had left her feeling no pain but somewhat stupefied. There had been no vermouth at all in the gin. Herr Perkheimer advised Signor Pignata to use caution in bribing the waiters, since they were still, as he pointed out, tied up to the pier. Now and then a few loafers put a head to the portholes to watch them eat. Miss Cynthia called Soby's attention to someone signalling to them from the back of the room. The elderly gentleman with the belted jacket, and the distinguished bearing, stood beside his chair, bowing. A gentleman, he was offering one of the ladies his place.

"No! No!" Miss Kollwitz objected. "Tell him to sit. We eat together."

Soby attempted to signal their thanks, and regrets, across the room. He motioned to suggest the good Samaritan should sit down. But he did not. No, from the back of his chair he took his cane, with the horn handle, from the rack beneath it his hat, then dropped his napkin like a soiled sock on the seat as he left. All eating stopped as he made his way toward them. Due to the scale of his figure it took some doing. Little Perkheimer called words of encouragement.

"May I 'pologize?" he said, taking Soby's hand, "for my gunthrymin? Dey are peex."

Did his gunthrymin understand him? There was no doubt that they heard him. He had the sonorous assured voice of a lecturer. Little Perkheimer begged him the honor of his name.

Hodler. Dr. Luther Hodler, of Basel.

Basel? Miss Throop intoned. Were the peex then his countrymen?

Dr. Hodler smiled a sad knowing smile. His hand raised, then fell heavily at his side. "Peex? Were they nod everman's gunthrymin?"

"How right you are, my dear!" Miss Throop replied, "but are not some pigs piggier than others?"

Perhaps the usage troubled Dr. Hodler. He tipped his head to put his best ear forward. Over his lowered head Soby gazed at the diners, the round faces of the women, the men bearded with napkins. They seemed to be waiting for his decisions.

"All little pigs are equal," Soby volunteered, "but some are more equal than others—if I quote correctly."

Dr. Hodler's cane beat a sharp tattoo on the floor. Was he delighted? His head pumped up and down. His freckled hand rested for a moment on Herr Perkheimer's head. Soby presented Miss Throop, who remained seated, Miss Kollwitz, who remained distant, then turned to present Miss Cynthia.

"No, no!" Herr Hodler interrupted. "You don't tell me—I tell you! I haf wait all my life to mitt Naw-si-ca!"

"Naw *who?*" replied the girl.

"Nausicaa, my child—" Miss Throop lidded her eyes. "You'll have the Odyssey your spring semester."

"Ah-HAAAAA!" Dr. Hodler boomed. "Now who iss Odyseeus?" He turned from Signor Pignata to Soby. "Led me guess. Don't tell me!"

"Do we have any assurance there was such a person?" Miss Throop inquired.

An Orphic smile showed the dimples in Dr. Hodler's cheeks. Did he exchange a wily glance with Soby? The reading glass on his vest, suspended on its cord, he flipped from side to side, like a coin.

"A-surance?" he echoed. "Wot assurance Odysessoos neet if he haf Naw-si-ca!" He bowed to Miss Cynthia, the hug of a corset showing across his back. "Eef I may zay so—" he began, but was interrupted by Miss Kollwitz. The blonde giant who had carried their luggage stooped over her with a napkin dangling from his collar. Was he bowing? No, there was no room for him to stand. Gathered around him were half a dozen or more of the Wandervogel.

"Bitte, bitte—" he said, and waved his hand at the table from which they had arisen. To clear the places they had carried away their plates of food.

Miss Kollwitz would have none of it. No, no, none

of such nonsense. The big fellow, however, like a hen shooing chickens, spread his arms and shooed them gently toward the table. Miss Kollwitz he lifted and sat on one of the chairs, like a child. Miss Throop was persuaded to sit on his left, Miss Cynthia at her side. And the gentlemen?—the sensible thing, since there seemed to be places, was to go along and get the matter over. Eating had stopped in both halves of the dining salon. Soby and Signor Pignata took places—but little Perkheimer inquired how many vacancies there were? Seven? Very well, then *his* would go to Dr. Hodler. It was unthinkable that he should not have a seat, having given up his own. All agreed, in particular the ladies, but the giant solved the problem by simply adding a chair, as he put it, for *der kleine*. The unseated Wandervogel joined those seated on the floor.

Dr. Hodler insisted on knowing the name of their benefactor, a man too large, both in body and spirit, for such a small dining salon. *Holzapfel*, it was, or something like it, since his tongue seemed too large for his mouth. Konrad Holzapfel, aus Steindorf, near Freiburg. As the head was not fully emerged from the shoulders, Herr Holzapfel's features had not emerged from his face. Under the shaggy brows were small, shoe-button eyes. Flat on his head, the smooth blonde hair seemed an extension of his forehead. A seamless veneer joined the head with the sloping back. Soby begged him to be seated—to spare him further stooping—while he introduced the ladies and Signor Pignata. Did he look puzzled hearing the name Perkheimer?

"Perkheimer?" he echoed, as if he couldn't believe his small ears. Would wonders never cease? That was how Herr Holzapfel looked. On *der kleine* he beamed the gaze of a St. Bernard on a toy poodle. Was he amused at the object or the name? It seemed hard to say.

Dr. Hodler interrupted to ask the steward for two bottles of champagne. Champagne? Not on the *Hephaistos*. But a sparkling red wine of Italian vintage. They were brought in a galvanized pail without ice, wrapped in a damp bar rag. Nevertheless it sparkled. Dr. Hodler walked behind them pouring it himself, with the twist accorded only the best. Forget the crowded table and the third class food. They had found good fellowship. Was it not in this way, he said, that great enterprises were launched. He said *lunched,* but never mind. It gave *this* enterprise its special flavor. Soby called for a toast, and Dr. Hodler, since they insisted, rose ceremoniously to oblige them. Of whom was Soby reminded? Was it Dr. Emil Ludwig, the deceased Latin department head? He too let his hair grow, and was sometimes likened to Wagner, sometimes to Goethe. He wore smoking jackets with velvet lapels at the dances he chaperoned. He might appear in his slippers, a green sash around his waist. With both affection and malice he was referred to as the *ancien regime*. Dr. Hodler held the glass so that the color of the wine stained his fingers, turning it slowly as if looking for what he might say. Were some things not always the same? he asked. Things like voyages? Were they not, each in their fashion, an Odyssey? Was it by accident or design that here in this room, at this crowded table, should be found the new actors for the old parts? Had he not recognized Nausicaa at first glance? And who should have come to their aid but the *great* Odysseus, himself? Dr. Hodler tipped his glass first to Miss Cynthia, then to Herr Holzapfel, who blinked his small eyes, and beamed his good natured smile. Never mind that he understood not a word. It was not so easy for Soby to follow Dr. Hodler's original syntax since his accent fell infallibly on the wrong syllable. In due time, he said, they would all take their appropriate places, the actors being new, but the roles being always the same.

Signor Pignata, too, had understood nothing, but he seemed pleased. The first to empty his glass, he held it forward so that Dr. Hodler could fill it, then hoisted it to make his own toast. After drinking to it, Miss Throop inquired as to what it was. Little Perkheimer, his eyes larger now that the porthole light seemed dimmer, volunteered a translation.

"He says that he hope a fine voyage for all!"

"That was all?" Miss Throop inquired. Since it had seemed to be more.

"He says it is the first time he is ever on a boat."

Was that possible? A son of Italy who had never sailed the seas? Trains and airplanes all over—he waved his arms—but not once on a boat! Did he look thrilled or apprehensive? He sipped more of the wine.

"AH-Haaaaa!" Dr. Hodler replied, "You see, choost as I zay!"

A quake-like shudder of the floor dropped him to his seat. Silver and glasses rattled on the tables, the surface of the sparkling wine vibrated. Soby felt the sensation of high altitude in his thighs. But it was nothing, no, nothing to beware of, being merely the throb as the motors started, and the first twists of the screw. The shaft seemed to pass under the table where they sat.

"Look, look!" Miss Kollwitz cried, popping from her chair to point a wagging finger at the portholes. The pier seemed to be drifting. The wine in Signor Pignata's hoisted glass spilled over its lip.

"Mama mia!" he exclaimed, but few at the table heard him above the full throated song that swelled from the lips of the Wandervogel: one of them Konrad Holzapfel himself. A heimat lied. The sweet sorrow of parting. Was it a strain to air such massive lungs through such a small mouth? His small eyes watered. A red flush spread at the roots of his hair. For all that effort the sound from his lips was hardly audible. As he sat at football rallies, respectful but silent, Soby waited for the lament to finish, his eyes on the porthole, the widening stretch of water between the boat and the pier. What led him to glance at Herr Perkheimer? From his lap, using a spoon, he flicked the seeds of the ripe olives in the direction of the gaping Wandervogel mouths. Owl-eyed, her mouth full of olives, Miss Cynthia supplied him with the pits, under the very blur of Dr. Hodler's nearsighted gaze.

At what point did the disturbing question arise? The elevation, or lack of it, when a man suspected that he might be a dwarf? Soby had once had a student, a tiny creature with a doll's small voice, hands and feet, who had collapsed like a rag doll having heard the rumor that she might be a dwarf. Until that moment she had merely been *mignon,* petite. Nothing had pleased her more than to be seen walking with Soby, or dance with one of the bruisers of the football team. Then that horrible word had been mentioned and she had collapsed, dropped out of school, to reappear a year later with platform shoes and weirdly high-crowned hats. Never before had she looked a little odd. Then she did. Were the arms a little short? The head a little large? The feet a little too small? She avoided walking, gave up dancing, and spent most of her time with her legs curled up beneath her in one of the darker window seats of the library.

Herr Perkheimer, his lathered face reflected in the bottom of the mirror, posed the same question of scale, but in reverse. The washbowl and the door were ill proportioned. Not Perkheimer. If a man from Mars should enter the room the outsize Soby, with his feet lapping the bunk end, would appear to be the abnormal specimen. Proportion. Perkheimer set the norm. His small boots, on the floor beside Soby's, resembled an amusing repair shop exhibit, with those of Soby representing some freakish missing link. In Perkheimer's face, however, there was a hint of the problem. The smear of lather exposed the wide mouth of a clown. The eyes were both expressive and large. One might think that Nature, in her sly way, had given Perkheimer the eyes and mouth of Holzapfel, and Holzapfel the features of Perkheimer. It seemed a strange wisdom. A misarrangement of parts. Even as he shaved, one of Perkheimer's eyes appeared to be wearing a monocle, the iris taking closeup snapshots of his face. His camera eye. He had described it as such himself. Herr Perkheimer was professionally engaged to supply an agency with colored slides of Greece—the one now awaiting, as he said, rediscovery. The cameras of the future would come loaded with Perkheimer's Greece.

Like a reasonably normal man Perkheimer cursed while shaving and bled where nicked. From the blood flecked lather his new face emerged. The corn silk hair, normally stroked back, lay forward to hang on his brows like bangs. He had the fresh un-kempt look of a rained-on bird. On the bridge of his nose, inclined to peel, he rubbed a drop of suntan lotion, then passed the oily fingers through his hair. Wearing his wash'n dry shirt, a Leica camera with a turret of lenses ready for action, he put a cigarette to the spout of his lip, used the towel on his shoes. Signor Pignata, lying facing the wall, turned sud-denly as if the boat had tilted, one hand to his mouth as if to stifle a yawn. Had he forgotten where he was? Pop-eyed he stared at Perkheimer. His hand moved from his mouth to his eyes. A bladder-like escape of air terminated in a moan. Did the ladies hear that? There was a rap of knuckles on the sliding panel. The voice of Miss Kollwitz said, "Hallo, you are awake?"

"Good morning, ladies!" sang Herr Perkheimer. There was a pause. It was not what Miss Kollwitz wanted to hear.

"A fine morning," Soby said. "How did you sleep?"

"Look!" she cried. "She is not here!" Her eye flashed at the crack in the panel, moved away.

"The cat?" Soby said, up on his elbow. He peered around as if he might see him.

"There is a cat also?" said Herr Perkheimer.

"No, no! The cat is here. The cat is not stupid!" Did that narrow the field? Considerably.

"The sunrise—" he said, blinking at the porthole.

"She's probably gone to the deck to see it."

"You think she gets up so early for the sunrise?" The moist eye of Miss Kollwitz gleamed at the panel. While it was there Soby did not move, nothing crossed his mind. *"He* is there?" Miss Kollwitz hissed. Soby did not say, he *who?* No, he knew that much, even so early in the morning. "If he is there, then who is up?" Miss Kollwitz asked. "You think she gets up for the sunrise?"

Not for the sunrise, Soby moved to get up. Herr Perkheimer, however, put up his small hand showing Soby the palm, shining with suntan lotion. Was it so unusual, he declared, for a young lady to be up so early? If not for the sunrise, perhaps for a glimpse of Greece. For that, one did not have to leave the boat. Wily Odysseus and his band of Greeks were encamped on the deck. He, Perkheimer, would be glad to see if the fair Nausicaa was among them. As he stepped into the hall he exchanged with Soby an enigmatic wink.

A discomfort not due to the movement of the boat led Soby to yawn, which he did not stifle, then roll, like Signor Pignata, to face the wall. At the first call for breakfast he pretended to sleep. Using the handle of her fruit paring knife Miss Kollwitz pounded on the sliding panel until Soby turned, saw her eye gleaming at the crack. On the tip of her wagging knitting needle she offered him a slice of pear.

* * *

Although the sea looked pond-like through the port-hole, the *Hephaistos* tilted, it seemed to Soby, as if Ulysses Holzapfel sported with Nausicaa on the deck. On the curved ceiling he heard the thump of galumphing feet. A large black beetle skied on the water that refused to drain from the bowl. Soby dipped his fingers, wet his eyes, then slipped on the jacket with the pipe burns, the shoes with the non-skid composition soles. A word to Signor Pignata got no reply. The morning light, perhaps, explained his unusual pallor: lint from the flannel blanket flecked his beard. The taste of pear in his mouth, Soby crossed the lounge where the marble faced steward sorted the usable butts from the refuse in the ashtrays. His laceless shoes were not mated. He wore no socks. Usable butts he stored in a tin for Black Currant lozenges.

A wind lifted the collar of Soby's jacket as he stepped on the deck. Members of the Wandervogel, their long hair blowing, stood along the rail facing the sunrise, their lips chill-blue as if they had been for a swim. Fifteen or twenty deck chairs, for the relaxation and convenience of the two hundred and eighty-five passengers, were occupied by Wandervogels still wrapped in their bedrolls, some of them in pairs. The pairs Soby looked at closely, but Nausicaa was not among them. Nor Herr Holzapfel, although Soby noted the case for his guitar. Up front two sailors with bare feet the color of a squid's belly swabbed the deck with a hose: the spray salted Soby's face. The coast of Italy was faint as a mirage. At the rear of the boat gulls dipped and soared in the windstream like kite tails, as if for the benefit of the miniature photographer. Little Perkheimer crouched as if in a foxhole, but he was not shooting at the gulls. At what then? The broad torso of Herr Holzapfel blocked the view. Since he had no neck, a heavy turtle-neck sweater pushed up behind his ears, the wind lifting his hair so that it stood up straight on his head. More like a tree than a man, he stood straddle-legged, his elbows out, as if to keep the wind from blowing the sea nymph away. Soby would have preferred it otherwise, but that was how she looked. Her hair streamed out in such a a manner it seemed to jerk at her head. She wore a raincoat, but in the wind it merely enhanced her figure, the cloth rippling as if a hand passed from her waist to her knee. Dr. Luther Hodler, wearing a beret, his cane hooked to the arm he held aloft, gesturing, stood to one side as if conducting a concealed orchestra. With one gloved hand he beckoned, with the other he dampered the wind's effect. The girl tipped her head now this way, now that, showing now her profile, with the hair streaming, now the full face with the slightly flared nostrils, the gold-flecked smile. Soby went toward them, pausing on the fringe of the operations. Dr. Luther Hodler, his right hand uplifted, held him at bay. A finger of cloud screening the rising sun gave little Perkheimer the chance he had awaited, shooting the nymph from below, with her hair streaming on the sky. Was this Perkheimer's new found land? Soby, the wind in his ears, was aware that with his arrival Nausicaa was host to a curious foursome, not one of them Greeks. The giant Holzapfel, the kleine Perkheimer, the scholarly Dr. Hodler —and Soby. What had brought them to this spot on the deck? A gift from the sea. A green-eyed sea nymph with a mocking gilt-edged smile. Dr. Hodler's mouth opened, wide, but the wind whipped the words away. Using his cane he called to their attention the gull that floated on the windstream above them. Plainly they heard his mournful, lovesick cry.

"Heem too!" Dr. Hodler bellowed, cupping a gloved hand to his mouth, turning on Soby the illicit, bloodshot leer of Gustave von Aschenbach. Did Herr Perkheimer get the shot? He had paused to switch lenses, then dropped back so that the huge Holzapfel, Dr. Hodler and Soby, along with the mournful gull, were among the beautiful and the damned.

twelve | A continental breakfast was served on the *Hephaistos* from 7:30 to 9:00. In the third class salon it featured baskets of bread with the taste of damp sea biscuit, sliced and sometimes buttered several days before. At nine o'clock a smattering of Wandervogel who had eaten at 7:30 were back for seconds. Konrad Holzapfel rose from the table to shoo them out. After several cups of coffee his voice was still hoarse. The night had been balmy, and Herr Holzapfel had spent most of it awake and singing, or pointing out the constellations to Dr. Hodler and Miss Nausicaa. Miss Throop had been there for a spell, but gazing upward fixedly made her dizzy. The movement of the sky upset her more than that of the boat. Dr. Hodler had helped her back to the lounge, where she had felt much better after a nightcap. Miss Cynthia had also taken part in the singing but showed no ill effects. It had been Dr. Hodler, an early riser, who had suggested she should see the sunrise. But she hadn't. All they had seen was clouds and clouds.

Dr. Hodler hung his head in shame, showing an area like the moon's surface. Hair rooted at his temple had been trained to grow over the dome, like so many fine cables connecting the hemispheres. How did one say it? That was life. One could be reasonably sure that the sun would rise, but that one would see it one could not be sure. Not on this earth. Spacemen perhaps, but for such men the sun would not rise. No, just one of the countless impersonal stars of the sky.

Better no sunrise on occasion than a sun that never set, that gave no warmth, only the deadly cosmic ray. Dr. Hodler was interrupted by a sneeze. The early morning air, he explained, made him subject to fits of sneezing: not a cold, he begged them not to be alarmed. A sprig of color, not particularly healthy, burned in one cheek but not the other. The wind perhaps. One might have thought that he had bruised himself, or been slapped. From Miss Kollwitz he accepted a piece of tissue, blew his nose. Dr. Hodler's discomfort, Soby gathered, was due to the interruption of his discourse, rather than to his sneezing and runny nose. Had he picked up where he had stopped the night before? Herr Holzapfel and his constellations had failed to present a balanced picture. The life of man, Dr. Hodler was saying, was here on earth. There was too much talk, these days, of something called space. And what indeed was space? An empty void. The stars were only of interest seen from the earth. Although an hour had passed since Dr. Hodler, his face a little windburned, had left the deck, there was about his forehead a feverish flush. He had eaten very little. His coffee had cooled in his cup. Although he mentioned no names, and glanced at them all in his near-sighted gemutlich manner, it was clear that his remarks had Herr Holzapfel in mind. A pity, since Herr Holzapfel understood not a word. To ease his throat he sipped coffee, holding the mug close to his face so that the steam left a film of moisture on his brow. When Dr. Hodler paused he hoarsely muttered *jawohl,* as if in complete agreement. No other speech had thawed loose in his throat. Amiably, he put up his huge paws for Miss Kollwitz to wind the yarn she had pulled from a by-passed double stitch. Soby's sweater was still the sleeve it had been when they left. Besides a slight migraine, that made her squint, Miss Kollwitz had other problems on her mind.

His sneezing stopped, Dr. Hodler inquired if they knew what they were approaching. He said *broaching,* which led Miss Kollwitz to exchange a glance with Soby. Little Perkheimer said, Was it not Greece? His head tilted in that characteristic manner, a smear of grease around his generous lips. Did he mean to be facetious? Wide-eyed, he respectfully awaited an answer, using his knife blade to pick up the crumbs on his plate. Alone, he had eaten half the basket of bread. Butter and jam were at the corners of his lips. Somewhere Soby had read of certain small creatures who, in order to live, were obliged to eat more than their own weight daily. Eating machines. Little Perkheimer seemed one of them. With a skillful stroke he rasped the blade of his knife on the prong of his fork.

"Greece tomorrow—" Dr. Hodler said, smiling at little Perkheimer, "but before lunch Brindisi." Did that word not ring in their ears? Brindisi, from where Caesar, at the summit of his power, sailed to Alexandria—

Miss Kollwitz flagged him down with the sleeve of Soby's sweater. She begged to differ. The reason he had sailed was that his power was threatened. She made this point, she made it clear, not to be picayune but for the sake of history and Miss Cynthia. These were matters she would take up in the fall at Oberlin.

Dr. Hodler smilingly stood corrected. The napkin at his throat he daubed at his forehead, his runny nose. Of political power that was certainly true, but he spoke of his power as a man. As a lover, if you will, rather than an emperor. Was it an accident he had waited for Cleopatra so long? History was full of similar passages, was it not? The mature, seasoned man she held in reserve for these special legendary occasions, for that moment when the woman in question was in the bud. Was that clear? In English he had problems with the metaphors. The opening flower and the seasoned man—was that contradictory to nature? Not—he took the liberty of saying—to the nature of man.

These remarks Dr. Hodler addressed to the ladies, in particular to Miss Cynthia, who sat eating jam from a spoon as though it was ice cream. Light from the porthole seemed to penetrate the skin of her face, the pink lobes of her ears. The stain of the jam heightened the color of her lips. What a pity Signor Pignata could not see her now, her hair tangled like seaweed, her flesh like a pink shell held to the morning light. And on her coral lips, for the moment, nothing more disturbing than grape jam.

"Look here!" Miss Kollwitz said, and took from the hands of Herr Holzapfel the skein of wool. To whom was she talking? To all mature, seasoned men generally, who were acting like fools. Through the loop in the wool she gave Soby a straight look.

"You like jam?" Soby said, to change the subject.

The head of Miss Cynthia slowly dissented. No, not so much. Not grape jam. What she *really* liked was homogenized peanut butter on raisin toast.

"Bitte?" Dr. Hodler queried, a stranger to the language.

Miss Kollwitz refused to carry it further. It was more than enough to hear about it. Talk about it she would not. On her own plate were heaped the discolored parings of the pear she had brought along with her, plus the small compost of pits she had removed from her mouth.

So much for Brindisi and today, said Dr. Hodler. What he wanted to discuss was tomorrow.

History was full of many things, Miss Kollwitz said, but tomorrow, thank heavens, was not yet history. She would be glad to let it take care of itself. This it would do since Miss Throop, Professor Soby, herself and Miss Cynthia were down for the guided motor tour of the island. It was open to all, although she could not speak for Herr Holzapfel. Deck passengers might be asked to pay a small fee. Dr. Hodler was perhaps too familiar with the island to pass his time visiting familiar sites, but. . . .

How clever she was! Dr. Hodler wagged his head at what he called a woman's tuition. Before it was on his mind, a woman knew what it was! If there was an island that Dr. Hodler knew like the back of his hand, it was Corfu. Every farm and hamlet. Every mountain path and inlet. Strange as it might seem the familiar landmarks might be the ones he had hardly set eyes on. Like the carpet, say, of one's room. He had walked it threadbare, one might say, looking for signs and footfalls in the sands of time. Why had he not found them? These footfalls were invisible. They were the tracks not of men, but men like gods. Here was this Corfu, the island on the map that they would all set eyes on tomorrow, ride around in cars, and when they left it would still be there. Then there was this other island. It would perhaps be there longer since it was a myth. On the shore of this island, so the story went, the wily Ulysses, his boat having floundered, his raft had been washed up on a beach. What beach? The exact location was not known. There were guesses, of course, as ~~and~~ Dr. ~~Hodler had his own map of the island. Thirty years of his life, give and take a few wars, had gone into it. On this map he had marked~~ the place where

Ulysses, strewn with seaweed, had been seen by Nausicaa and her maids. Was it not childish? Mapping these invisible tracks in the sand? That Nausicaa or Ulysses had ever lived was a matter of conjecture— a matter of conjecture, that was the important point. All other things passed. Conjectural matters did not. Otherwise Luther Hodler, who might have passed his life among sensible people, doing profitable things, spent it wandering along the shoreline of a myth. Noting where Ulysses first floundered, where Nausicaa had found the courage to face him, the road along which she had led him to meet the king, her father. Mad, was it not? Yes, and he had even cheated playing with himself. Of all this nonsensical speculation he could not have cared less. No, he cared for one thing only—the first glimpse of Nausicaa, one of man's primal visions of loveliness. Did they recall it? Hardly a specific word was said. No, and therein was the poet's genius. Homer knew that each man must paint her for himself. Helen he saw dark, with the melancholy gaze that mirrored her fateful attraction, but Nausicaa was fair as the first dream of life. Nothing clouded her brow. Nothing corrupted her innocence. It was Nausicaa, over so many centuries, who had beckoned to Dr. Hodler, had called him each summer to the shores of Corfu. Island or myth? For thirty years he had told himself it was the myth that mattered: he had been relieved to know she would not materialize. What if one day he should find her tracks in the sand? What would he do? Run and hide with shame as Ulysses had done? No, there was reason in this madness, and thank God she was only a myth. One that never grew old, as man must himself. Was it not then passing strange that Dr. Hodler, about to wind up thirty years of research, and making, for reasons of health, perhaps his last trip to the island—was it not passing strange that before his eyes, while they were good enough to bear testimony, this mythic creature, this Nausicaa, should materialize?

There Dr. Hodler paused, feeling, as well he might, the fixed stare not of Nausicaa, but Miss Kollwitz, her cheeks so full of wind her eyes almost popped. Not only Dr. Hodler, however, felt their gaze. Once he had sensed the gist of his matter Soby had settled his eyes on the porthole, where the sea, scuffed with whitecaps, alternately appeared and receded, putting to Soby the question of now you see it, now you don't. Did she feel that Soby had been his collaborator? More was passing strange than Dr. Hodler had dreamed of in the voyage of the *Hephaistos*.

"Pish Posh!" she said, but Dr. Hodler was too far advanced to retreat. He put up his hand, the thumb and forefingers twitching as if he held a piece of chalk, and would now explain what he had written on the blackboard. Would Miss Kollwitz be so kind as to let him continue? A rhetorical question. He did not wait for her consent. What he proposed, in the light of what he said, with the kind cooperation of Adrien Perkheimer, and, of course, Herr Holzapfel, was to go to this site, this mythic location, and photograph the great Ulysses rising from the sea, with Nausicaa—for the first time in the flesh—on the shell-strewn beach. Not like Helen, in her tower, or Penelope at her loom, but on the beach, one of the shell-like gifts from the sea. Once more the poet's instincts had proved to be right. What more fitting climax could be imagined to thirty years of research than to see it realized, so to speak, in the flesh? To get there was a matter of perhaps two hours, most of it along the shore line, but they were scheduled to stop in Corfu for more than six. The ladies were welcome, but they might find the walk severe. Dr. Hodler could lead them to the spot blindfolded, but it was not of easy access. The beach was rock strewn. There was the matter of the tide. Most certainly some of them would end up with wet feet.

Dr. Hodler paused, blinking his eyes at the space where Miss Kollwitz had been sitting, her head below the table level while she stuffed her knitting into her bag. Was there to be a scene? They heard the clasp snap on her purse. Her head appeared in the light long enough to blow her nose. With the calm deliberation of a UN delegate exercising his right of veto, she picked up her bag, her tin of mints, the napkin in which she had wrapped food scraps for Aschenbach, and with her shawl looped over her head made for the door. There she turned and said, "Look! You are coming?"

From her lips the girl drew the spoon, still filmed with the jam. "You hear!" cried Miss Kollwitz. "You see what you have done?" Was she questioning the girl or all mature, well-seasoned men? There was no focus in her shadowed staring eyes. "Passen sie auf!" she cried, shaking the hand in which she gripped the cat scraps. "Nausicaa my foot. She does not know who she is!"

A length of yarn from her bag followed her up the stairs to the deck. From Herr Holzapfel, so long silent, came sounds as of plumbing thawing. Lumps of speech clogged in his throat would neither go up or down. Finally it came. "Was ist los?" he inquired. He looked at Dr. Hodler for an answer, but his gaze, like that of Soby's, was on Miss Cynthia. Little Perkheimer, his turret of lenses held to his face, like a machine gun, was focusing the one with the shortest focal length on her face. What was she doing? Merely returning the lenses' bold stare. The tremor Soby thought he observed in her lips, sealed with the mucilage of jam, might have been the flutter in his own lids. Had she no nerves? Were the eyes of men so much alike? Was it because, in truth, she did *not* know who she was? Staring at her shamelessly Soby wondered if what he felt was desire—mature, seasoned desire—or something more on the order of cannibalism. The coral lobes of her ears. The grape-stained flesh of her mouth. To eat the beloved. Certain celebrated lovers had tried. That hooting pack of goat-skinned barbarians who had streamed down the slope of Aschenbach's dream—where had they been headed but for just such a barbecue? Aschenbach had not faced it. No, poor devil, he had closed his eyes. He had fled from the sight like a man running for his life. By the light of the burning torches what had been seen? A bacchanal? Merely the same old fertility rites? Or had that first glimpse of beauty, the word made flesh, established in man the two poles of his nature—to materialize or to spiritualize? To pass away in a delirium within sight of the beloved object, like Aschenbach, or to sit and stare like cannibals at the grape-stained lips.

"Hold it!" Little Perkheimer's command led Herr Holzapfel to open his small mouth, close his eyes as if someone had sprinkled him with salt. Little Perkheimer snapped it before the eyes opened. A face emerging, foetus-like, from the lump of head.

"Make it vun of itch," said Dr. Hodler, showing Perkheimer two fingers, like the letter V, then took from the bread basket his first slice of the morning, eating it dry, as Miss Kollwitz had advised him that all of them should.

With black coffee and dry toast for Signor Pignata, Soby made his way back to the cabin. The sallow-faced young man with the bushy hair less than a finger's breadth from his eyebrows sat on Soby's bunk, turning the pages of one of his paperback books. His soiled steward's jacket, without buttons, opened on his hairless, tattooed chest. No expression perceptible to Soby showed in his face. He put the book down, stood up to finish the half made bunk of little Perkheimer, picked the soiled rag from the sink, and without comment stepped into the hall. The door he left open to give Soby an insolent view of his back.

Signor Pignata lay facing the wall, his sleep undisturbed. Soby's sense of outrage was diminished by the fact that the hooligan had sat there going through his books, not his pants. Was it the higher life he aspired to? Closer examination showed that he had sat there smoking one of Signor Pignata's filter-tipped cigarettes, the ashes on the floor at his feet. And Herr Perkheimer's cameras? They hung by their straps from hooks above his bunk. Even as he formed a proper warning statement Soby sensed that "loot" was not what he was after. Books? He could taste the wryness of his smile. With limited experience in these matters, the eyes that had returned the gaze of Soby, like those in a trophy, had put away childish things. Short in the leg, but too long in the waist for the jacket he was wearing, the back of his head was more expressive than the front. How did one explain it? An animal that turns knowing he has nothing to fear. Nothing from Soby, that is. In the mirror below his eye level Soby saw the coffee and toast on the tray he was holding. He lowered it to the bunk, wiping the damp palms of his hands on the sheet.

In the room at his back the voice of Miss Kollwitz said, "Look here!" as if speaking to Soby. "My dear—" Miss Throop sighed, as if weary of the subject "—old lechers never die, they just degrade away." There was a pause while Miss Kollwitz puzzled it out. "I find it curious," Miss Throop continued, "that what is so admirable in Goethe, is so lamentable, let us say, in poor Aschenbach."

"But Goethe ist Goe-the!" cried Miss Kollwitz. "He is nod Dr. Hodler!"

"Suppose we ask the child which she prefers. The live one, or the dead one?"

"Good!" said Miss Kollwitz. "A laughing stock! What pictures does he want? Without her clothes!"

"My dear, I hope we can get one. Nothing would please her mother more."

The door closed with a slam that jarred the key to the floor. Signor Pignata, rising on his elbow, peered around wildly but recognized nothing. To put it away he placed a hand over his eyes.

"How are you?" Soby asked, placing a hand on his shoulder, but Signor Pignata was not responsive. He yawned. A coated tongue passed dryly over colorless lips. "Fresh air," Soby said, "you need some fresh air!" He gestured at the ceiling to indicate the deck.

"My dear Soby—" The voice came from behind

the sliding panel, but it was not the characteristic voice of Miss Throop.

"Good morning," Soby replied, "how do you feel?"

"Wicked," was the reply.

Before Soby commented, little Perkheimer, wearing sunglasses that cast green shadows on his cheekbones, put his head in the door to cry "Brindisi! Brindisi! Corfu next stop!"

Did he mean to be funny? Soberly he gazed at the sallow face of Signor Pignata, that of a corpse on which the beard had continued to grow. "Herr Julius Caesar?" he asked, getting no answer, then closed the door and repeated the cry in the hall. "Brindisi! Brindisi! Calling Herr Julius Caesar!" As the cry receded Signor Pignata, in a half crouched position, put out his hands like fins and slowly rose from his bunk. A silence, as if the boat had sunk and the green light at the porthole was water, proved to be nothing more than the calm of the harbor, the throbbing of the screw having stopped. As if no interruption had occurred the voice behind the sliding panel continued—

"If one determines not to save it, my dear, should one give it away or sell it?"

Was she speaking to Soby? Sensing danger, Signor Pignata had put out his hand to Soby's shoulder, his lips moving but no sound escaping his mouth. Two or three times the *Hephaistos* shuddered before expiring like a monster. The voice of Miss Kollwitz could be heard on the deck. Beaming, the pedlar on the pier held aloft his clusters of grapes, his roving eye on the porthole framing Signor Pignata's land-hungry face.

The sight of land got Signor Pignata, with Soby's assistance, to the crowded deck. Herr Holzapfel's Wandervogel, like gigantic children with their bottom-soiled lederhosen, lined the rail where two pedlars sold them Japanese lighters. In the water a boy waited to dive for anything that was dropped. On the pier side, Damen und Herren leaned over the rail to buy chocolate, tossing their coins to a monkey who caught them in his bellhop hat. Damen, with the expressions of troopers manning foxholes, occupied the steamer chairs forcibly taken from the Wandervogel, a sign chained to a ventilator describing the chairs as for *first class only*. With Herren who had gone to buy chocolate, the Damen exchanged places. They did it quickly to keep the seats warm, without a loss of heat. Herren only, fifteen or twenty, were gathered at the fantail where little Perkheimer appeared to be firing his sawed-off shotgun at the cruising gulls. There was no sound, however. The birds dipped and soared undisturbed. Dr. Hodler, holding the velvet lined case, stood to one side as if out of harm's way. Hooked on his arm, his cane cast the shadow of a wagging tail.

Where was the land? Over the roofs of the pier, the roofs of the town, trees plucked by the wind showed its prevailing direction. "Caesar, yes—?" said Soby, hoping to arouse in Signor Pignata a sense of history. But he took no interest. The light of Italy seemed to hurt his eyes. He turned from the land to look up front where Herr Holzapfel, hulking like a ship's prow, stood like an awning for Miss Kollwitz as she peeled and quartered a pear. To shade her face she wore her muffler looped over her head. Herr Holzapfel accepted a slice of the pear, but the Wandervogel at his side declined. Her hand, as if already sticky, went to the hip of the shorts she was wearing, then pushed downward as if to wipe the juice from the palm. The movement continued till both fingers and elbow bent the wrong way.

"Mama mia," Signor Pignata said, but without an exclamation. His eye for the characteristic detail was a shade ahead of Soby, whose eyes had been on the girl's long legs. They looked thin in the heavy shoes, the ample-bottomed shorts. A short sleeved peasant blouse exposed both her tanned and her pale arm. The tanned one she raised, bent in such a manner Soby winced to see it, ignoring the fact that it seemed to be waving at them.

"Cee-Pee!" she called, pronouncing it in such a way one might wonder if she meant Soby, coming toward them all legs, the shoes clopping, the overample seat of the pants hanging, to stand before them with her arms down straight, like a girl scout, her tummy thrust out. Her knees and calves touched, but a juvenile gap separated her thighs. An expectant smile widened her mouth. Was it to Soby or Signor Pignata she presented herself? Soby smiled, but Signor Pignata, without comment turned on his heel, not too sharply, and walked off. A pinfeather from the pillow he had hugged all night was tangled in his thick hair. Soby felt—never mind in what order— admiration for Signor Pignata's standards: shame and relief that he had none of his own. He stood there, brazenly smiling, the illicit thoughts of a man with designs on children plainly on his face.

"Look here!" Miss Kollwitz gripped his arm as if he had been caught at something, holding him till Herr Holzapfel, his lederhosen whining, could see for himself. Dr. Hodler, however, came up first. A little winded, he wagged his cane toward the bridge of the *Hephaistos,* where Herr Perkheimer, with his gun-like camera, sighted at him through the telescopic sight, aiming the barrel like a single cyclopean eye.

"Bang, bang!" he cried, like a small fry shooting Indians, and took another shot. If Miss Kollwitz understood it, the humor of it was not to her liking.

"No, no!" she called, "no pictures!" as Soby, smiling, faced the camera, Herr Holzapfel's shadow falling across his face. Between them, the girl smiled her golden sunkist smile.

thirteen | Miss Throop was at the table when they appeared for lunch. Her flowered print, with its satin lining the color of the upholstery in the old Pullman coaches, her face shadowed by her flop-brimmed hat, gave her an ample but dated elegance. Dr. Hodler commented on how well and rested she looked. A paisley shawl, of the size that once covered the ends of grand pianos, passed around her shoulders, the ends loosely coiled about her freckled forearms. Rested she looked indeed, her jowls powdered, the dolphin earrings dangling to tap at her throat, with just a hint that she had stopped for a moment at the bar. Involuntarily the gill-like pouch of one eye flicked Soby a wink. And where, she asked, peering around, was Miss Cynthia? Was there more than humor in her performance? Miss Cynthia was there, in her borrowed shorts, her peasant blouse, and her Wandervogel hair-do, but Miss Throop saw her not. Nor did she return the girl's gilt-edged smile.

"Ah-HAAAAA!" boomed Dr. Hodler. "You see? She is Miss Cynthia no lonker!"

Dr. Hodler's wide, encompassing grin was sometimes hard to tell from a grimace. A side to side movement of his jaws had perhaps overdeveloped the muscle. A marble-like protuberance, white as a knuckle, appeared on one side, then the other. "You do nod recognice Nausicaa?" he said. "No wonder. This is how she fool so many pipple. If she did nod fool pipple you know what happen?"

"I do indeed," Miss Throop replied.

His head forward to hear his own answer, Dr. Hodler was not listening. "You know wod happen?" he repeated.

"I do," Miss Throop replied, "would you like her to tell you?"

Dr. Hodler paused as if he found the language strange.

"If he does, I do not!" Miss Kollwitz barked, "I have heard enough already!" The chair Herr Holzapfel had pulled out for her she sat down on, her legs swinging. Soby slipped the seat of her chair under the borrowed shorts of Miss Cynthia, noting the whiteness of her scalp where her hair was parted. Dr. Hodler remained standing, as if he meant to speak. The wide curve of his lips was now a little painful, since they were chapped. It was characteristic of him to wait till he had their attention before speaking, blowing on his fingers as if they were dusty with chalk. Had Miss Kollwitz unnerved him? No, it seemed to be his intention, in the pause, to put that small incident behind them, to turn their eyes, like his own, to the prospect of Greece. Attentive, Soby observed the crumbs of the morning in the folds of his vest, the impress of the pin in his four-in-hand on the fold of his neck. At their tables near the portholes Wandervogel thanked the Lord, in song, for their daily bread. Perhaps Dr. Hodler joined them. Little Perkheimer broke the silence by putting a question to the air beside him. "Signor Pignata?" Something seemed to have happened to his place. There was no extra plate at the table, no empty chair. Was he not well? Soby hastened to explain that Signor Pignata had been well enough to get a breath of air, but the smell of the fuel oil slightly nauseated him. It was just as well he avoided the smell of food. Dr. Hodler agreed, also suggesting, as he lowered himself to his seat, that a few hours on shore was the thing for him. He would get that tomorrow on Corfu. He would like to suggest Signor Pignata join them on their little tour to Nausicaa's beach.

"I beg your pardon?" Miss Throop said.

It was what Dr. Hodler had been preparing to come to. He straightened to smile at her over the steam rising from his soup. With the ladies' kind permission, he said, Herr Holzapfel, Perkheimer and the Wandervogel—Herr Soby also, if he cared to join them—would make an excursion to where Ulysses set eyes upon Nausicaa. With the ladies' permission— he bowed to Miss Cynthia—for once she would be there. A myth would have become a reality.

Miss Kollwitz would have spoken, but a napkin was clapped to her mouth. Inhaling, she had burned herself on the soup.

"My dear Soby," said Miss Throop, "I hope Miss Kollwitz and I will not interfere with this historic occasion." She sipped her soup with the lips of a flute player.

No, no. But the simple fact was that Soby was no hiker. No, not of that sort. Nor had he come prepared with the proper shoes. He would have to leave history in the capable hands of Dr. Hodler, Perkheimer, and Miss Nausicaa. Perhaps Herr Perkheimer would supply them with a picture of the great event.

So much for that. Soby reassured them all, impartially. Dr. Hodler who seemed pleased, Miss Cynthia noncommittal, Miss Throop resigned, Herr Holzapfel puzzled, Miss Kollwitz hissing like an adder at her spoonful of hot soup. If the ladies so desired he would be delighted to take the shore excursion listed in the brochure, the Villa Achillaeum built by the empress of Austria, was it not? A melancholy spectacle, Dr. Hodler observed, but in such bad taste it was of some interest. Statuary in the garden. But the views were splendid. Along the road one would see handsome peasants. Would it interest them to know how they measured distance? With cigarettes. Was the island as small as all of that? Miss Throop inquired. Dr. Hodler did not mean as a ruler. No, no, not end to end, not even the peasants. But how long it burned, or rather how many one smoked, walking from place to place. Three cigarettes to Canoni, perhaps about seven to Nausicaa's beach.

When in good form Dr. Hodler spoke English in the manner of a smiling ventriloquist, the lips slightly parted. Some of the words materialized, some did not. He urged them to try the local wines, tasting of resin, and see the archaic inscriptions in the museum. The view from the Canoni was world famous, thanks to countless bad water colors. They hung everywhere. It was perhaps what they would see if they stopped to look. On that point, and many others, he was in complete accord with Herr Perkheimer who believed that Greece lay buried beneath a mass of photographic ash. A vivid and telling phrase. He had asked for the loan of it. In Herr Perkheimer's opinion, as well as Dr. Hodler's, Greece awaited rediscovery. Not that Dr. Hodler was Schliemann, no, but he hoped in a small way to be instrumental, with Herr Perkheimer's assistance, in penetrating the wearisome clichés. What had ruins to do with Greece? Ruins had only to do with themselves. The living proof, not the dead reminder, the living flesh, not the mutilated marble—for this one journeyed to Greece, or one was deceived. What better place to begin than on that beach where Nausicaa had sported with her maidens. If Dr. Hodler had to choose he took the side of those sailors with their cheap pinups over those of the scholar with his bits of bone and stone. It was Nausicaa one wanted, not tracks in the sand. With Miss Cynthia's permission, it was Nausicaa they would find.

Did Dr. Hodler pause expecting some comment? A fly crawled on the cooled surface of his soup. Miss Cynthia watched it with the absorption that kept Soby from commenting, favorably, on what Dr. Hodler had said. The fly moved about cautiously, as if testing thin ice. Was it absurd to think she heard the tamp of his small feet? Did that explain something odd about her face? The Wandervogel hair-do? Or simply that she did not smile. The wide generous mouth had contracted to a small neutral position—the one from which one started, so to speak, to make a new face. As on Signor Pignata's canvas, part of the one seen earlier had been erased.

"Look here!" With a flap of her napkin Miss Kollwitz shooed the fly toward the porthole. Through it they saw the pier drifting away like a ferry slip. The fruit pedlar had sat down on his box to eat his own pears. The land Signor Pignata had not set foot on seemed to drift away, like floating islands, and Miss Throop, her eyes lidded, stoically waited for the shuddering throb of the screw. As if he saw it emerging from the ashes where Dr. Hodler had left it, little Perkheimer said—

"Ahhhh Greece!"

Did he mean to be funny, that fellow? One never knew.

The food was not bad. A little grudgingly, perhaps, Dr. Hodler felt obliged to admit it. One had to be grateful for small favors on such a boat. Dr. Hodler made the comment as he peeled the foil from a bar of Swiss chocolate—extending it toward the ladies to help themselves. Miss Kollwitz sniffed it, a surer test of the quality, she observed, than tasting, since one caught the delicate aroma of the vanilla bean. Miss Throop took hers straight with a chaser of black coffee, her pleasure visible in the way she lidded her eyes. Miss Cynthia, like Soby, let the wafer dissolve like a lozenge, black on the tip of the tongue she put to her lips. Herr Holzapfel put his piece away for another time. Little Perkheimer took no sweets of any kind. His share of the bar he presented with a bow to Miss Cynthia. "Swedes to the sweed!" Dr. Hodler quoted, over the hand he cupped to his mouth he gave Soby a penetrating look. Behind it, he used a piece of the tinfoil he had peeled from the chocolate like dental floss, to clean between his front teeth.

"My dear—" Miss Throop said, a napkin to her lips, "if I were you I would present it to Signor Pignata."

"If I were *you*, Aunt Winnie," the girl replied, "I would too."

Without perceptibly flinching, Miss Throop smiled. The veined lids of her eyes were like transparent leaves. The wars of women, Soby observed, as if watching a crucial skirmish, featured internal bleeding, the surface reserved for the wars of men. Miss Cynthia arose, the napkin full of tidbits for Aschenbach spilling to the floor, followed by charms from the unfastened bracelet on her wrist. Dr. Hodler, Soby and Herr Holzapfel pushed their chairs back at the same moment, but Herr Holzapfel collided with the chair of Fraulein Kretschmar seated directly behind him. She too was rising, and it was Herr Holzapfel who remained in his seat.

"Setz dich!" she said, using the familiar form, but with something like authority in her voice. Although only second in command, it was Fraulein Kretschmar who wore the Wandervogel whistle, the pitch-pipe, and under her voluminous skirt, the pants. She did the mending, she called the tunes, she sang the loudest, she played the B flat recorder, and from her bag of emergency materials Miss Cynthia had been supplied with her Wandervogel outfit—most of it rather large. Wandervogel with personal problems came to Fraulein Kretschmar for aspirin, sulfa-capsules, and candid advice.

In this present crisis Fraulein Kretschmar's voice reassured them all that accidents would happen— the soothing monologue of a clucking hen.

From where he sat—Soby had sat down when he saw so many standing—all that he saw of both Frauleins were their extremely contrasting bottoms, a lean and fat hog eating from the same trough. Miss Cynthia was the first to stand up, a blurred radiance in her throat and face. Fraulein Kretschmar, her dirty tan a mottled color, begged the Damen und Herren alike to sit down. Herr Holzapfel, so long getting up, remained standing. Against orders? No, it merely took time for orders to penetrate. Fraulein

Kretschmar wagged her finger at him, as if she meant it to be amusing, but Herr Konrad Holzapfel did not smile. No, he stood like a dancing bear for whom the music has stopped. Between them there was surely more than met the eye, but what met the eye was more than enough. Down he sat. The girl gripped by the arm, her thighs impressed with the cane bottom of the chair seat, Fraulein Kretschmar marched her off. Did something need mending, or was that an example of Fraulein Kretschmar's foresight? A little bit of this Nausicaa business went a long way. As a Wandervogel, Fraulein Kretschmar had it under control.

Was it by way of distraction that Dr. Hodler tapped his spoon on his glass, invoking silence, rising from his chair for the second time? His resemblance to Goethe was not striking, but there were other and stranger lovers, mature and well-seasoned, who came to Soby's mind. Gustave Aschenbach, for example, would have worn such a smoking jacket, the satin lapels bearing the imprints of his shapely hands. The silk shirt dated from another time, and another neck. The hand he raised, then let fall to hook the finger in his vest, had a perceptible tremor when it stroked his face. With the meal over the touch of color in his cheeks was less artificial, but he had lost some of the carmine from his lips.

With Herr Perkheimer's permission, he said, he wanted to make an announcement. Those who had missed his photographic lecture and demonstration of the morning, would have another chance to consult Herr Perkheimer in the afternoon. Dr. Hodler advised all interested parties to be there. In his opinion Herr Perkheimer was the first to bring light to the camera obscura. His approach was simple. To take *no* picture rather than one that had been taken before. A hard saying, since it might well lead to the retirement of the camera. One saw, it seemed, only what had been seen so many times before. In this connection Dr. Hodler would welcome those who would like to join tomorrow's excursion, by foot, to what was believed to be Nausicaa's beach. Where else might one more profitably begin a search for the true Greece?

With somewhat strained attention Soby had followed the gist of Dr. Hodler's remarks, his eyes on Herr Holzapfel's impassive face. Slow to emerge, as in a darkroom solution, had been the expression of a tricked bird dog—the bird gone, but the taste of the feathers fresh in his mouth. It crossed Soby's mind that Herr Holzapfel was one of nature's triumphs: a perfectly scaled metaphor of the obvious. The *Rise of Man* in one impressively scaled figure, Ur-mensch to the eyes, a suggestion of Spate-mensch above the ears. Being obvious, he was unfathomable. The simple fact was the hardest to grasp.

The chair Fraulein Kretschmar had just vacated moved as if by an invisible hand. Soby, along with those facing the portholes, leaned forward as if to peer out. The white sky gave way, like a rising curtain, to the white capped sea. Just as they had leaned forward they now tipped back as if to get away. An empty bottle tipped over. Cups rocked in their saucers, silver on the plates.

What had happened? Merely a touch of the open sea. They were crossing—Dr. Hodler put up a calming hand to reassure them—the Adriatic from Italy to Greece, in a boat not much larger than the one that had taken Caesar to Cleopatra. They should be grateful. In just such a boat one should sail for Greece. Better yet if the men among them had a seat at the oars! Dr. Hodler squared his rounded shoulders as if he was about to be summoned, but a slight pitch of the boat dropped him to his seat.

"My dear—" Miss Throop began, but she was interrupted by the rise of Miss Kollwitz, a quartered pear, peeled, on the plate she extended toward Soby. Before taking his seat at the oars, would he deliver the pear to Signor Pignata? In the opinion of Miss Kollwitz an empty stomach—at sea—was worse than a full one. In case one had to, there should be something in it one could throw up.

"Might I quote you, my dear?" Miss Throop inquired. Miss Kollwitz had no time for banter. Another errand of mercy—the scraps for Aschenbach that Miss Cynthia had failed to deliver—she wrapped in her napkin, adding a safe-type bone. Miss Throop went along with her to avoid a scene. Soby remained to smoke his pipe, sip his coffee, and eat one-quarter of the pear. Herr Holzapfel, his head tilted like a badly repaired statue, dozed off with the *angst* of an outwitted bloodhound on his huge face.

Signor Pignata did not look up to see who had entered. He sat on his bunk, his head in his hands, but the long fingers parted so that his eyes spied on the object against the wall. The portrait of Primavera sat, as Miss Cynthia might, on the armless chair, her eyes level with his own. Did he feel an inspiration? Had he made up his mind about the mouth? In the porthole light the goldleaf smile dazzled like the harness in the mail order catalogues overpowered the shadowy horses. The mouth, lip sketched over lip, seemed to suggest that it was speaking, the expression changing each time Soby blinked. Holding the tray with its peeled pear, already discolored, the coffee with the lipstick smear on its rim, Soby stood half in, half out of the room, not wanting to interrupt. For his part, Signor Pignata let him stand. His raw silk pants were neither off nor on. They hung below his knees, as far as he had managed since the narrow cuff would not go over his shoes, and his shoes, the laces knotted, were still on his feet. At that point he had glanced up at the portrait to see the girl looking at him. Little wonder he had put his hands to his face. "Per favore—" Soby said, crossing the room to put the tray on little Perkheimer's bunk. In the porthole the sea rang hollow as it did in a large shell. The smell of the pear disturbed him more than the roll of the boat.

"Domani," he said, "Corfu domani!" to turn Signor Pignata's attention to other matters. How did he take that? Behind Soby's back he laughed. A musical, strained, villainous, operatic laugh. This was followed by several terms new to Soby, but they needed no translation. Sounds pronounced with relish, universal as the hiccup, the hiss of breaking wind. In case there was some doubt in the matter these words were accompanied by gestures, a movement of the lips as if rinsing out the mouth. So much for women. One in particular. Propped on his knees, his elbows wide, Signor Pignata leaned forward to make the wide-mouthed, AHH sound of the caged tiger at its trainer. A curious sight, his pants down, crouched as if for other matters, Signor Pignata, his fangs exposed, expressed his contempt.

From behind the sliding panel, a little weary, Miss Throop spoke as from a sealed tomb.

"My dear Soby," she said, "I hope you are grateful."

"Grateful?" he repeated, curious.

"One is only young once," she said, "heaven be praised." Another word, needing no translation, Signor Pignata pronounced with syllabic slowness. The face in the portrait might have read it on his lips. It seemed to enhance the mocking curve of her smile.

"Eat," Soby said, "you must eat!" and put the quartered pear on the berth beside him, then turned to face the portrait to the wall. On the reverse side, however, something had been roughly sketched in. A fish? No, a mermaid. It seemed to be crossed with golden bars of light. Only when he stepped away did Soby recognize the smile. No face at all, merely a curving mouth, the lips parted as if to sip a film of goldleaf from the sea. This smile was neither mocking nor ambiguous. A siren, she openly leered at Soby. Quickly he turned it back to face the wall, as Signor Pignata, slapping his bare knees, rolled over on his back like a cat with his paws in the air. The plate slipped off on the floor, but the slices of pear stuck like snails to his jacket collar. Had he been tippling? Nothing more potent than a lover's revenge. "Prima %$&*#%!" he roared, lashing her with words. Soby left him coiled on his back, pawing the air.

"Where *is* the child?" Miss Throop called. "I must say she might adore him if she could hear it."

Where was she? Damen und Herren occupied the lounge, the chairs on the deck. At the fantail, straddle-legged, a score or more windwhipped Herren formed a semi-circle around Dr. Hodler, whose broad back sheltered little Perkheimer. He held his camera gun to his shoulder, sighting down the barrel. At what was he aiming? On the horizon nothing but white caps were to be seen. He appeared to be shooting at the invisible coast of Greece. Hatless, his cornsilk hair blowing, held to the deck by the weight of his cameras and gadgets, Herr Perkheimer aimed and fired at what could not be seen. The Herren stood attentive, waiting for the scene to materialize. Soby too waited, but rested his eyes on the canvas covering one of the lifeboats, an end of it blown loose, flapping like a sail. Beneath it, just their eyes showing, the blonde heads of Wandervogel huddled out of the wind, their mouths full of windblown song. Among them Fraulein Kretschmar, and Nausicaa of the one white arm. In the shadow of the canvas her mouth seemed full of golden coins.

Soby turned, a hand gripping his arm, to see the tam-o-shanter'd head of Miss Kollwitz. The pom-pom dangling on its cord whipped in the wind. She wore a button sweater, of her own knitting, one pocket with a pear, the other wadded with tissue, both hanging just below the reach of her short arms. What did she want? To measure his *other* arm. The left was frequently shorter, as he must know. From her reticule she took the sleeve that one day, God willing, would be a sweater, moved windward so it would flap the length of his arm.

"Look here!" she cried, pounding on his chest, "Look, look, you are on fire!"

Soby threw up his arms, like wings, to make room

for Miss Kollwitz, fire fighter. With her pocket guide
to Greece she slapped the front of his jacket where
his blowing pipe ashes had burned several new small
holes.

"Did you not smell?" she cried, sniffing the air. Up
where Soby inhaled there was no touch of smoke. It
was all down on her level, blowing into her eyes.
"After dinner I mend it, you hear?" She seemed to
feel he had lost more than his hearing. Using the book
she slapped him in places where there seemed to be no
fire. "I don't like it, you hear?" she said, but whether
it was the fire, in particular, or just life in general
was not quite clear. She continued to slap him in
places where no smoke nor fire was apparent, but
might, at any moment, break out. Flecked with oil
soot, her lips chapped, the small hairless face of
Miss Kollwitz bore witness that a woman's worry was
never done. With a seaman's squint she scanned
the white capped sea where Caesar, mature and well-
seasoned, had proved himself as big a ninny as the
rest of them. What she saw out there did not seem to
please her. Not one bit.

fourteen | Soby, the sun of Greece in his eyes, squinted at a prospect laden with history but felt only the pressure of current events. Signor Pignata had been up at dawn to pack his bag, tie up his equipment, and inquire of little Perkheimer when the next boat for Venice left Corfu. A week, he had answered. And what boat was that? The one he was on. In six days it would stop in Corfu on its way back. It had taken Soby, the ladies, and Dr. Hodler to persuade him that it might be wiser to stay on the boat, than sit waiting for it.

Flanked by Miss Kollwitz, in her tam-o-shanter, and Miss Throop in the shade of her parasol, Soby watched the Wandervogel, male and female, the sleeves of sweaters looped at their waists, go down the gangplank at the heels of Herr Holzapfel, unmistakably golden the fleece on his head and his enormous thighs. Fraulein Kretschmar, her bosoms lobbing, one hand in her blouse front pulling up a bra strap, wore a skirt imprinted with the flags of all nations, a few of which had run. A pouch containing aspirin and a kit for snakebites hung on a strap from her shoulder: the dirty tan on her legs called attention to the white hollow at the back of her knees. She was followed by Miss Cynthia, a long-limbed colt harnessed to a draft horse, her hair gathered so it wagged like a pony tail. Her short-sleeved blouse exposed the healing vaccination scar. She carried a red plastic purse containing gum, lipstick, and a pocket radio.

Dr. Hodler, a folded kerchief protecting the collar of his belted jacket, wore the knickers buckled to reveal his shapely calves. One hand kept the binoculars from bobbing on his paunch. A panama straw, limp as cloth and the color of old newspaper, cast a shadow on the pier like a flapping parasol. Whether little Perkheimer brought up the rear of one safari, or led off another, was not clear from Soby's position on the deck.

Outweighing, if not outnumbering the Wandervogel, a line of Herren, with several sturdy Damen, hung with pouches, cameras, and several water bottles, were prepared to penetrate the photographic ash that had buried Greece. Two wore lederhosen, one a pair of blue jeans cut off at the knee, one a pith helmet, several carried bowie knives attached to their belts, one a geologist's pick. Single file, Holzapfel led his charges through the clutter of a used car lot— or so the scene appeared from the deck of the *Hephaistos*.

Fifteen or twenty cars of the sort from which used parts were taken, or new parts added since they had become antiques. Touring cars, with and without windshields, some with a soft blue exhaust, since the motors were running, the drivers having learned it was not wise to let them stop. An elderly man, one who had learned to wear everything he owned and leave nothing behind him, shouted directions through a small megaphone. Soby gathered he exhorted the chauffeurs to be calm. Not all the passengers would go off on foot—no, there were many who would ride. A chauffeur with a drayman's cap, a jacket with brass buttons, stood up in his car to flag his arms at Soby—he seemed to be beside himself at the sight of a long lost friend. He knew Soby? No, he merely knew his *business*. He leaned in to the back of the car to show that the seat had springs. Also a top that would go up if it rained. The wheels were of wire, the radiator wore an ornament to indicate the heat of the water, and in both fenders there were dents once occupied by tires. As Soby nodded, smiling, he used both hands to squeeze the red bulb of the horn.

"Look here!" Miss Kollwitz cried, "do not overdo it!"

Did she mean the horn? No, she meant the figure in white suede sport shoes bringing up the rear of the line on the gangplank. Signor Pignata looked every inch the sensitive, consumptive artist: he carried a sketch pad, a stool with collapsible legs. Neither the Wandervogel expedition, nor the motor excursion, appealed to him. He was in no condition for the former, and the latter, on narrow winding mountain roads, merely brought to the land what he left boats to get away from: the rock and the roll, the smell of oil, the sight of Damen und Herren sharing picnic lunches.

For the shore tour Miss Kollwitz wore her green tam-o-shanter, a brown wool scarf long enough to fold under her armpits, a plaid raincoat, with a hood attached in case it rained. In the pockets her pocket guide to Greece, a banana and a pear. A parasol of pale green silk hung from a cord in the fold of Miss Throop's right arm, two long pins with eyes like cats held her wig to her crownless hat. Black kid leather shoes, laced higher than the ankle she exposed on the gangplank, were tipped with snap-on rubbers. The car tilted as Soby gave her a hoist to the running board.

A spare rear seat being available, Soby took it to avoid overcrowding. It set him a little high, due to his height, so that members of the motor excursion gathered around the car thinking he might be the guide. He wore his corduroy cap, with the strap adjusted, the tweed jacket Miss Kollwitz had mended with the yarn that proved to be quite noticeable in the light. Dr. Hodler had suggested a cane but Soby had left it at the breakfast table, the handle hooked to the back of his chair. While they waited for the caravan to start moving Miss Kollwitz stuffed small wads of cotton in her ears, advising Soby, whose ears were bigger, to do the same. Miss Throop had fortified herself with two grains of aspirin, one of neutral spirits.

The city of Corfu, which the guide advised them had suffered considerable war damage, reminded Soby, as he told them, of Mexico. Shuttered windows, faded colors, an air of apathy. Miss Kollwitz, the cotton in her ears, begged him to speak up louder. The chauffeur, driving with one hand, waving at the points of interest with the other, repeated each observation in German, Italian and demotic French. When Soby questioned him in French he said, "O-kay, you bet."

The countryside was surprisingly lush and beautiful. Along the black-top road well-fed peasants worked in spring-green fields or held plump, waving children. Miss Kollwitz shouted that what they smelled on the exhaust-blue air were raisins drying. Olive, orange and lemon trees crowded the slopes. On the curves they could see the winding caravan behind them, the tranquil sea, and snug in its harbor the SS *Hephaistos*. The Wandervogel were no longer in sight. The beach of Ulysses? The chauffeur took his hand from the wheel to fling it backward, over the mountains. His eyes, however, remained on the diesel-like plume of the car ahead. Now they were climbing, he leaned forward as if to give the motor some assistance, his eyes on the heat indicator on the radiator. Climbing faster than they were was the column of red. Up ahead, somewhere, a blowing horn stuck, they swung wide on a curve to pass a car with a tire flat, the gentleman with the megaphone rising to shout and wave them on. Behind them, now, was the point of no returning, the red could go no higher, and the road turned black where the motor hissed and bled to death. A sound so familiar Soby seemed to smell not drying raisins, but steaming alcohol, blackening the road like rain and rising in a cloud of steam from under the hood.

"Look here!" Miss Kollwitz cried, leaning forward to grip the seat back, but the worst was over. Up ahead where the grade levelled off, they coasted to a stop. In the shade of a tree droning with bees they sat silent in a cloud of steam, the motor hissing like a dragon at the pedlar who approached. He supplied Soby and Miss Throop with a beverage, but Miss Kollwitz, her cheeks puffed, warned them that the altitude itself had all but deafened her. Half shouting, she advised them to go easy on the native liquids, and with the cotton bulging from her ears peeled, quartered, and ate her pear.

The Villa Achillaeum, built in 1891 by the Italian, Carito, for the late Empress of Austria, had been sold in 1911 to Wilhelm the Second, Emperor of Germany. Miss Kollwitz paused in her reading to lid her eyes, removing a pear seed from her lips. Of pseudo-Greek style, it had been decorated with more luxury and profusion than taste. She read on, while Soby removed their lunch boxes from the front seat, the tops spattered with rusty water that had geysered from the radiator. Behind them, the caravan of cars formed a line that disappeared around the curve. Damen und Herren sat in the droning shade, waiting for what next. Since they had passed their guide on the way up, helping his driver to change a tire, Soby suggested that rather than sit and wait they might browse around. The huge gate to the Villa was closed, but a footpath curved about the summit on which the Villa had been erected. It opened out on sunning slopes of olive trees and curved away in the direction of the sea. Why didn't they follow it to some attractive prospect and eat their lunch? Miss Kollwitz thought it a fine idea since she had never cared much for Wilhelm the Second. Miss Throop, likewise, had not come to Greece to look at ruins she might have seen on Long Island.

With the lunches, Soby led the way. Miss Throop's shawl was inclined to snag in the vines that trailed from the Villa wall, but the delays gave her a moment to catch her breath. Wisps of her auburn hair crossed on her forehead like veins in weathered marble, a warm scent rose from her body that attracted the bees. Miss Kollwitz fanned them away with her book. Below them a she-goat, hung with a bell, stood

poised on a stump like an ornamental corkscrew—
Miss Kollwitz hissed them quiet to hear the tinkling
of cattle bells, the bleating of a lamb. The path
dipped, curving toward the sea, then rose up a flight
of steps cut out of the rock to a bower, a flowered
alcove with stone benches and miniature columns,
the vine-tangled archways framing the view. They
stood apart, as if for more air. Miss Throop's shawl
had darkened where it clung to her shoulders. The
hairless brows of Miss Kollwitz glistened as if with a
film of oil. Soby had words appropriate to the occasion, but the climb had left him winded. The drone of
bees seemed a dubbed-in sound effect for the sweet-
smelling air. The prospect looked toward Greece,
lost in a haze, but also took in Corfu, the Shrine of
the Canoni with its jewel-like monastery, and a wide
expanse of pond-tranquil sea. Miss Throop was the
first to speak. She begged him to please put the
lunches down. Before Soby complied a sound from
Miss Kollwitz, stopped by a hand clapped to her
mouth, led them to make a half turn, standing with
their backs to the view.

They faced a formal garden, informally gone to
seed. A nude figure of bronze, twice-life-size, even if
one thought of Herr Holzapfel, stood on a marble
base itself ten or fifteen feet high. A Greek unquestionably, thanks to his helmet and shield, and the familiar aspect of nude physical perfection ornamenting bookends, lamps, trophies, and awards for excel-

lence. Exposure had blackened the bronze, but the base had bleached to a drugstore marble, white as the sandblasted stone of a city library. On it was engraved—

A C H I L L E S

To the Greatest Greek
from
The Greatest German

"No, no!" Miss Kollwitz cried, "Goethe is greater!" She turned to Miss Throop for confirmation. Speechless, Miss Throop scanned the ruin for a bench. On the one behind her, beside the box lunches, she lowered herself. To keep the bees off, as well as the sun, she let the parasol rest on her shoulder, a filtered light tinting her face a marble-green. From beneath it she smiled like an overripe, comical valentine.

As if learning the parts of speech, she said, "Goethe, goether, goethest, my dear, which is it?"

Soby would have spoken but the face of a Damen, streaked with cobweb and beet colored, peered up at him from the steps leading down to the path. At such an angle Soby had seen it, or one like it, manning the steamer chairs on the *Hephaistos*.

"Bitte?" she croaked, "ist hier frei?" as if she peered into a train compartment.

"Ja-ja," Soby replied, his head nodded. She came up, gripping two lunches, to stand in the bower like a cage. The jacket she had taken off was folded across her arm. Two more, one a Herren with glasses, showed their heads, then climbed to stand beside her. Still another somewhere below called, "Gibt's platz?"

In the alcove there was kein platz, but platz there was in the garden. The Herren stepped forward to gaze at the statue, the Damen trailed along. "Noch platz?" Another Damen, elderly, her sleeves rolled, fanning her face with a piece of lunch box. Yes, there was still place, but for how many? A Herren in lederhosen and heavy ribbed half hose blocked the stairs while he steadied for a snapshot. Soby, leaning over the wall in order to see down the path behind him, saw a solid line of Damen und Herren leading back to the road. What had happened? The Deutsches volk had tagged along, following the leader. Without comment Miss Throop moved the lunches so there was room for Soby on the bench beside her. The parasol, with the movement of her shoulders, let off the pressure of her laughter. On they came, crowding the tangled paths, the weedy lanes of the garden, standing in a respectful arc around the base of the monument. There was no laughter. Those with guidebooks read the descriptions aloud. The whirrr of winding camera shutters blended with the insects. Soby occupied himself with the knotted cord on a lunch box, opening it to see the pear, the pickle, and the unwrapped sandwiches. The pear he gave to Miss

Kollwitz, who peeled it with her back to the Damen, the Herren, and Achilles, her gaze across the noontide listless sea to the mountains of Greece. Bees gathered on the parings, the sticky blade of her knife, and with some apprehension Miss Throop, coolly sucking on the pickle, watched her pop the quarters into her mouth. About her head, like a hive crowned with a tam-o-shanter, they spun a humming web as if she stood there napping on her feet.

The voice of the guide, tri-lingual, spoke to them from a cornice where the stucco was peeling, a slotted window framing his megaphone. The encampment in the garden stirred, opened lunch boxes were shut. Napkins, crusts, and scraps were picked up, a moment of indecision ended when two lines forming were known to be one. Miss Kollwitz took her place in the line to the left. Miss Throop, feeling no desire to know the Kaiser Wilhelm any better, begged Soby not to deprive himself of such knowledge just because of her. Soby preferred to sit in the alcove and smoke his pipe. Her finger wagging, Miss Kollwitz warned him to be more careful with his ashes. This time she would not be on hand to put the fire out. Miss Throop sat so that she faced the empty garden, the weeds trampled in the paths around the statue of Achilles: Soby turned on the bench so that he faced the island view.

"What do you see, my dear—" she gave her parasol a twirl. "Achilles sulking in his tent?"

Soby did not smile: his gaze had drifted toward the other end of the end of the spectrum, Ulysses Holzapfel sporting with his maidens on Nausicaa's beach.

"If you mean Signor Pignata, I can't say I blame him. If she had so little interest—"

"My dear, she has always had little interest. If the interest is giving out it is his, not hers. I'm afraid the interest came from her Aunt Winifred Throop."

"Hasn't that given out too?"

From her skirt, spread out on her lap, Miss Throop plucked the seeds and burrs she had gathered along the path. With an exaggerated girlish gesture she tossed them to the wind, like petals plucked from a daisy. "Don't you think Signor Pignata is an ass, my dear?"

"Whatever I think," Soby said, "I didn't persuade him to come on this wild goose chase—"

Miss Throop put up her small freckled hand to stop him, blowing the seed she held with a puff of air. "A wild goose chase?" she repeated. "You think it is?"

"It certainly is for *him*," Soby said with some conviction. Then he added, "As well as some of the others."

"A wild goose—" Miss Throop pronounced the word with her pleated lips puckered, as if cooing.

"Her mother would love it."

"Too bad her mother is not here to enjoy it," Soby replied. He puffed a cloud of smoke and ashes from his pipe bowl.

"I've been thinking that—" Miss Throop tipped to dust the ashes from the sleeve of Soby's jacket.

"One wild goose at a time is enough?" said Soby.

Like a bird, Miss Throop's small hand plucked at his sleeve. "There's not much to a goose, my dear," she observed, then, "—just what part of the bird would you like me to save you?"

The match Soby cupped to the bowl of his pipe did not conceal his face. Inhaling the cloud of smoke he had just exhaled, he coughed. "That's very kind of you," he said, fanning the air, "but goose, wild goose, has never been to my taste. There's always the chance of biting down on some of the shot."

Considering the situation—he was flabbergasted— Soby thought his quick recovery worth noting. Miss Throop, however, seemed indifferent to what had been said. Her hands crossed in her lap, she put her feet out before her, like a child with new shoes. Did she expect Soby to comment on her trim ankles, laced in the pumps like a corset? "He says I have *an intellishunt fooot!*" She put her hands to her lips, giving the parasol a twirl.

"Signor Pignata?" Soby stood up as if he could bear to sit no longer.

"*Him?*" Miss Throop rocked from side to side,

swinging her legs, as if amused by the idea. "You think it is a woman's foot he has eyes for?"

"I have not given it much thought," said Soby. Without noting the time he gave a twist to the stem of his watch. No thought at all seemed necessary for him to recall, without prodding, the sallow-faced cabin steward with the finger-width brow, glancing up from the paperback volume of Soby's. *An intellishunt foooot.* Was that the culture he mined from books? The flat back of his bushy head blocked the corridor of Soby's vision, his pants cuffs rolled to show that he wore no socks.

"My dear, you should be flattered. We've all taken your advice."

"My *advice*—?" Soby queried.

"Everyman his own Pygmalion," replied Miss Throop, "if you don't care too much about what sort of Pig."

Soby wore a totally baffled expression but to no effect. "To give credit where it is due, it was Miss Cynthia's idea before it was mine."

Miss Throop smiled as if it had been her, and not Miss Cynthia, who had sat for the portrait. The heat, perhaps, gave her face a healthy glow.

"My dear," she said, extending her hand, "do you feel that youth is wasted on the young?"

Soby bowed, his heels together, in the manner of Signor Pignata. The plump freckled hand of Miss Throop he raised to his lips.

"I've always thought so—" he replied.

"It's comforting, isn't it, my dear, to know that some of us are old enough to enjoy it?" As she arose the twirling parasol concealed her face. In its green net two bees, droning like hornets, crossed the empty garden with her to where Miss Kollwitz, framed in the door of the Villa, waved her pocket guide.

"Look here!" she cried. "They are leaving! It is time!"

The caravan had departed by the time they got back to the car. A delay of ten or fifteen minutes followed while Soby sat at the wheel, manipulating the spark, and the chauffeur, his hat on the fender, spun the crank. Once—he took pains to explain—it had knocked his hat off. He made a gesture with his hand to show the crank passing his eyes. In his gaze, his wide teeth-clenched grin, Soby sensed the humor of desperation, ready to backfire at some whimsy of the spark. It was Soby who inquired, just in passing, if he had added water to the radiator, to which the answer was no, since the return trip was mostly downgrade.

The delay—it came to twenty minutes since he allowed the car to coast on the grades—took up more than half the time they were allotted for the Canoni, where tea would be served while they sat and enjoyed the view. Miss Throop considered it a small loss, since a member of her family, one who painted on china, had already spoiled it for her with water colors so well described by Dr. Hodler. Confident she would never see it again, she had painted all of Greece on her honeymoon.

Why didn't they, Soby suggested, take a quick run over the mountain to see how Dr. Hodler's expedition was getting along? The breeze flapping her hat concealed the glance Miss Throop intended for Soby. From Miss Kollwitz there was no comment. Deprived of her tea she remembered her banana. The chauffeur, however, even when plied with a tip, merely wagged his head. There was no road for a car. One could go little more than half way. To go half way made no sense at all but Soby thought it better than nothing. From the mountains there might be a view of the beach.

The value of the bill Soby passed to the chauffeur he did not not realize until he had released it: he grinned like a bandit, tooting his horn at everyone they passed. His delight, however, led him to forget about the radiator water. In the mountains behind the city, trailed by a half a dozen boys, one of whom hitched a ride on the fender, they came to a bucking, dry-gasping stop. The view was splendid, a fine view of the city, the *Hephaistos* snug in the harbor, as well as the Canoni, the road lined with the waiting excursion cars. Miss Kollwitz, her breath scented with banana, leaned over Soby's shoulder to point out the hikers, five or six blonde heads going along a trail on the canyon's far side. Wandervogel, unquestionably. Miss Kollwitz squeezed the red bulb of the horn as she waved. Farther back on the trail there were others, not all of them Wandervogel, the sun glinting on the chrome and lenses of their cameras. Not visible, however, was the huge figure of Herr Holzapfel. Nor the colt-legged, loose limbed Nausicaa. In the random retreat of the expedition Soby sensed a non-Wandervogelish disorder. What had happened? Where was Dr. Hodler and little Perkheimer?

"Do you see our goose?" Miss Throop inquired, placing her glasses on the bruised ridge of her nose. No, Soby did not. Nor the ample lobbing charms of Fraulein Kretschmar. Up ahead, however, where the cobbled street narrowed to grass ridged path, a horse-drawn cab, the horse at a slow clop, came into view. The driver flicked the tassel of his whip, toying with the flies. Room had to be made for the cab to pass by letting the boys push the car backwards. Unable to ride in *anything* backwards, Miss Kollwitz was allowed to climb out. Until the cab came alongside they were unable to see Dr. Hodler, sprawled low in the seat, with his right leg hoisted to the seat rail. The shoe was off, the ankle swollen tight in the heavy sock. It resembled nothing so much as a padded club. On his back, the sun in his face, Dr. Hodler's eyes were closed until Soby signalled the driver to halt.

"In heaven's name!" Miss Throop cried. "The poor dear!"

In his characteristic manner Dr. Hodler raised his hand, enjoining silence. His coat was folded as a pillow beneath his head. His eyes were brighter than usual, due, perhaps, to the burn on the eyelids, but his grimace indicated that even the smile cost him some pain. His lips were dry and chapped. A creamy suntan lotion had caked on his nose. One arm white as a woman's, the sunburned one he raised to caution them not to panic. No, it was nothing. Nothing more than a little sprain. A short cut suggested by Herr Perkheimer had been inadvisable. One of the Wandervogel had gone for help, which proved to be the cab in which he was riding. And how had *their* day gone? He beamed a cracked, grimacing smile.

Their day had gone fine, just fine, Soby allowed—but how about Dr. Hodler's expedition? That he couldn't say since they had gone on without him. Little Perkheimer would have news of it. His photographs would tell the story that Dr. Hodler, unhappily, had missed.

And Nausicaa? Soby would have asked if Miss Kollwitz, familiar with sprains, had not diagnosed Dr. Hodler's as a severe one, that should be treated by a doctor as soon as possible. So he was transferred against his wishes from the cab to the car. There was no water in the radiator, but from where they had stopped it was all downgrade. Soby took the seat beside the driver, Miss Kollwitz moved to the spare where the swollen foot of Dr. Hodler rode in her lap. Thanks to the boys who had followed them out of town the car was turned about and headed down the grade.

In town there were doctors, but not, it seemed, during the siesta. While they discussed the matter, parked where the chauffeur could fill his radiator at a public fountain, the warning whistle of the *Hephaistos* could be heard. Was there a doctor on board? There would have to be. On their way to the harbor they passed Wandervogel powdered with dust, shaggy as satyrs, eating grapes as they sauntered along, singing their songs. Two horse-drawn cabs, crowded with lame members of the photographic expedition, raced them the last hundred yards to the pier. Crowded with caravan cars, souvenir pedlars, and two or three hundred Damen und Herren, there was not room on the dock for the car with the ailing Dr. Hodler. He had to be assisted—largely by Soby, with the advice of Miss Kollwitz—through the crowd and up the gangplank to the deck. The first mate, supported by the steward with the finger-width brow, a hand at his armpit, nodded amiably, repeating oui, oui, oui at Soby's requests for a doctor until two members of the crew came to bear Dr. Hodler away.

For air, Soby remained on the deck. Herr Holzapfel, his huge shoes dangling from his neck by their laces, waded along the shore with Fraulein Kretschmar and a remnant of the Wandervogel. His lederhosen were wet. He had the sallow look, in spite of his tan, of an oversoaked skin-diver. And Nausicaa? Soby almost overlooked her as she came up the gangplank. Her wet hair hung lank to soak the shoulders of her blouse. A rill of water glistened in the fuzz on her thighs. She came toward him head down, eating ice cream, her scalp bone-white where her hair was parted, a film of chocolate cream coating her long tongue. Where were her shoes, her purse, her pocket radio? She was preceded by two Damen, in souvenir straw hats, followed by one Herren and three shaggy Wandervogel. Was the *Hephaistos* some species of Ark? Was Soby there to identify the surviving animals? Little pigs, big pigs, shaggy goats, fat hens, and one wild goose with an ice cream sandwich, the cat-like tongue honing the rim like a potter's wheel. She came toward him without lifting her eyes, absorbed in her work.

"And how was Nausicaa's swim?" he said, smiling.

The mouth that Signor Pignata despaired of painting widened as if she had hooked her fingers at the corners. But what had changed? The upper lip exposed the chocolate film on her teeth. But the familiar mocking smile no longer had its golden lining. Did Soby look startled? His pipe hung loose at his mouth.

"Your braces—?" he said. She curled her lips to show him they were missing. Gone. A film of ice cream in their place.

"And that's not *all* I lost," she said, lifting her arms like wings to show him they were empty. Gone, too, were several buttons from her blouse. "But *look!*" she cried, and popped the last of the ice cream sandwich into her mouth, crunched down on it, then stared at him happily, without a grimace. "Look doll, no pain!" she cried, and threw up her hands. Miss Kollwitz, coming up the plank behind her, took her firmly by the hand that was still sticky, leaving Soby with no more than the ring of the word *doll* in his ears, the scent of ice cream in his nose, the taste of goldleaf in his mouth.

fifteen | A wind that smelled of Africa, in Fraulein Kretschmar's opinion, the enervating sirocco, left particles of soot in her blonde eyebrows and smeared the wings of her porous nose. In profile Fraulein Kretschmar was generously handsome, with a fine brow and rather small ears, but viewed from the front—as Soby was obliged to view her—the face split into unequal halves, each with an eye, one nostril, a common mouth. One of Fraulein Kretschmar's eyes was that of the sly fox in the fable, upturned to watch the clustered grapes. Pins taken from her hair were stored in the fold between her breasts, an effect hardly calculated to put comrade Wandervogel at their ease. Speaking in udder confidence, as she said, Fraulein Kretschmar thought it wise to tell him that the American Fraulein, although charming, seemed to be ill-informed concerning the ways of European men. She was pretty in that girlish, immature way older men like Dr. Hodler were apt to find attractive. Fraulein Kretschmar did not want to be misunderstood. In the States teen-age girls had a freedom that was not customary in Europe. Fortunately. For her own peace of mind, as well as everybody else's, Fraulein Kretschmar had cultivated her acquaintance with the object of keeping things under control. Unfortunately, on a day long excursion—with Dr. Hodler among others to look after—she had not been able to be everywhere at the same time. An incident had occurred, or almost occurred—the reports naturally varied—shortly after they had reached Nausicaa's beach. From what she could gather Dr. Hodler wanted a scene with Herr Holzapfel, as Ulysses, dragged from the sea by Miss Cynthia, as Nausicaa. Herr Holzapfel had been ashamed to admit that he did not swim. In spite of his great strength he was frightened by the sea. Had Miss Cynthia sensed that? One never knew. Although an excellent swimmer herself she had pretended to be in trouble. The reports varied. Some say she took advantage of him. Some he of her. In either instance he had almost drowned. It had taken Fraulein Kretschmar—a trained swimmer and a lifeguard—along with several Wandervogel to get him ashore. The scene had certainly been more dramatic than planned. Nothing serious had occurred, fortunately, except for the loss of Miss Cynthia's braces—a small thing when one considered what had been at stake. She might very well have lost what could not be replaced.

Fraulein Kretschmar's recital left a froth on her lips she did not trouble to lick off. Her concern was for them all—a large number if one added Dr. Hodler to thirty-three Wandervogel, a child like Miss Cynthia, plus the fact that Herr Holzapfel could not swim. As experience had proven, he could not even float.

The day's excursion—Soby noted, as Fraulein Kretschmar left him—had cleaned the dirt from her feet and the cracked polish from her nails. White fingernail scratches brightened up the bites on her brown legs. A pedlar with scarves, stamped with scenes of Corfu, sold them to Damen who had gathered at the rail, passing them up attached to clothespins on a fishline. They tossed him Greek coins he caught in his upside-down parasol.

A draft that smelled of soap more than Africa, and of disinfectant more than soap, came toward Soby with the voice of Miss Kollwitz faint with hoarseness. The door to the cabin had been propped ajar. Her face in shadow, Miss Kollwitz leaned out to psst at him as he passed. He saw only the almost hairless crown of her head. Without a by-your-leave or comment she took him by the sleeve and drew him into the cabin. Miss Throop, her windburned face glistening with lotion, faced the mirror, her eyes closed, a towel wrapped like a turban about her head. Miss Cynthia sat in the shadow of an upper bunk. Through hair combed down over her face she peered at Soby as from a thicket, a small plastic comb snagged in the tangle at the back of her head. Miss Kollwitz waved a brush tufted with hair under Soby's nose.

"Look!" she hoarsely barked, "an outrage!" and turned to Miss Throop for confirmation.

What was? Soby looked toward the shower and said, "No hot water?" That hardly seemed likely since a film of steam smoked his glasses.

"No, no!" Miss Kollwitz slapped him with the brush. Peering down at her Soby had the impression of a child in her mother's nightgown.

"Something is missing?" Soby asked, since it seemed likely.

"That remains to be seen," Miss Throop replied, "all we have are the fingerprints at the moment." The girl's head bobbed, shook with a stifled sneeze.

"Look here!" croaked Miss Kollwitz, wagging the hairbrush.

"Show Watson the evidence, my dear," Miss Throop said.

Soby turned to see Miss Kollwitz thrust her hand through the girl's hair to the towel around her shoulders, folding back one corner to expose her bare arm.

"Will you lay off!" said the girl. "I'm not dead yet!"

She stepped back, speechless. On the girl's soft upper arm were faint bluish bands. "Both arms!" Miss Kollwitz barked, shaking her brush at Soby. Water from the bristles prickled his face.

"What happened?"

"For crying out loud," cried the girl, *"noth-ing hap-pent!"*

"That is *nothing?*" Miss Kollwitz put her nose within sniffing distance. Then she wheeled, still gripping the comb, and with her small hands tried to get a grip on Soby. "So that is nothing!" she cried, trying to shake him like a child.

"You should see *his* arm," the girl said.

It was strange how well Soby could. The massive limb with its crisp golden hair, the imprint of her vanished braces.

"Just what is missing is conjectural," Miss Throop intoned, "pending a more complete inventory. If swallowed, the brace is not a total loss. My own concern is more in the way of the intangibles."

The towel, perhaps, gave her mirrored image something of the look of a Rembrandt self-portrait.

"Talk! Talk! Talk!" Miss Kollwitz thumped her brush on the mattress of a bunk, dust rising. "Do we nothing but talk?"

"I understand he had something of a scare?" said Soby.

"Look here! They are already talking?"

"If you don't dry up," cried the girl, "I'll give you something to talk about!"

She rose from the bunk, thumping her head on the frame of the one overhead. Raising both hands to her head the towel slipped from her shoulders and there she stood, a lank-haired lady Godiva with little on but the bruises on her white arms. Miss Kollwitz made a sound as if punctured, her cheeks sucking in. Did she know she stood before them like Eve in a pair of soiled shorts? "You want something to talk about!" she said, "your big baboon is scared of more than the water. If he wasn't maybe there *would* be something to talk about!" She turned, showing her back with the faint outlines of her bra strap, the shorts dropping at her feet as she kicked them off, stepped into the shower. They heard the water come on, but it was cold, not hot. They heard her gasp, then yell "Cold as a witch's tit!"

Miss Kollwitz turned slowly, as if the room was dark, to face the eyes glowing in the corner. They closed as Aschenbach exposed his wide toothless mouth.

"How's mama's lover-boy?" Miss Throop hiccuped as she leaned forward to stroke the head of Aschenbach.

"Lover who?" The girl's wet face peered at Soby from the shower. Did she think it was *him?*

"I've always found the term more picturesque than accurate," Miss Throop observed.

"You *would!*" cried the girl.

A draft down the hall led the cabin door to drift open, thumping Soby, who stepped outside before carefully drawing it closed. The boat was moving. Behind the door of his own cabin the voice of Signor Pignata, in the shower, sang *Come Prima* with a fervor that left some doubt as to his meaning. The air in the cabin, up where Soby breathed it, was largely steam. The sound of steam escaping, however, came from little Perkheimer, sprawled on his bunk, his face down in a pillow he had tucked up around his ears.

*   *   *

Was he weeping? His small feet thumped the foot of the bed like a child with a tantrum. On Soby's bunk, like so much tangled harness, he had dropped his arsenal of camera equipment. Had the expedition failed? Had he failed to penetrate the layers of photographic ash? Soby opened the porthole near his head to get a little fresh air into the cabin. Ostrich-like, Perkheimer continued to conceal his head.

"Look here," Soby said, taking a cue from Miss Kollwitz, and placed his hand lightly on his shoulder. A tremor passed through his body, into Soby's arm. "Now, now—" Soby said, giving him a pat, as one corner of the pillow flattened out on the bunk, one large tear-magnified orb of little Perkheimer looked at him. Into the tissue Soby proffered he blew a wet nose. No sooner cleared, however, than he turned a masque-like face on Soby, the large eyes wet, the mouth in a wide, grinning leer.

"You're sick?"

His head nodded, up and down like a puppet's.

"Too much sun?" Soby suggested.

Little Perkheimer's tear streaked face was flushed, but it was not the sun. No, no. He wagged his head as if the brains might rattle. No, no. He put his face forward till Soby caught the scent of his hair oil. "Seek from laughing!" he said, then rolled over to face the wall. A little crazy, perhaps? Soby stared at the sea, light-smeared with every color but that of water. "Excuse, excuse—" Little Perkheimer rolled back to face Soby, his eyes swimming. "A choke, I have a little choke, yes?" He raised his head to check the door to the shower. Signor Pignata had stopped singing, but the shower drummed on the wall. "A little choke, yes," he repeated, and gave Soby the leer of a collaborator.

A little dirty choke? Was that what he meant? He curled a finger to beckon Soby closer. "No ruins, no broken columns, no broken statues, no peasants, no nursing babies, no goats, no—no nothing!" Little Perkheimer plopped his face into the pillow. The humor of it escaped Soby.

"Maybe no ruins," Soby said, "but there were goats and peasants."

"Yes, yes, all over! But no pick-churrrs!"

No pictures? Perkheimer's small head wagged as if it hurt him. Tears of a more familiar sort brightened his eyes. "Dumbkopf!" he said. "Why they come to Corfu?"

A glimmer of light, no more, led Soby to blink his eyes. Not so much from what he had said, as the word *they*, and how he had said it. The day's outing had ripened his hair: one more day would see it blooming. Through the tear washed eyes did Soby catch a glimpse of the wings of his mind? "Ex-cooosay," he said, aping Signor Pignata, and turned to reach one of his cameras. Tenderly he slipped it out of the case, unhinged the back. What was there? Nothing. Neither a strip of film nor a film cartridge. He did this with a second camera, then a third, and finally took from the rack his "cannon." The camera attached to the stock was empty. Not even a spool. Was that the way Perkheimer hoped to penetrate the layers of photographic ash?

A cloud of steam poured into the room as Signor Pignata stepped out of the shower. He wore a blue robe, initialled on the pocket, and a light sunburn that made him look almost healthy. On the fingers of the hand he ran through his hair, as if he had the Midas touch, there were flecks of gold leaf. The towel looped about his neck, he ignored both Soby and Perkheimer. From the shadow of his bunk the portrait of Primavera returned his gaze. Her lank hair was now green and hung like seaweed to drip on her shoulders. The cloth of gold covering her breasts had been removed. Gold remained to cap the nipples of her breasts, fleck the corners of her mouth. What Signor Pignata had done pleased him so much he held it up for them to see it. A sea-green siren with gold tipped breasts. The smile he had despaired of painting, however, seemed to have been transferred from the portrait to his own face.

"Come Prima!" he sang, tossing his head so that water from his hair sprinkled the mirror. Did it make him dizzy? He put his hand to the wall for support. The flush of healthy color drained from his face. "Mama mia," he whispered, crossed himself in the manner of Signor Lipari, then closed his eyes as the

Hephaistos first pitched, sea spraying the portholes, then rolled to show that they were once more in the open white-capped sea.

They found most of the chairs in the dining salon unoccupied. Little Perkheimer and Miss Cynthia—like two children of a large but ailing family—faced each other, alone, across a large display of food. How explain it? Had so many tourists stayed on at Corfu? No, no—Perkheimer advised them—more had actually come on than gotten off, deck passengers for Athens—but the day had been exhausting and the *Hephaistos* had a disquieting roll. Did they not feel it? Miss Throop commented that she compensated with a roll of her own. It was noticeable as she took her place in the seat usually occupied by Miss Kollwitz, who had sent her regrets, the day's outing having brought on one of her migraines.

The day's outing had revived Miss Throop—or perhaps a better word would be restored—her face glowing in the manner of an old painting expertly cleaned. Soby had found her at the bar, sipping liquid in which a wick appeared to be floating. *My dear;* she said, *you must have one. It's embalming fluid.* Behind the bar, his soiled jacket exposing his disturbingly hairless chest, the browless steward with the bushy hair rinsed a glass in dirty water, filled it with gin, and dunked a peel of onion with his thumb. Soby had observed no other finger on his hand was clean.

Jokingly, of course, little Perkheimer commented on the disappearance of the *suitors*. Where were they? Off battling among themselves? He hoped so, since it had left *him*—had it not—as heir apparent? Not too apparent, but apparent enough to be heir? Herr Doktor Soby—if he saw matters clearly—was the umpire in this contest, being too wise a man to make, like Perkheimer, a fool of himself.

Little Perkheimer paused there to pour wine he had taken the liberty to order, Liebfraumilch, in order to celebrate his triumph, however short lived. His head tilted so the bangs dangled slantwise on his forehead, he peered at Soby under the bottle as he poured. One could see the bright satin-smooth lining in the spout of his lip. Had Soby detected a lift in his voice when he said the word *fool?* Was that not precisely what he was? A courtless fool, a kingless jester, with his nightbird's eyes, his silken hair, his smiling clown's mouth as he leaned forward to pour them Lieb-fraumilch? The red lining of his lips showing, he sipped the faintly amber liquid. Liebfraumilch. *Echt Deutsch.* Who else would give the juice of the grape such a name? He put his tongue to the lingering taste of it on his lips. A suggestive, disturbing pucker, like that of a child nursing. Liebfraumilch. Was it not a wondrous word? What else—if he, Perkheimer, might say so—should bear such a name but wine and women. What else was it that so drew a man on? In the courtly manner of Dr. Hodler—his glass, of course, on a lower level—Adrien Perkheimer rose to toast Miss Liebfraumilch. With all respects to Dr. Hodler, Herr Holzapfel, and Signor Pignata, he thought the image more suggestive of the *ewig weibliche*, the eternal woman, the *je ne sais quoi* that drew a man on.

Was he playing the fool? Miss Cynthia gave him a blue tightlipped smile, as if she had lost her teeth, rather than her braces. Before Perkheimer sat down, or went on, Fraulein Kretschmar, a little winded, the pulse in her bosom showing, brought the news that Dr. Hodler was indisposed with overexertion, as well as a sprain that seemed to be steadily getting worse. She had left him with his foot, like a bottle, in a pail of ice water. She also bore the regrets of Herr Holzapfel, whose presence was needed on the deck, and in whose chair she took the liberty of depositing herself. The situation on the deck, she was sorry to say, was far from clear. In addition to the peasants there were innumerable animals, geese and pigs. The practice of the company to sell deck passage whether space was available or not, made it necessary for all the Wandervogel to remain on the deck. In theory they were assured priority to the deck accommodations, but in practice it was first come first served. To speak frankly, Herr Holzapfel was now holding down Fraulein Kretschmar's bedroll, while she rounded up what food she could for *all* of them. One flannel covered canteen, and three of the pans from Herr Holzapfel's pack, Fraulein Kretschmar filled with bottled water, antipasto and fish while she described the situation, now and then pausing to have a bite of food herself.

In spite of the day's adventures, on sea and land, Fraulein Kretschmar had gained more than she had lost, with the exception of an earring on Nausicaa's beach. Her dirty tan had a polish, like brass, and the blouse that had dried on her body gave assurance that what met the eye was more than enough. Her hair in braids, the tufted ends on the slope of her bust like tassels, it was hard to tell if Fraulein Kretschmar was the somewhat older sister, or the mother of Miss Cynthia, seated on her left. She saw to it that the girl had food on her plate. With her own knife and fork she sliced up a piece of tough meat. When one hand was not busy Fraulein Kretschmar would toy with the wet ends of Miss Cynthia's hair, using her napkin to soak up the moisture, protect the collar of her blouse.

And Miss Cynthia? She sat like a pet in the hands of the clipper, or a woman under the hood of a hair dryer. Was it the day's events or Soby's imagination that led him to feel this, too, was a portrait? Fraulein Kretschmar's version of the growing child in its proper place? The coolness, perhaps, explained the gooseflesh on her arms, the sealed blue line of her lips, and the button-like prominence of the tips of her breasts. That was due to the cold shower, of course, but Soby could not resist the impression they were tipped with gold.

Fraulein Kretschmar, beaming and scolding, let the tassels of her braids drag in her soup as she leaned forward to ladle more to little Perkheimer. One must eat! That was a Wandervogel rule. Fraulein Kretschmar did not say so, but if little Perkheimer had been in her care one would not now be wondering if he was merely stunted, or a real dwarf.

Were they not marvels—little Perkheimer cried—all of them? He meant women, of course—Miss Throop, Fraulein Kretschmar, and the newly crowned Fraulein Liebfraumilch, her brow with more than a touch of the blue of skimmed milk. But no—no, he meant more than the ladies, he meant the *ganze Deutsches volk*. Were they not incredible? Laboring, as they did, under such a strange curse. A curse? Fraulein Kretschmar begged him to be more explicit. Little Perkheimer, in turn, begged her not to take offense—did not all men labor under some such portent, wear on their souls the faint shadow of some small leaf? The curse he spoke of, to say the least, had the virtue of being the curse of perfection. Yes, that was what the German wanted. It was what led them like geese to Greece. Not to *see* Greece, no, no, Greece lay buried under their own fall of ashes—but to gaze into the Grecian mirror for the one perfect German. What a strange curse it was. Could they bear to hear it? Never to be German enough! What an absurd thing it was to criticize such people for being *too* much German, when they were doomed to fail because they could never be German enough. He, Perkheimer, could say so, since he, too, was doomed to eternal disappointment. *Echt Deutsch* he was, seven parts in ten, but on his mother's side he was one part Jewish, one part Polish, and one part midget. Data was lacking, but he was presumed to be Austrian. Hearing the guide cry *"sind wir alle"*—are we all here?—Herr Perkheimer had cried Jawohl from the bottom of his soul. *Ja, Ja, sind wir alle nicht Duetsch genug*—not German enough?

There little Perkheimer paused to uncork his bottle of Liebfraumilch, sniff the cork, then lean forward to add a bit to Fraulein Kretschmar's glass. But she detained him. Her plump brown hand covered her glass. No, no, let Fraulein Throop have it, since she had no time left her to drink it, with the Wandervogel waiting for her, as they were, up on the deck. Fraulein Kretschmar was German enough to know that *sind wir alle* did not apply, as some seemed to think, to everyone on the boat. Using the tassels of her braid she dusted the crumbs from the slope of her bust. Could they assist her? No, no, she was German enough, was Fraulein Kretschmar, to carry a few small pans, the canteen in its flannel cooler jogging on her hip. They were able to judge the roll of the boat from the way her braids, tossed over her shoulders, swung their tassels in the small of her broad back.

sixteen | From the sea Piraeus, the port of Athens, smoldered like the wasteland of Jersey marshes, or, more poetically speaking, the gates of hell. Undecided, Soby leaned on the rail rather than risk an early commitment. Behind the sulphurous cloud, on good authority, was Greece. A wind smelling of diesel fuel held the ship flags taut as fraternity pennants, puffing the cheeks of Miss Kollwitz with more than words could express. One sleeve of Soby's promised sweater was looped about her neck; the other, on which she had just started, was coiled around the knitting needles in the reticule with her supply of fruit. A babushka, souvenir of Corfu, flapped about her face.

"Look! Look!" she cried, "we are here!"

Assembled at the waterfront were motor busses, pedlars, loafers, natives, exiles and a peasant with cages of small birds in tiers on his back.

"Do you know the Southwest, my dear?" Miss Throop inquired. "I hadn't thought of Greece as Arizona flooded."

Fraulein Kretschmar, begging their pardon, called their attention to poor Dr. Hodler, his right foot in a sling, one arm around the column of Herr Holzapfel. The other arm, his cane crooked at the elbow, he waved to them. In the dipping shadow of his panama straw his face had the pallor of Signor Pignata. The glow of health, some of it applied, had been bleached out of the fabric. For them, he forced a

244

grimacing, blue-lipped smile. Miss Kollwitz would have gone toward him, but Fraulein Kretschmar calmed her. He had old friends in Athens. He needed professional care. He would join them, it was hoped, when the *Hephaistos* returned from the trip to Rhodes.

Soby and Miss Throop waved, Miss Kollwitz shouted words of good cheer and advice. Dr. Hodler's head wagged, but Soby noted that his roving blood-shot eye was elsewere. Up front, where a few stray Wandervogel, with a loyal corps of Perkheimer's Ex-pedition, received their last instructions before the rediscovery of Greece. *Der kleine* was not visible, but Miss Liebfraumilch, alias Miss Nausicaa, alias Miss Primavera, could be seen in a purple beret, with a not-quite-matching sweater, ornamented with two, or more, college fraternity pins. Since the sweater had not been washed Miss Throop had been forced to the conclusion that the child was still growing, or at least filling out. In any case, she would appear safe in Herr Perkheimer's hands. At breakfast he had sug-gested—in default of more substantial suitors—that Miss Liebfraumilch should join the Perkheimer Acropolis Expedition. Up there, their paths would cross. On the map it appeared to be a small and open place.

And Signor Pignata? Fraulein Kretschmar peered around the deck as if she might see him, comradely concern, no more, certainly, on her flaking face.

About the wings of her nose, beneath her eyes, her tan was like something cleaned with artgum. It had been a mistake to wash her hair. Her braids, hung in loops, were like frazzled pieces of rope. Belted at the waist, the long sleeves rolled, a sweater of Herr Holzapfel draped her like a sheath. The small slit in her pitch pipe was smeared with a lotion for chapped lips. As for Signor Pignata, Soby might have advised her that he lay in his bunk, a pillow wrapped about his head, but with something more than a touch of nausea in his bearded face. Happy dreams? Evil deeds? The sulphurous smell of land seemed sweet to him.

As an economy measure the Wandervogel would go to Athens by public transportation, not in the middle class busses with American hubcaps and German motors. With Herr Holzapfel busy with Dr. Hodler, Fraulein Kretschmar had her hands full. The Fuehrer's whistle hung on a leather thong from her neck. Soby watched them file down the gangplank, that roped incline where the dreams crossed: for *echt* Wandervogel the only natural habitat. Fraulein Kretschmar, without breaking her stride, led them through the seaside ways of temptation, food, souvenirs and postcards, to where the stream of traffic halted their progress. As they gathered around her and she scanned their faces she was possessed by her *heimat* instincts.

"*Sind wir alle?*" she cried. Too late she heard what she had said. From the gangplank little Perkheimer called "Jawohl!" and waved his small hand. Unsuspecting Wandervogel turned to stare at him, several smiled. Herr Holzapfel supported Dr. Hodler as he bargained for a taxi. Fraulein Kretschmar, however, did not lift her eyes, and waited serenely for the signal that came when the policeman beckoned to her with his white gloved hand.

Four busses, each supplied with a guide who spoke French, German and English, according to the brochure, transported them to the Acropolis. There were no French in Soby's bus, but never mind, it was the language favored by the guide, a small woman with a hoarse but powerful voice. Behind her memorized harangue Soby felt her hate as well as her impersonal passion for survival. To eat this busload of carrion she needed no more than a shaker of salt. She weighed them, smiling, like a shipment of hogs. Through the barred bus windows, the disorderly traffic, he glimpsed the familiar ruins of history. From a rise he saw new buildings, old graves with new ornaments. Miss Kollwitz leaned to grip his arm and shake it—

"Look, look!" she croaked, pointing skyward. Fleeting but familiar Soby saw the marble symbol on its pedestal, drawing the eyes upward to Truth, Beauty, Law and Order, the Pure Food and Drug Act, Long-Life Insurance, Protected Savings, Foundation

Garments, the marble ash filling the chunks in the modern mind. Her eyes level Miss Throop said,

"My dear, why is the upward gaze always so idiotic?"

They rode in silence, apprehensive that something might be missed. The wider view seemed as barren as the backs of cattle picked clean by birds. On a curve, as if the bus had tipped, those on one side filled the aisle to be near the windows. The bow on a woman's blouse covered Soby's eyes, her bust pillowed on his head. The bus stopped while the guide shrieked them back to their seats. At the remove of a dream, framed by the window, the Acropolis emerged from a smoking pyre. That was dust. A gale-like wind levelled it over the smoldering city. As if to protest Soby arose. For three thousand years Greece had been serene and windless in the soul of Arnold Soby. How explain this gale? The guide begged him to please resume his seat.

On a rise, barren as a cinder, the wind blurring the view like drizzle, voices shouted through megaphones that there would be five minutes for the taking of pictures. Had the road been built with this in mind? The site was barren as a sacrificial mound. Adrien Perkheimer took one look then ordered his corps to put away their cameras. Had they come here, he cried, to praise Greece or to bury it? Like a gadfly he harried them, shooed them back to their seats. A Greek boy, plump and dark as an olive, with the body of a teen-

age Ajax, his hair a freshly mowed flat-top, bullied
them all into buying and eating his wares. Pistachio
nuts. He was, he said, working his way through high
school. He singled out Soby to receive his blessings.
He inquired about jobs in Chicago, the price of shoes.
The last of Soby's features to be scrutinized was his
face. His gaze, impersonal as the gale, scanned
Soby's face but passed no judgment, leaving on his
brow dust from his first close brush with Greece.

Nevertheless, it left him unprepared for the Parthenon.

"Look—" Miss Kollwitz said, but to no one, as if
she had left her keys somewhere. Was the problem
scale? Or the years Soby had spent in the tombs of the
library basement, the walls cluttered with the sepia
murals of the glory that was Greece. He stood staring, suitably ironic comments drying in his mouth.

The hour and forty minutes allowed for Athens
gave them an hour—the brochure said—free to wander, rediscover Greece with Perkheimer, or listen to
the windblown lectures of the guide. Miss Throop
thought it better to follow, as did Soby, their inclinations. And what were they? To get out of the deafening wind. A round column—Miss Throop observed
—had that one lamentable imperfection: it was
round; the wind lapped it like water, stirring marble
dust. Soundlessly, her voice windstrewn, Miss Kollwitz read to them from her guidebook. Miss Throop
commented on the sensation of being *within* a picture

she had so long known only from the outside. Soby
tried and failed to light his pipe. Battles had raged
within these halls of marble, powder kegs had ex-
ploded, cannon balls had rattled, but Soby had the
impression that the wind alone, given time, could
have produced such a ruin. In his hair he felt the
rain of marble dust. A grey sunless sky cast a hardly
perceptible shadow, but the windless side of the column was warm to the touch. They huddled with their
backs pressed to it. Now and then a word, or a sta-
tistic, flicked from the chapped lips of Miss Kollwitz.
From a crevice, using his pipe stem, Soby excavated
chips of marble. Seaward, the sulphurous cloud hovered over Piraeus. Within the Parthenon Damen und
Herren formed a dark clot in the vein of marble, the
Herren hatless, the Damen keeping to the windward
of the hoarse-voiced guide. Little Perkheimer, giving a false scale to the porch of marble maidens,
took shots from below of what appeared to be Miss
Liebfraumilch. Did she make a strange Greek? She
had too many legs and arms. One she waved, showing
its flexible marble joint.

Miss Kollwitz, her map of Greece flapping, called
their attention to a covey of Wandervogel. They had
gathered, like gulls, on one of the lower slabs of rock,
overlooking the footpath that led up from ancient
Athens. Along it, surely, came Hercules. He paused to
tilt his huge head, show his small face. The perspec-
tive exaggerated the impression that the head had not

fully emerged from the shoulders, an Ur-mensch climbing from the dark into the light. Upward and onward, however, was his near-sighted, button-eyed gaze. To the Wandervogel he waved a huge ham-like hand. Moments later, their chanting voices wind-borne, they appeared at the heels of their leader, crossing the marble square like Athenians bearing gifts. Their marching stirred up dust that pricked Soby's face. He had the taste of it on his lips, the grit between his teeth.

Miss Throop, a thumb and finger on her eyelids, dozed in the shelter of the voice of Miss Kollwitz, her subject being what conquering Xerxes carried off to Susa. Did it seem nearer? What had been ravished, who had been carried off? Down the drafty corridors of Soby's mind lined with the shrouded marble fig-ures the wind blew unobstructed, opening, as it did, room upon room, door upon door. At its end a prob-ing shaft of light spilled into the open, the world be-fore marble, the deep forest night cloudy with smoke, lit up here and there with flares, the air vibrant with a sound too high to be heard. About a smoking pyre goat-skinned men with sputtering torches could be seen dancing. Women too, Soby could see, but never mind. What disturbed him was that the faces sweating in the torchlight looked familiar. Very. Ur-mensch all of them, the fathers of forefathers, but wearing the masks of unmistakable spate-mensch—if that was how Dr. Hodler and Signor Pignata might be classi-

fied. Not to mention others. No, not to mention the
bearlike Holzapfel, with his cookie face, on the leash
of a capering midget like a gargoyle. Not to mention
the figure on the smoking pyre. A white goddess with
gold tipped breasts and other females, pelted and
painted, sprinkled the sacrifice with an appropriate
sauce. Soby may have strained to see them, tilting
his head in the manner of Dr. Hodler, a smile or
grimace on his face, a little hard to say which. To get
his attention Miss Kollwitz had to grip and shake his
sleeve.

"Look! Look!" The arm with which she pointed
puffed out like a balloon. Soby, in turn, took a grip
on her as if she might blow away. The court of the
Parthenon was faintly striped with the light that fell
between the columns. Otherwise it seemed empty, a
vast scene painted on canvas, or done with mirrors, to
serve as a backdrop for Isadora Duncan or Cecil B.
DeMille. Little Perkheimer, swinging his photo-
cannon, appeared between two columns like a midget
guerrilla, wheeling to aim and fire as if at a pursuer.
A fleeting moment, but long enough to give the scene
a spectacular grandeur, the columns pushing up like
pillars to support the sky. Then he was gone, and that
frame was filled with the ponderous hulk of Holzapfel, arms spread as if he meant to pull the pillars
down.

Were they playing cops and robbers? So it seemed.
From behind a toppled column little Perkheimer put

up his head to fire another volley, then duck as the huge Holzapfel headed for him. A moment later he was back in the spot Holzapfel had left. He hooted to attract his attention, fired at him as he charged. Nothing more comical could be imagined, but that was not their intention. No, that was soon obvious. Holzapfel's rage led him to charge with his arms spread wide, crab-like, as if he thought to catch the minnow Perkheimer in his net. The uneven terrain was not well suited to his lumbering gait. He tripped on the boulders, slipped in the marble dust. Nimble as a chipmunk, little Perkheimer was up and down, in and out, popping up to fire a volley at Holzapfel's broad front, his humped, bear-like rear, or sneaking up to shoot an arched volley between his straddled legs. Cool as it was, sweat darkened the hump of the giant's back. His arms hung as if he might get down on all fours. Unless the mouse ran into his mouth, he would not be caught. Fraulein Kretschmar, if unobserved, would have run forward to his assistance, but that—as she may have realized—would have made matters worse. Smaller, nimbler Wandervogel too might have done better, but they had not been fired on. After all, a lion should not need assistance in battling a mouse. He did, however. His arms dangling he stood and stared at the midget seated on the boulder, his gun in his lap, his small legs insolently crossed. That was too much; Herr Holzapfel stooped as if he might pick up one section of a broken col-

umn, leaned on it a moment, then lowered his bottom
to one end of it.

"Now, now!" cried Miss Kollwitz. "Do something!" and urged Soby to go forward. Do what?
Were there no other volunteers? At a safe distance, between the columns and at the far ends of the arena,
Wandervogel, Damen und Herren remained in their
places. What were they waiting for? The next round?
What had happened? Had Fraulein Kretschmar in-
sinuated that in the opinion of Herr Perkheimer even
Fuehrer Holzapfel was not German enough? It
seemed likely. Would it help matters if Soby pointed
out that Herr Perkheimer was shooting only blanks?

"Look, look!" Miss Kollwitz flapped her arm to
where Miss Cynthia, swinging her purse like a sling
shot, made her loose-jointed way across the rubble
to head them off. Little Perkheimer she let scoot by
—like one of her offspring dodging trouble—but
Herr Holzapfel, ducking the swing of her purse, let
his arm sweep her aside like a tangled vine, Miss
Cynthia collapsing like a stick-figure toy on stilts.
Propelled from behind, Soby sprang forward as the
wind made off with his cap. He turned to see Miss
Kollwitz flailing her arms and Miss Throop, the veil
across her face, calling advice the wind blew over
Athens, at the same time making inscrutable gestures
with her left hand. Little Perkheimer ran along a toppled column like a Disney squirrel. Fraulein Kretschmar, the wind puffing out the sleeves and skirt of

Herr Holzapfel's sweater, first swooped to the left, then to the right, uncertain whether to attack one flank or defend another. And Miss Cynthia? She was back on her wobbly legs. The purse dangling, she took off, but not on the heels of Herr Holzapfel. As Fraulein Kretschmar headed for little Perkheimer, Miss Cynthia took after Fraulein Kretschmar, and Soby, stretching his legs, took off for a point somewhere between them. It left him with Miss Cynthia coming toward him, Fraulein Kretschmar moving away. Miss Cynthia, the gale in her face, looked up to see Soby, hatless and smiling, his arms spread wide to block the path. Did she recognize Soby? He was smiling when the purse looped in his direction, circled her head, then came back at him as he put up an arm and ducked. It struck him with no more force than a bean bag, but as the strap slipped between his fingers he grabbed it, and she in turn gave it a jerk. The howl he made startled them both. Up went his hand, the buckle fast where it had dug into his palm, and when she jerked on the strap to free it, brought the purse down flatside with a smack on her face. Could one believe the howl she made? The way she stamped her feet? Soby had to grab her, hug her, that is, one arm tight around her wriggling body, and with the other try to control the whipping strap of the bag. Supple as a cat she dipped her head and bit his hand, the soft flesh of his thumb, as he took a handful of her hair and jerked her head with a snap. Might he have killed her? The thought struck them both. For a moment she hung on him limp as rope. Over her head, the grip he had on her hair, Soby saw the figure of Fraulein Kretschmar, pleasure, fear and stupefaction on her face. The girl was sobbing. Soby shook her like a child in a tantrum.

"You pick a *red* bag with this in mind?" he yelled, and put the bleeding cut to his mouth. It pleased him to see the tear-streaked dust on her face. A crazy childish tantrum? Had she bitten her own lip? From her purse she took a mirror, smeared with chocolate, and curled her lips to examine her teeth. Was she looking for blood? He had forgotten the way she clamped down on his thumb. Where he had slapped her with the purse her face glowed with some of its color.

"May I ask what the hell got into you?" he said.

Like a cat, she was preoccupied with her own wounds. The lower lip sucked in, she looked at the marks of her own teeth.

"When you're through with your own," he said, "I have some others you can examine."

She did not ask to see them. He controlled the impulse to let some of his blood drip on her.

"May I ask whose side you are on?" he said. Was it a smile on his lips, or a grimace?

"I'm not on *your* side! I don't sit and smirk when a big bully picks on somebody."

"I see," said Soby. "You'd like to see a real fight.

You'd like to see Goliath crack a few real skulls. Is that it?"

The way she looked, her lip sucked in, one might have thought it was Soby who had bit her. Was it in her eyes, or the hint of her smile, he saw the slogan on the seat of her bathrobe, *What a Way to Go*.

He looked up, hearing a cry, for some sign of Herr Perkheimer. Fraulein Kretschmar stood between two columns, like a wingless victory, one arm upraised, the gale puffing out her sleeve. Off where she gazed the great pursuit continued, both a way to go and a way to stay, but only Fraulein Kretschmar seemed vitally concerned. Most of the Wandervogel, a few Damen und Herren along with Miss Kollwitz, her clothes flapping like a scarecrow, seemed to be concerned with the survival of Soby. He put his bleeding palm to his mouth.

"You don't *do* that!" she said, "that makes it infected." She reached to tug at his sleeve. Soby lowered his hand to where they both had a look at it. Along the back of his thumb her teeth had left their imprint.

"Fraulein Kretschmar has a snake bite kit," he said, "think that would help?"

"You think I'm a *snake?*" she eyed him with interest.

"I think you've got quite a bite."

"What sort of *snake* you think I am?"

"I think—" Soby replied, taking a breath, "it's

time you stop this damn nonsense. I don't think you're a goose, and I don't think you're a snake."

"What *do* you think?" He did not reply. "You know what I *used* to think? What I *used* to want to be?" Did she think he was hard of hearing? She put her face so close her blowing hair brushed his cheek. "I *used* to want to be so beautiful everybody who saw me would just fall down *dead*." Her arms had raised as if she thought she might soar, then flapped at her sides. Did she perhaps expect Soby to be the first? He thought he might.

"You don't want people to fall down dead *now?*" he smiled.

"Not *every*body," she replied, "just *most* people."

"My dear—" Soby began, but the wind spared him, words to the effect that *some* people, if not most people, in one way or another did just that. Fell down dead—in order to arise, like the phoenix, from their own ashes. The sunned smell of her skin, lightly salted, seemed to be on his lips.

"Yes?" she asked. Strands of brown hair blew across her face, the lips parted.

"My dear Miss Cynthia—" he said.

"I'm *not* Miss Cynthia!" she interrupted.

"Very well, then who are you? Make up your mind."

"What if I *have* made up my mind?"

That surprised him. "Very good," he said, "so you have made up your mind." She let him wait. He released the limp arm he was holding. "Very well," he repeated, "so who are you?"

"Wouldn't you like to know!" she cried.

Was her smile at what she knew, or what she saw in his face? The white part in her hair directed Soby's gaze to where Miss Kollwitz wagged her guidebook to catch his eye. Beckoning, she pointed to the watch strapped to her wrist. Soby, too, checked the time, giving the stem of his watch a twist, then let his hand fall to take the girl's arm. Several whistle blasts, windborne, preceded the appearance of the Wandervogel, orderly as quail, with Fraulein Kretschmar bringing up the rear. Their safari passed through the rubble to march in profile on the horizon, then go over the rim as the unheard music seemed to taper off.

And little Perkheimer? Members of his Expedition, sans their Fuehrer, were gathered on the steps below the Beulé gate. He appeared to be missing until Miss Kollwitz, following the downward trek of the Wandervogel, saw him like a gargoyle on a small jut of rock. There he sat shooting down Wandervogel like sitting ducks. Miss Kollwitz hallooed to warn them, but the wind, plus the fact that they were weary, kept all but Fraulein Kretschmar from raising her eyes. If there had been film in Perkheimer's gun he would have caught her gaze, not on himself, but the humped Hercules behind her who took from her hand his share of Wandervogel pistachio nuts. On his slab-like brow nothing had disturbed the film of marble dust.

seventeen | A pharmacist in Piraeus dressed Soby's hand while Miss Kollwitz inquired about lockjaw, and Fraulein Kretschmar took all the blame upon herself. It had all begun, had it not, the moment she had turned her back? Like two boys fighting at recess with sticks and stones. As to *what* had happened, opinions differed, but Herr Holzapfel was not a man to hold a grudge. Let bygones be bygones Herr Holzapfel said. And so they would, if Herr Perkheimer would merely give up the pictures he had taken. An understandable request, considering what some of them had been. Would Soby—Fraulein Kretschmar pleaded—speak to him concerning this matter? Otherwise Fraulein Kretschmar could not openly vouch for his safety, the deck of the *Hephaistos* not being that of the Acropolis. The matter was urgent since the *Hephaistos* was scheduled to sail for Mykonos at midnight, where the Wandervogel, along with Herr Perkheimer, would leave the boat. A small island. There were few marble columns behind which he might hide. Little Perkheimer—Fraulein Kretschmar darkly hinted—might not leave the isles of Greece until the matter was settled. For his own sake she begged Soby to speak to him.

All Soby had to do was explain that Herr Perkheimer was a little peculiar, loading his camera not with film, but with blanks. But he didn't. First of all, it was hardly likely Herr Holzapfel would believe it. Second, little Perkheimer might prefer burial in Greece. Side by side with his worthy adversary, Ulys-

ses Holzapfel. One stone would read, *echt Deutsch.*
The other *nicht Deutsch genug.*

His hand bandaged, Soby went aboard to find little
Perkheimer singing in the shower, the cabin full of
steam but little else. Signor Pignata, his luggage and
his easel were gone. In Soby's bunk, however, as if
she lay under the covers, was the girl's gilt-lipped
portrait. Her head rested on his pillow, her eyes on
the door. Was that the work of Perkheimer or
Pignata? For a moment Soby felt a kinship with the
rage of Herr Holzapfel. Perkheimer was inclined to
carry things just a bit too far. He placed the portrait
on the suitcase under his bunk, then turned to see Miss
Kollwitz, her face glowing with windburn, peering at
him through the crack in the panel. What had she
seen? Only into the wings of her own mind.

"Look!" she said, and opened the panel to reveal
what she was holding. A lifebelt? It was streaked
with cat fur where Aschenbach had been sleeping
on it.

"I've never questioned he's a smart cat," said
Soby, and smiled. Miss Kollwitz did not return it.
No, that was not the point she wanted to make.
"Look," she repeated, and turned the object so that
Soby could see the underside. There were holes as if
mice had been sleeping in it. As she gave it a shake
some of the stuffing poured out. A finger to her lips
she hissed, "He is smarter than you think! We have
one only!"

"One only?" Soby had let his gaze settle on the

figure in the berth behind her, a seal rolled on its side, a towel over its face. A corner of it rose and fell as Miss Throop snored. "I don't think—" he began, but Miss Kollwitz interrupted.

"No? Did you not hear?"

Hear what? The wind in his ears, Soby had heard nothing. Miss Kollwitz turned to glance at Miss Throop, then beckoned Soby to come closer. Down to her own level she lowered his ear. "There is a storm!" she hissed. "On the boat from Rhodes everybody is sick!" The flavor of her lozenge sprayed his face.

"We're in the Aegean now," Soby replied, "we may roll a little but—" he smiled his reassurance.

But that was not for Miss Kollwitz. "You have them?" she cried, and shook the shabby lifebelt at him. Soby had no idea: he turned to peer around as if he might see them ornamenting the portholes, or like reassuring trophies on the walls. The screw of the *Hephaistos* turned, stopped, then turned again. The light, the mirror, the glass at the bowl, the lifebelt held by Miss Kollwitz sympathetically vibrated. Miss Throop rose from her bunk as if summoned from the grave.

"My God, what's that?" she cried, her eyes on the lifebelt.

Too late Miss Kollwitz tried to conceal it. Pointing at the cat she said, "For him. A bed for him!"

Miss Throop was not deceived. "Isn't it women and

children first, my dear?" she replied.

From behind the shower door the girl cried, "First for *what?*" There was no comment. Her head wrapped in a towel, she peered at them from a cloud of steam. Miss Kollwitz held the lifebelt like something strange fished from the sea. "*Life* savers?" she barked, "what for?" The sarcasm was not lost on Miss Kollwitz.

"Not for you!" she cried. "Better for *him*, than for you!" She wagged her finger at the cat house, the shabby tail of Aschenbach visible.

"I can take care of myself!" she yelled. "Don't you worry about me! You hear?" The door of the shower closed with a slam. Miss Throop sat plucking cat fur from the lap of her skirt. Calmly she said—

"We won't, my dear. That is now Professor Soby's department."

There was a silence. The screw of the *Hephaistos* thrashed like a dying dragon. When it stopped Soby said, "Lifebelts?" as if someone had just asked him. "Let me go inquire," he added, and fumbled at the door with his bandaged hand. No, no—Miss Kollwitz objected, and dropped the lifebelt to open it for him. Waiting there, two dirty glasses of embalming fluid on his dented tray, the steward with the pitted face, the hairless chest, returned Soby's gaze. How explain that now, at this moment, Soby should think of the dark thatched face of his wife, the impersonal gaze as she listened to his counsel, her mouth full of grapes.

"Ex-coosay," he said, as if waiting to be introduced.

"Wait! Wait!" Miss Throop cried, "don't let him in!" she rocked to a squatting position, knees spread, one small foot grubbing for the pump on the floor while she fumbled at her wig. "My dear boy—" she called, "un momentito!" squashed the crownless hat low on her head, pulled the spread to cover her knees but leave her feet exposed. "Come in, come in!" she called. Miss Kollwitz let him in as Soby, seeing the passage was empty, stepped into the hall and crossed the lounge for a breath of fresh air.

A joke. A little joke on himself. The head of Perkheimer wagged to think about it. Konrad Holzapfel lifted his gaze, no more, to look at the face of little Perkheimer, his mouth full of olives, but a confession on his lips. Could they bear to hear it? If one allowed for the tilt of the boat he seemed a man without a care in the world. Bygones were bygones. Anyhow, that was how Perkheimer looked. He had run his fingers, not his comb, through his silken hair. Still moist from the shower he wore a face towel around his neck, like a boxer, a light sweater with tassels on the zipper, leather patches on the sleeves. He let them wait while he worked over the olive seeds. Would they promise to keep it a secret? The head of Miss Cynthia nodded. His head so low it seemed to

lie on his plate little Perkheimer whispered hoarsely
that the hood had been on the lens of his camera all
the time. Could they believe it? A necessary precau-
tion in a wind full of marble dust. A telephoto lens
worth many hundred dollars might be destroyed in a
few moments. Perkheimer's trained hand had remembered what his mind had overlooked. Was that
not some joke? All the film in his camera was
blank!

Herr Holzapfel listened without comment to Fraulein Kretschmar's laughing translation. It happened,
she said, to the best of them. Fraulein Kretschmar
herself, in moments of excitement, invariably made
many double exposures, being more anxious to get
the picture than wind the film.

Herr Perkheimer smiled, slowly wagging his damp
head. No, no. Quite the contrary. Would they believe that it was perhaps more painful for others than
for himself?

"Look here!" Miss Kollwitz barked. "Do not speak
in riddles!"

Riddles? Little Perkheimer paused to muse over
the word. Was it a riddle, he asked, if only Germans
understood it? He beamed a smile at Fraulein Kretschmar, who did not return it. Did Soby sense trouble, or merely the porthole draft on his neck?

Did the ladies feel the draft, he asked, and half
turned as if to check it. Not Fraulein Kretschmar.
No, she felt no draft, but there were beads of mois-

ture in the fuzz on her lip. Would Herr Perkheimer be so kind as to explain just what he meant?

He would indeed. But he let her wait while he selected and chewed an olive. He let the pit drop like a bad tooth on his plate.

Was it not characteristic—little Perkheimer said —for all those who were not German at all, to feel more pain than those who were not quite German enough? To feel no pain—was that not quite an accomplishment? Little Perkheimer took off his hat to all those who felt the pity and concern of others, but were German enough to feel no pain themselves. No, that took talent. One he sadly lacked. There too he fell short of the ideal sadly—he did feel some. A Saul Perkheimer, an uncle, had been instrumental in Perkheimer's career, leaving to him the camera he would find no use for at Auschwitz. He paused to beam.

Fraulein Kretschmar, clutching her napkin, pushed back her chair and rose from the table—but Herr Holzapfel put up a heavy hand to her shoulder, held her to the spot. Leaning forward he forced her back to her seat. Fraulein Kretschmar had stood all she could stand, but she would not be leaving. No, she would stand, as would Herr Holzapfel and anyone else he had insulted, but he would, and quickly, be leaving the table himself.

Little Perkheimer cocked his head to one side, like a listening bird. Absently, as it had, no doubt, placed the lens hood on his camera, his hand went to his hair and raked strands of it forward. A curious gesture. One felt that it might not be his own. Had Herr Holzapfel not heard, he said, that he took off his hat to the almost-German people? Herr Holzapfel had indeed. He wanted nothing from him, least of all his hat. He would be much obliged, however, if Herr Perkheimer would be pleased to leave the table.

Leave the table? Perhaps there was some mistake. Herr Holzapfel should be advised that he, Perkheimer, was also German, if not—as was so often true—quite German enough. But who was the least? Should *he* not be the first to leave? In mere size, in quantity, in avoirdupois as one described it, he, Adrien Perkheimer bowed to Herr Holzapfel, a mighty German indeed. But these were secondary matters, were they not? The German soul was the question, wasn't it? Let them bare their respective souls, so to speak. No one would know so well as Herr Holzapfel that the soul's cage was the body, so let them bare it, and see how matters stood. So saying little Perkheimer rose from his seat, but not to leave. No, he pushed his chair aside to make a clearing, and to use it, so it seemed, for a clothesrack. Over the arm he placed the towel he took from his neck, then unzipped and removed his sweater. Beneath it he wore a T shirt, clean white against the tan of his small body, the arms of a well developed teen-age boy. There he paused, as if surprised to see that Herr

Holzapfel was still seated. His huge hand still held Fraulein Kretschmar in her place.

"Bitte, bitte!" little Perkheimer said, flicking one small hand like an orchestra leader wanting more sound out of one section of the horns. Herr Holzapfel made no sound, nor did he move. The impression that his face seemed to shrink or the head itself grow larger, was perhaps due to the closeness of the eyes. They did not blink, nor return Perkheimer's gaze. Fraulein Kretschmar muttered *bitte,* as if to rise, but the weight of Holzapfel's hand seemed to hold her to the seat.

"*Sind wir nicht alle?*" asked Perkheimer, peering around, as if to lead them in a sea chanty, at the same time pulling the tail of his T shirt out of his pants. "My friends," he said, "what a small thing it is to take off one's hat to something. If one admires it—and is German enough—let him take off his clothes!" He bowed to Fraulein Kretschmar.

Clay-colored, except for his ears, Herr Holzapfel's hand still rested on Fraulein Kretschmar as if the arm was powerless to remove it. What terrified him? Was there simply too much German to expose? Little Perkheimer without further comment slipped his T shirt over his head, shaking it out neatly before placing it over the chair. A silver chain dangled a charm in the few hairs on his chest. He took it off, slipping it into a pocket. And now his pants—no, first his shoes—since the cuffs were narrow—unlacing them carefully, placing them on the seat of his chair. And then a sock with a hole in the heel, just as Fraulein Kretschmar cried "Stop him! Stop him!" as if shouting at a thief. Nobody did. Little Perkheimer removed the second sock. As if she meant to do it herself Fraulein Kretschmar arose, tipping over her chair, a napkin pressed to her face as if she might be sick.

"Are we not all here?" little Perkheimer repeated, loosening the buckle of his pants. Fraulein Kretschmar dropped as suddenly as she had popped up. Without a sound, little more than the whoosh of a coat falling off a hanger, the cry escaping from Miss Kollwitz on whom she leaned. One might have thought she had cried *"Fire!"* Damen, including some Herren, arose as if at a signal: two or three breathed the air at the portholes, others headed for the stairs. Herr Perkheimer, with a child's wide gaze, peered around as if at a circus, his eyes coming back to the stupefied face of Herr Holzapfel. Was he paralyzed? The eyes did not blink. His mane of hair, the tufted blonde eyebrows, appeared to be pasted on the face of a child. From the back, an emergency exit, one steward and three members of the crew, as if headed for the galley, came up behind Perkheimer. And that was that. There was no scuffle. No, he went along peaceably. The steward carried his clothes, including his pants, going ahead to make way at the gangway, clotted with Damen und Herren, for the members of the crew who carried him.

"What a way to go!" cried the girl, but Soby, as usual, may have missed her intentions. Herr Holzapfel, intent as a sleepwalker, made his way as in darkness to a porthole, where he took in gulps of air like a surfaced fish. It was not presence of mind that led Soby to offer his brandy to Miss Kollwitz, her brow glistening as she fanned Fraulein Kretschmar's sea-green face. Miss Throop intercepted.

"My dear Soby," she said, "women and chillun fuss." The lolling movement of her head was not due to the roll of the boat. She was tight, the sound that escaped her was that of a tire deflating, as if a hole had been punctured in her corseted bust. From the bowl of withered olives she took a handful, letting them fall into her gaping purse. "For Aschenbach," she muttered, "he thinks they're mice!" then she lifted her arms like wings, waiting for Soby to come and hoist her from the chair.

Passengers, in particular the ladies, would be pleased to stay in their cabins, due to the roll of the sea and the slipperiness of the decks. This announcement, in German and French, and what Miss Kollwitz identified as English, found them seated in the lounge in chairs chained to the floor. To combat a tendency to yawn Miss Kollwitz sucked on the seed of an olive: to combat her state of mind she allowed herself to cheat at solitaire. Not that it was the slipperiness of the decks that troubled her. No, nor was it Miss Cynthia, at the moment, with the Nausicaa nonsense now behind them and Signor Pignata happily off the boat, nor was it Herr Perkheimer who was mad as an owl.

Who could imagine what such a creature might do next? Miss Kollwitz recommended that Soby pass the time in the lounge with her, smoking, rather than risk sleeping in a cabin alone with him. At Mykonos —she had it on good authority—they would put him off. They would reach it by midnight, so he would still have a good night's sleep. But even that was not why she felt obliged to cheat at solitaire. No, it was her colleague, Miss Throop, giving in not merely to her lust for martinis, but inclinations of the sort that Miss Kollwitz preferred not to think about. That cabin boy with the hair growing out of his eyes who made her shudder just to look at him, brought Miss Throop coffee in the morning and gin in the afternoon. Would Soby believe she had twice found the door locked? The room full of the smell of the cigarettes he always lit the wrong end of? How explain it? Miss Kollwitz could tell him it was something evil on the boat. One could smell it. It led Dr. Hodler to behave like a child: Herr Perkheimer appear to be demented. Before she did something peculiar herself Miss Kollwitz was determined to leave it. At Rhodes. At Rhodes with Soby's help. They would stay over several days and leave on another boat. It would mean the loss of several hundred dollars but better that than something one could never recover. It was Miss Throop who was retiring; Miss Kollwitz still had to return and face Winnetka, Cynthia's mother, and the world.

It had been a long day, Soby said, why didn't they see how she felt in the morning? Many people would be leaving the boat at Rhodes. It would be more relaxed. The worst was over—was it not?

Miss Kollwitz let the cards spill into her lap. Had he failed to notice Miss Cynthia with certain members of the crew? The tall one, teaching her to sing in Greek, the old one who looked like a fish? A man like Soby, one with so little interest in girls was, alas, a mixed blessing. Had he no eyes? Did he not know that she had been actually *pinched?* His pipe inverted, Soby puffed hot ashes into his lap. Miss Kollwitz, her mind on hotter matters, let them lie. From the floor, her backside topside, she stooped to pick up her cards, then went off hardly caring if he burned to death or not.

Most of the lounge chairs were empty when Soby went along the wall, damp from the drip of the portholes, down the gangway to the door of his cabin. It was locked. He rapped but got no answer. Was Perkheimer asleep? He rapped again and said, "It's me, Soby." At his back a door opened, the head of Miss Kollwitz in its flannel nightcap.

"Look here, you will wake her!" The snore of Miss Throop was audible. Soby muttered he was sorry, but that he had no key. Signor Pignata had left the boat with it. Miss Kollwitz drew his head down to hiss that she had heard nothing, no nothing. What did she mean? She feared the worst, whatever it was. The tilt of the boat widened the door, freshened the sour smell of the draft. A towel lay on the floor where Miss Throop could reach for it.

Perhaps it would be quieter, Soby suggested, if he went in through the sliding panel. Perkheimer might not even be there to wake up. Miss Kollwitz let a moment pass. Before letting him in she picked up the towel and pulled the sheet higher on Miss Throop, moved the girl's arm so it did not hang from the upper bunk. The panel opened perhaps a foot, there it stuck. Through it Soby could see the porthole like the foaming window of a washer. "Perkheimer?" he whispered. No reply. Something loose on the floor rolled away, then toward him. Soby took off his coat, handing it to Miss Kollwitz, then inched himself through the opening. Miss Kollwitz passed through his coat, then closed the panel herself. From behind it she called, "He is there?"

Soby struck a match. As it flared he could see that the upper bunk was empty. "No—" he said, cupping the flame, and crossed the wet floor to his bed. Drip from the porthole had soaked the blanket at the foot.

"Look here!" she hissed, "what did I tell you?"

Soby used the match to light up his pipe, then turned to flip it toward the bowl. The eyes of a bird, a trapped animal, stared at him from Pignata's corner. Herr Perkheimer? As the match burned his fingers Soby said *ouch*. In the darkness the sea washed the portholes, the room glowed with a cold bottle-green light. The mirror, the washbowl, the wet floor, the figure in his trench coat, his beret, his boots with the cleats on the soles, his cameras, and gadgets, the straps criss-crossing on his chest. Would it speak? No, it did not speak. One was meant to pretend it was not there. Soby took off his shoes, his pants, and lay with the blanket over his legs. He did not yawn, nor notice the pulse in his sore hand. A palpable terror shared the room. Was it the sea? The screw throbbed loose, with a shudder, when the *Hephaistos* pitched.

"He will kill me," the small voice said flatly. "You watch."

Soby did not contradict it, nor rise on his elbow to shake his head. He was thinking that the night is different indeed from the day. The facts were different. Only by night was terror palpable.

As in a dream? No, seldom had Soby been so wide awake. Perhaps that was the trouble. The unreal and the sur-real were much alike. A roll of the boat, for example, had loosened the luggage under his bunk, so that it skidded across the room to thump the door. The portrait of the girl had gone along on top of it. As the boat tilted in reverse one of the bags skidded back across the floor, but the portrait, propped on the door, remained. On a level with Soby were the eyes, the parted lips. Either the eyes were closed or she had none, the frothy phosphorescent light changed her complexion to the green of bronze long at the bottom of the sea. Gold capped were the nipples of her naked breasts. Her hair seemed to be powdered with marble dust. A jumble of eerie and disquieting sensations led Soby to lie there, smiling, as if the antique mermaid would speak.

Was this Davy Jones' locker? Was it here one heard the song the sirens sang? Like that haunting long drawn out *u*-sound that had chilled the blood of Aschenbach but left him perspiring, Soby felt himself pleasurably doomed. In a moment, in a tilt of the boat, he would feel about him the clutch of her bronze arms. He would taste in his mouth the cold metal, the marble dust. One day, in a fisherman's net, this awesome spectacle would be brought to the surface, a flesh and blood man in a mermaid's arms. The fishermen would be Perkheimer, Dr. Hodler, Signor Pignata and Herr Holzapfel. On the deck Miss Kollwitz and Miss Throop would lid their eyes. Separate the lovers one could not. There was nothing but to dump them back into the sea, a point midway between Scylla and Charbydis. Like a lover he toyed with the gold nuggets that tipped her breasts. He rolled with the roll of the sea. He felt no pain. When Perkheimer asked him for the time he thought with relief that his watch, with its luminous face, was guaranteed to be waterproof. What time was it? Soby replied it was either quarter past eleven, or five to three: he, Perkheimer, could take his choice. Perkheimer, with the eyes of a trophy, peered from his silken bangs as though from an ambush.

Three o'clock? Then where was Mykonos? Mykonos? Was it not a small island? Soby replied. He had even had difficulty locating it on the map. Did Perkheimer expect any Greek sailor to do it on such a night? Herr Perkheimer did not—not any longer—he sat as if strapped to the corner of the bunk, a filter tipped cigarette, long out, dangling at the spout of his lip. Now and then a film of water brightened the floor. The roll of the boat filled the washbowl with a black, sour-smelling slop, then sucked it empty with a gasp. Behind the sliding panel Miss Throop wanted to die, but could not. At intervals she repeated O my God! without her usual accent. The hand of Miss Kollwitz could be heard slapping her broad back. The sea frothed and glowed at the porthole, where the light seeped in like water, the room like a fishbowl full of odds and ends. A mermaid medallion, a sleeping doll with the face of a gargoyle, a man lying contentedly in a water soaked bunk. From the hall seeped a strong disinfectant smell. The slap of a swabbing mop, the strings under the crack in the door. Without warning the sliding panel opened on the sea-green face of Miss Kollwitz, a wet face towel clamped to her mouth. Perhaps the sight of the room disturbed her, the floor wet, the luggage scattered, the layers of filth in the washbowl, the face that looked up at her from the sea-washed floor. Her cheeks filled, but perhaps it was more than wind. She moved from the panel without a sound. Through the opening Soby dimly observed the form of Miss Throop, a corpse waiting for burial, and that the bunk above her was occupied only by Aschenbach.

"Look here!" Miss Kollwitz cried, but she made no appearance, water sucked and slurped at the washbowl, and Soby would have sworn he heard the muffled bark of Miss Cynthia. He didn't, however. No, Miss Kollwitz had awakened—if that was the word—to find the cat, Aschenbach, in her bunk, her shoes on the floor, but Miss Cynthia Pomeroy, of Winnetka, gone. In the manner of a man whose time had come, Soby arose.

Mykonos? The mate assured Soby that all was well. A collar stud had left its green imprint on his neck. The twist of his head had worn the cloth from his jacket collar. The celluloid stiffener was exposed like a bone. From exposure his flesh had the color of fire blackened metal, the eruptions like blisters under paint. He reeked like something pickled, dropped in the street. The blackness ahead was Rhodes, not Mykonos—they would touch at Mykonos going back.

The storm had made it inadvisable. The crown of his mate's cap was discolored like a rag for swabbing machinery, the bones of the head were plainly visible. They stood in the hatchway, facing the spray that swept the deck. The *Hephaistos* pitched but there was less roll, the black sea had a light tracing of foam.

And Miss Cynthia? Under the flapping canvas of a lifeboat Soby saw the drained faces of Wandervogel, as if they had been swallowed by a whale. The face of Fraulein Kretschmar faced the new day with a stiff upper lip. The tousled heads of Wandervogel, along with that of Herr Holzapfel, were dark with spray. At the fantail, alone, a barefoot member of the crew swabbed the deck. Sweater and pants were of the color of the deck, or a rainsoaked tree. Drawstrings dangled from the flaps of a seaman's oilskin hat. Not the legs, white as a fish belly, nor the marble feet, but the arm that curled behind her, the gloved thumb probing an itch between the shoulder blades, held Soby's eye. One knee and one elbow arched like a bow. In the shelter of a ventilator the steward who had supplied her with the outfit waved his arms to suggest how to use the mop. Soby came up behind her, bringing his sore hand up firm into one armpit, spinning her around as she dropped the handle of the mop. Was he surprised to find her lips sea-blue, and not gold? Without a word he pushed her toward the hatchway, one shoulder high, her feet flapping, the smell of a wet dog rising from her clothes. At the stairs, one step above him, she turned to swoop his cap from his head, and with a wide, boom-like swing sail it over the sea. Soby grabbed her, that is he gripped her in the manner of Herr Holzapfel, shaking her so that the cap rocked over to conceal her face.

"Stop this clowning!" he yelled. "You hear me!"

The hat covered her face like a helmet visor. She made no sound. He whipped it off and with a swing that hurt his arm sailed it over the rail. The hair stuffed into its crown fell wet and lank about her shoulders, framing the parted lips, the runny nose, the mocking smile.

"You're going to get into trouble!" he yelled, shaking her. "You hear me?"

"You scared for *me* or *you,* doll?" she replied. Without a moment's hesitation Soby slapped her with the palm of his bandaged hand. It popped her eyes, her mouth opened wide. The slap had cleared her cheek, veined with strands of her hair, as if to buff up the flush of color, but what she saw in his eyes led him to ignore what he saw in hers. He closed them, making a face like Miss Kollwitz to see no evil, but she did not slap him back, as he hoped. No, she let him stand there, gripping her arms, his hair dripping with spray, as if he meant to kiss her for the first or the last time. Her arms hung limp, she would have leaned against him if he had not held her firmly. The voice of Fraulein Kretschmar, her head peering from the lifeboat above them, led Soby to tip his head and open his eyes. She wanted to call his attention, no more, to the phantom figure of Miss Kollwitz who stood in the hatchway like a pillar of salt. What had she seen? Worse, what had she feared she *might?* Happily the wind blew off the sounds in her open mouth. As one of Soby's hands fell to his side the girl waved. "Hi!" she cried, then walked like a sailor across the deck to the door of the hatchway, Miss Kollwitz leaning on the wall to let her pass.

eighteen | Under beach umbrellas that shadowed the white sand, bathers watched the *Hephaistos* enter the harbor, tranquil as a pond in a medieval courtyard, which was how it looked. Soby returned the wave of a child on the beach. If swimming shorts could be bought he would soon be there himself. Under one of those umbrellas, or perhaps two, for the sake of appearances, Soby and the ladies would spend a few days recovering from a voyage by water. There were tours to be taken. A medieval castle to explore. The Knight's castle of Rhodes seemed to be waiting for the arrival of Connecticut Yankees, Wandervogel, and cinema crews from Hollywood. But better if they had not come by boat. Aside from Wandervogel, there were few Damen und Herren on the deck. They looked at the scene a little skeptically, with compressed lips. Where was the wine-dark, white-maned sea they had just crossed? Still out there, and if anything perhaps a little worse. Rather than behind, it now lay ahead of them. Soby heard this news from strange Wandervogel, assembled on the dock, long-haired and shaggy as goats, waiting for a boat to take them to Athens, Mykonos, and Corfu. In two hours the *Hephaistos* would make another stab at Mykonos. But not with Soby. If for nothing else, he had the ladies to thank for that.

Miss Cynthia, wearing a middy blouse with anchors on the sleeves, blue sneakers with white laces, and a Camp Fire Girl's expression, came to tell him that Miss Kollwitz said to tell him that Aschenbach had disappeared. Was she pleased? Soby kept his eyes on the sea. Like a sling, hanging below her knees, she swung the plastic bag with his dried blood on it. "Aschenbach?" he said, as if recalling the face, and stared at the white part in her hair. Pigeon-toed she went before him, her hair parted to show the two peeling vertebra divided by the green line of the gold chain she had bought in Florence.

Herr Perkheimer, smiling, met him at the door with the cat house in his arms, the dutch door open. Miss Kollwitz insisted Soby peer in, to make sure for himself. When Aschenbach had turned up missing the first thing she had thought of was the sliding panel, open during the night, which had led her to disturb Herr Perkheimer. Herr Perkheimer begged to disagree. Clutching the cat house he said it was a pleasure to be of service, since he, too, planned to spend a few days at Rhodes. Did he exchange a wink with Soby, or was it the ribbon of cigarette smoke? Anyhow, there he was, attached to the house of Winifred Throop. If the door were larger he might have crawled into it.

Miss Kollwitz cried that she would not leave the boat without Aschenbach, not for one moment, having heard in what way the Greeks were fond of cats. They ate them. Actual mention of it was there in her book. Soby said he could appreciate her feelings, but the situation was complicated. If she would leave the boat, it would have to be without Aschenbach. The rules were strict about dogs and cats. They should be grateful that he had decided to shift for himself. *No, no!* Miss Kollwitz cried, and turned to Miss Throop, her wig puffed through her hat like a bird's nest. She had not spoken. The wide limp brim of the hat concealed her face. Propped erect by her corset, her knees spread, her swollen feet stuffed into her unlaced shoes, she sat with her small, puffy hands palm up in her lap.

"I think we better get going," Soby said, but Miss Throop did not seem to hear him. Herr Perkheimer's smoke seemed to tangle in her hair like a web.

"Aunt Winnie, you tight or asleep?" asked the girl.

In the pause a yawn escaped her. "My dear Soby —" she said, putting up one arm, "I am not tight, but I wish I was."

"The luggage!" cried Miss Kollwitz.

"I'll come back for it," Soby replied.

Little Perkheimer, with the cat house, followed by Miss Cynthia with her flight bag, went ahead of them, single file, with Soby bringing up the rear.

A taxi, with Soby posted up front, the cat house between the hood and the fender, took them along the fortifications in the direction of the Hotel des Roses, situated on the beach. Wandervogel, led by Fraulein Kretschmar, could be seen on the road on top of the ramparts. A brisk offshore breeze flipped the pages of the guidebook Miss Kollwitz used as an eyeshade.

Since they had so little time before the siesta, when everything official would close its doors, Soby suggested that the ladies relax at the hotel while he, and Herr Perkheimer, made the necessary arrangements. They would pick up the luggage, they would go to the bank. They would inquire about visas and the next boat to Athens. Miss Throop made no comment. Miss Kollwitz seemed to feel events were out of her hands. Herr Perkheimer remained in the taxi while Soby, carrying the empty cat house, escorted the ladies to a table with a view of the harbor. Was that white boat the *Hephaistos?* Apparently it was. White as a seabird with its head under its wing.

It led Miss Kollwitz to wonder aloud if they might be hasty in abandoning the tour. They were on an island. Would they ever get off it? Soby reassured her it was better to be on an island than on the *Hephaistos;* he drew out chairs for the ladies, but Miss Cynthia remained standing. Miss Kollwitz turned as if to question her.

"I'm going with Mr. Soby," the girl said.

There was no comment. "You hear?" Miss Kollwitz cried. "You hear her?" She leaned forward to grip the arm of Miss Throop.

"Make mine the usual," Miss Throop said. From

her bust, higher than usual, she plucked invisible flecks of lint.

"I'm going to look for Aschenbach," she said.

"No, no!" Miss Kollwitz popped up. "You stay. I go."

"Aschenbach?" Did Miss Throop bark or hiccup? The shawl vibrated on her wide shoulders. "My dear," she said, "I thought you had found him."

"No, no!" Miss Kollwitz cried. "You stay. I know him." From her bag she drew the sleeve of Soby's sweater, looped it about her head.

"My dear Soby," Miss Throop said, "would you care to join me? I'm sure that Miss Cynthia and Miss Kollwitz—"

"I think—" Soby stood blinking at the glare over the harbor, "Herr Perkheimer and I had better go alone. There are complications. I'll take a look around for Aschenbach."

"You hear?" Miss Kollwitz shouted at the girl. "He wants to go alone, you hear!"

"*He's* not crazy and *I'm* not deaf!" she replied.

Soby went off, the voice of the ladies like birds trapped under the awning. In the street, however, neither the taxi nor Herr Perkheimer were where Soby had left them. He checked the hotel lobby, the bar, the gentlemen's room. Was he looking for something? A boy with many cameras, perhaps? The driver of a horse-drawn cab pointed his whip in the direction of the harbor. He shouted at Soby the need for haste.

They went off at a walk. Citizens on bicycles tooted their rubber horns as they pedalled past. Along the road assorted Wandervogel sat along the sea wall, but no Perkheimer. Tranquil as a seabird, the *Hephaistos* floated in the bay. Along the rail Damen und Herren with new Wandervogel who had come aboard at Rhodes.

Soby leaned forward to speak to the driver, but his attention was on the ramparts. Herr Perkheimer, his arsenal of cameras and pouches flapping, went along the rampart wall in the nimble manner of Douglas Fairbanks. Insolently he turned to jeer at the giant pursuing him. Behind the lumbering Holzapfel Fraulein Kretschmar waved and screamed encouragement. Before Soby was out of the deep seat of the cab they were gone. How did one get up there? The driver took a moment to think it over. Ten minutes, perhaps. His glance advised Soby to relax in the cab. At the port of entry Soby asked him if he would help with the luggage. He would, for a consideration. They found the deck of the *Hephaistos* clear, but below, the cabin doors propped open, scores of Damen und Herren sprawled on unmade bunks. An odor like that of soiled diapers soured the draft. In Soby's cabin the beds were unmade, but the beds of the ladies had fresh linen, and the floor had been swabbed. The bowl smelled of disinfectant, clean towels hung on the rack. Not one to underestimate the power of a woman, Soby wondered if they were a bit hasty. Perhaps the worst was over? By tomorrow noon the *Hephaistos* would be back in Athens. Goliath would still be pursuing David on the isle of Rhodes. Soby hesitated, but the driver made up his mind. He went off with all but one of the ladies' bags.

At the gangplank Soby explained that the ladies were staying over; for a consideration, not particularly small, he was allowed to pass through with their luggage. At a milk-horse clop they headed back for the hotel. Returning Wandervogel smiled and waved. The ramparts were quiet. The siesta had begun. From a pedlar, as a little surprise, Soby bought three odorless nosegays, which he delivered to the ladies, leaving the driver with the bags. Miss Throop sat alone, a withered olive in her empty martini glass. The nosegay Soby proffered, with a bow, she placed in the glass, then topped with the olive. Her tic, not her wink, flicked the lid of one bloodshot eye.

"My dear Soby," she said and hiccupped. "What is it?" Her head lolled back to see him better.

"I'm afraid—" Soby began.

"Tut, tut, darling." She put her fingers to her lips. Dim but perceptible Soby felt a pleasurable twitch of guilt. Had the girl told all? Had Miss Kollwitz described what she had seen? Miss Throop flapped her fin-like hand. "Evelyn's law, my dear. If you can't sell it, give it away, but for godsake don't save it! May I suggest Corfu? Her mother would love the ring of it, especially by wire. Just be kind enough to let us know when we might expect you in Venice. Miss Kollwitz will be living in sin with Aschenbach."

Miss Throop plucked the olive from the nosegay and popped it into her mouth, biting down on the stone. Was there about to be a scene? A film blurred her eyes. Behind her the beach umbrellas vibrated in the offshore breeze that blew the hair of Miss Kollwitz over her face. She came toward them waving a key, followed by a hotel porter.

"Look!" she cried. "Where is she?"

Soby's head shook, he said, "I've no idea."

"She went to look for *you!*" Miss Kollwitz gripped his arms as if to shake him. A bag of grapes she was holding spilled to the floor. She released Soby to stoop for the grapes and he went off, still holding two nosegays. Her voice followed him across the verandah into the street. In the back seat of the cab the driver took his siesta, the horse tossed the feed-bag, then lowered its head. Before the driver's eyes Soby wagged his last bill. "The boat! Subito!"

Leisurely they went off. The deafening clop of the nag, her mane blowing like a merry-go-round charger, kept him from hearing the warning whistle, but he saw it. The nag also, since she increased her pace. Wandervogel, including Herr Holzapfel, lined the rail facing the ramparts. Like Hercules, he raised a huge fist to shake it at the walls of the city. Did they seem higher than ever? Little Perkheimer, looking no larger than a seabird, sat there with his short legs dangling, a thumb to his nose. He lowered it to aim his gun, strafe the crowded deck of the *Hephaistos*. From where Soby passed beneath he looked like a child playing with a toy gun.

One hand stretched out before him, waving, Soby ran for the boat. Cheering Wandervogel urged him on to where, wheezing, he reached the tilted gangplank, raised his eyes to scan the faces along the rail. What if the girl was not on it? The mocking smile was not there. No Fraulein waved a boneless arm. Was the giddiness Soby felt over-exertion, fear, or relief? A member of the crew dropped a coil of rope in order to prop up Soby, a hand at his armpit, until the gangplank could be steadied on the pier.

"Look who's here!" cried a voice. Did that mean Soby? Level with his eyes the girl's head was framed by the open porthole, a Sailor's Valentine, a life preserver around her neck. Before Soby could speak the hole emptied, was then plugged with a shabby fur piece. It proved to have a top, the cactus-jowled, toothless face of Aschenbach. From the deck Fraulein Kretschmar beckoned, smiling, but Soby went forward propelled from behind, light-footed, lighthearted, the smile of the anointed on his sweaty face.

nineteen | Occupado? As if troubled by
the missing purdah, Madame Sambar cupped a hand
to her mouth. At her back three moon-faced daughters
sat on their luggage as if to protect it. All chewed
gum. All wore black stockings and patent leather sandals.

"There must be some mistake—" Soby said, but
there was no mistake about it being occupado. Fresh
towels hung on the rack. Fresh linen occupied the
berths.

"Occupado, occupado!" Madame Sambar chanted,
and flipped her plump hand to shoo him away.
Bracelets clinked on her arm. A respectable mous-
tache occupied her lip. A piece of luggage rope, her
own, secured the knob on the sliding panel to the
bunk post where Miss Kollwitz had draped her knitting. Madame Sambar had possession, nine points of
the law. The door closed with a snap. The bolt
clicked.

"I guess that's *that*," said Soby, and turned to see
how Miss Cynthia took it. Had she understood what
had been said? She seemed unconcerned. Half
turned, she gazed down the passage to the smoky
light in the lounge. Was it now Soby's problem? So it
seemed. Someone would always turn up—as so many
had—to look after her. One of the blessings of Soby's
life—momentarily suspended—was that the younger
generation was never his own, and after a four-year,

qualified loan were shipped back where they had come from.

"There's no problem—" he said, widening his smile, "since you and Aschenbach can have *my* cabin."

He waited for her to say, "But Mr. Soby, what about *you?*"

She let him wait. As they entered the lounge the marble faced steward with the hairless chest, his tattoo showing, said "Hi, bebe!"

"Hi," she replied. Unmistakably he gave Soby an appraising leer as he rang the bell for lunch.

Madame Sambar and her daughters, from Lebanon, shared the table with Miss Cynthia, Soby, and a young man from Nacogdoches, Texas, Orien Reefy by name. "Ah can't tell yoh wah tut means to heah mah mothah tongue!" Mr. Reefy said. As a matter of courtesy he included Soby, but directed his remarks to Miss Cynthia. "Ah wutof swan yoh was a suthun cul til yoh opnt yoh mouf!" Even with her mouth open Mr. Reefy felt things were looking up. "Yoh-all excuse the expression, suh, but yoh dawtuh is the fuss white woman I set eyes on in five weeks!" Where had he been? "To tell the truth, suh, dam if I know. One eye-land looks to me lak another eye-land!" Mr. Reefy had given up his position with a textbook company in Nacogdoches just to see what all the fuss about Greece was about. They said to him, Mistuh

Reefy, yoh take as much time as yoh like. The moh yoh see the moh yoh'll love Nacogdoches.

"Na-co *what?*" said the girl.

"I wuss waitin foh yoh to ask me that, Miss," he replied.

"Sounds Spanish," said Soby.

"Yoh doan say? Everywheah I go peepul say Na-co what? Then I wuked out this way to help'm. Yoh-all remember Con-stan-tin-ople?"

"I'm afraid we've not been there," replied Soby.

"Ah mean the song. Yoh-all remember the song? Connnnnnn-stan-tin-OOOOO-pulll, C-o-n-s-t-a-n-t-i-n-o-p-l-eeee!" he sang.

The Sambar girls covered their faces with their napkins. Miss Cynthia lidded her eyes and spelled it out with her lips.

"Na-co-do che-" she recited, "it doesn't work out."

"Suh," said Mr. Reefy, "yoh dawtuhs a smaht cul. Yoh know who yoh dawtuh reminds me of, suh?"

"*Who?*" put in the girl, one eye on Soby.

"Yoh dawtuh reminds me—"

But Soby interrupted. "If you don't mind, Mr. Reefy, I'd rather she reminded me of anybody but my daughter."

That was so unexpected Soby doubted what he had heard. So did the girl. Mr. Reefy had just time to glance from father to dawtuh, a tongue to his lips, when the boat shuddered as if the screw throbbed out of the water. A wall of sea, white as a snowslide, frothed at the portholes, followed by a muffled silence. As if their names had been called Damen und Herren stood up. Water flooding the deck spilled into the hatchway where the mate, soaked to the knees, pounded with his fist on the latch that held the door ajar. Invisible arms circled the waists of Madame Sambar, her daughters, and Mr. Reefy, drawing them from the table as they leaned forward, grabbing the cloth for support. Cups and saucers, china and silver, the bowl of fruit and bottles of mineral water, along with Mr. Reefy's camera, spilled into their laps, and from their laps to the floor. Soby leaned on the table as from the ledge of a window, watching it all. Trays of glasses on a stand near the door went over slowly, as if suspended in water, covering the floor near the exit with glass like pieces of ice. Was that all? One moment it seemed so, as the center of gravity shifted, the toppled pieces were frozen as in a still from a Mack Sennett comedy. Then the arms that had seized Madame Sambar took a grip on Soby and the chair beside him, but there was no longer a cloth on the table for him to grab. His arms went up, but they were short of the long disjointed arms reaching for him, her face white as if the pull of the sea had drained it of blood. Arms extended, his feet in the air, Soby went over as if tossed in a blanket, the porthole sprinkling him with the sea. Did he black out? Seldom had his mind seemed so clear. The hubbub and confusion were curiously unconfused. The hairy legs of Holzapfel, streaked with spilled beer, the whistle of Fraulein Kretschmar staving off panic, and the voice of Mr. Reefy, envious but unruffled, "See who *huh* Daddy-O is, ah can tell yoh!"

And who was it? The head of Soby was in her lap. She clutched him like a teddy bear she might be deprived of, a blank whiteness in her startled face. Not knowing where it came from Soby cried "Ouch!" From his fall? No, from the way her nails dug into his flesh. The voice of Fraulein Kretschmar begged the Damen not to panic and ordered the Wandervogel to restore order. First aid she brought to Soby, personally. She described his condition as shock. The best place for his head was where it was, in a woman's lap. A wet napkin was applied to his forehead, the collar of his shirt unbuttoned, but the arms around his head did not relax. His ear pounded with the beating of her heart.

Mr. Reefy said, "If ah fall on *mah* head, will I get fust aid like Daddy-O?" But only Mr. Reefy understood that. What had happened? Some said the rudder had broken. Another said that an earthquake commonly produced such things. All admitted that no man knew the sea, or what it might do next.

Was it over? One could not say it was over if the crew went about chaining down the tables. Mr. Reefy went away and came back with the word that the passage to Mykonos would be rough. Passengers were advised to stay in their cabins and clear of the decks.

Was Soby all right? With Miss Cynthia's permission, Mr. Reefy helped him to his feet. One arm and one leg seemed splintered with sleep. The girl on one side, Mr. Reefy on the other, they stopped at the bar for bottled water, then went through the lounge where the Wandervogel were gathered. The sea kept them off the deck: they sat on the floor singing heimat lieder. A few Herren, smoking pipes, sat in the chairs. To Soby's credit let it be said he suggested that perhaps *they* would like to join *them*. The girl and the boy. Birds of a feather, that is. What was her answer? That shrill bark said to be from her mother. In her flour-white face her lips looked black, like the Rawley girls under the prom lights. Among other things Mr. Reefy showed himself to be a good loser.

"See who *huh* Daddy-O is," he repeated, and went ahead to open the door to the cabin. Before the lights switched on they saw the eyes of Aschenbach like coals blown alive by the draft through the door. "Gawd a-mighty!" Reefy said, stepping back, but as the lights came on he saw the cat, the empty luggage racks. "Yoh folks sho travel light," he said, "doan you?" Was it light in the head Soby felt? He made no comment. He stood with one hand on a bunk for support watching the girl move the cat from a pillow. Without turning from the bunk she said, "Daddy-O, why yoh travel so light?"

The tilt of the boat closed the door Mr. Reefy, departing, had left open, and sucked out, with a slurp, the dirty water that had filled the bowl. Her loosened hair screening off her face Miss Cynthia threw up what she had eaten, put a towel to her face, and with the roll of the boat sprawled out on the bunk.

Was the child sick, sobbing, or a little of both? Oddly enough Soby felt relief, as if the food had been on his own stomach.

"Cynthia—" he said.

"Don't call me Cyn-thi-aaaa!" she shouted. The hand Soby had extended toward her shoulder he jerked away, as if she might bite it. "Look—" he said.

"Look, look, look, look!" she cried. "You and Miss Nowits!"

Before Soby could reach out for the post, a tilt of the boat toppled him against the door. Water poured from the cup of the porthole to the foot of the bed. She glanced up, white-faced, to see if he was hurt, sniffled.

"When you're through with that towel," he said, "I suggest you put it at the porthole." He took his raincoat from the door, as he opened it she cried, "Wait!" He stood there, waiting. "Where are you going?"

"I'll drop back when you feel a little better," he said, and closed the door with a snap. If she had called he might have opened it but all he heard was the wash at the porthole. He slipped the raincoat on, found his pipe, and stood in the dark striking wet matches. The pipe unlit he went down the hallway to the lounge. Mr. Reefy, surrounded by Wandervogel, was teaching them the words of *Git Along, Little Doggie, Git Along*. He plucked Holzapfel's guitar, and sang it in the manner of Burl Ives.

"Daddy-O!" he called. "How you feel?"

Soby felt fine, just fine. Three Herren and one Damen played cards on a table covered with a cloth to keep the cards from sliding. They swayed in a slow dance to accommodate the roll of the boat. With the hatch door closed the oily smell of the diesel sweetened the air. Water dripped on the stairs leading up to the deck. The bar—cleared of the dirty glasses, and three or four bottles—was open. The sallow-faced steward sat on a stool sewing a button to the fly of his pants. Soby did not interrupt him. He waited till the button was attached, the fly buttoned up.

Was there anything to drink? Gin served in a brandy glass. Soby sipped it, one eye on the clock, one on the kerosene tinted liquid that kept a level he could not keep himself. The steward had nothing, good or evil, to say. By the dim barlight he thumbed the pages of a German movie magazine. Soby tipped him, asking for the loan of an opener for his bottled water. He bought matches, but none of them would light. A little after eleven the Wandervogel stopped singing cowboy ballads, formed a clearing at the center of the room for their sleeping rolls. When Soby brought up the word Mykonos, the steward merely shrugged.

For a pillow—and to see how the girl was now feeling—Soby went back down the gangway to the cabin. There was no answer to his knock. Would he find it locked? The door sucked inward, pulling him with it as the floor tilted, the porthole luminous with a sudsy, glowing froth. In the corner of the lower bunk, the goldleaf shimmering, was the portrait. What made it so lifelike? Goose flesh formed on Soby's hands, his mouth dried. Lifelike it was, indeed, since the girl's head stuck through it, the lips smiling, the eyes rolling as in the comic snapshots of the penny arcade.

"Daddy-O," she drawled, "why doh yoh-all trafful so light?"

If his head had not been in it, the roll of the boat would have closed the door in Soby's face. He saw no stars, no, rather a burst of light as if a flashbulb had popped in the darkness. Once more the tilt of the boat opened the door. As if various lights played on it, he saw the portrait approaching, the white arms spread wide as she tripped and toppled toward him. Did she cry his name? He heard the gasping slurp of water from the bowl. Clamped in her arms, his own flat at his sides, they careened from the door to the wall, from the wall back again to the door. Through her wild hair he saw the porthole like a wad of clothes wheeling in a washer. Was he the first to laugh? Laughing, his knees sagging, he was held upright by the weight of her body, the belt of his coat hooked to the knob of the door. Behind the sliding panel the light blinked on and off as Madame Sambar calmed her daughters. Were they crazy? He felt pleasantly remote from the disorder, safe in his front row seat at a Mack Sennett shipwreck scene. What next? His arms were free and she was trying to remove them from the sleeves of the coat. He laughed as if tickled. Free of the sleeves he threw his arms around the girl. She turned to see the cabinet mirror slap on the wall, crashing like a cymbal, pieces of the glass dropping into the frothing bowl. The light went out. As they reeled, toppling, Soby was certain the boat had capsized. Behind the sliding panel Madame Sambar's daughters screamed. Nothing held him, or supported him, but Soby could not move. A weight like an illness pressed on his chest, his diaphragm. Then, like a sleeper stirring, the *Hephaistos* righted, the light came on, water spilled from the bowl, and Soby saw the face below him as if by moonlight, the eyes like those of a cat. Had the light, or the darkness, widened her eyes? Nothing Soby would call an expression showed in her face. Nothing but terror so free of complications it had no name, but more of an odor. She seemed unaware of the pool of water in which she crouched, her legs coiled beneath her, one tapered foot showing like the tip of a fin. In that shallow pool she was more fish than fraulein—more a creature of the bottomless sea than one of land. For such occasions the mind of Soby searched for an appropriate quotation. Oddly enough, one came to mind—

> *Or is it of the Virgin's silver beauty*
> *All fish below the thighs?*

Was it the unexpected silence that brought her around? The mask of terror cracked, the wide mouth trembled as if uncertain about the expression: as one coming out of ether she wondered who and where she was. Did Soby speak to reassure her? What she heard, or saw, made her laugh. The shrill unholy glee of someone trapped in a looney bin. Had the child lost such mind as she had? Soby stood up, found the glass still in its rack above the bowl, dipped it into the water, then spilled it into the girl's white, hysterical face. The laughing stopped as if he had struck her, the eyes remained wide. He wet his hands, rubbed her cheeks between his palms, then half lifted, half dragged her from the corner to her bunk. The stiffness left her body, she sprawled out on her face. A breath neither sweet nor sour, but cave-like, exhaled from some unexplored region of her body where it had been stored. He sat on the wet floor at her side, warming her hands. The froth at the porthole, the tilt of the floor had let up for some time before he knew it. The stillness called his attention to the fact that the screw had stopped. He pushed up to stare through the porthole at the harbor of Mykonos. Few lights. The feet of Wandervogel thumping the deck.

"What a way to go!" she said, her voice hollow. "Was I out *cold?*"

"Not cold," he said, "just cool." The familiar mocking smile toyed with her blue lips. "That's better, that's more like it."

"Like what?"

"Like Miss Cynthia Pomeroy," he replied. Did that disappoint her?

"You mean I wasn't any *more* than that?"

He shook his head slowly. "Maybe quite a bit less," he smiled.

"I hope I wasn't somebody *naughty*," she said, "but if I was I don't suppose I need to worry." In the worldy arch of her brows Soby gathered that he saw her mother, still a formidable sight. She pursed her lips. It brought to Soby's mind how they might taste.

"A girl can be as naughty as she likes," he said, "if she has just vomited."

Her head raised from the pillow, she drew the soiled back of her hand across her face.

"In case you pass out again," he said, "I can assure you there is no cause for worry."

Did she lift her hand to strike him? Her eyes stared as if the light had gone out. She sat up, pushing away the hand he put out to calm her, then stood up, straddle-legged, propping herself on the rim of the bowl. Where the mirror had been two or three small fragments remained. She pried one loose, wiped it like an apple on her thigh, then stared into it like a pocket mirror, one eye at a time. Her mouth, the lips curled back, she examined last. With the broken mirror had she lost a familiar part? Turning suddenly she said, "Why don't *you* like me?"

It cost Soby little effort not to smile. "Like *who?*" he said, "Miss Cynthia Pomeroy, Miss Primavera, Miss Nausicaa, Miss Wild Goose—"

She interrupted. "Don't you like *any* of them?"

Why, he wondered, had he looked so little at her eyes? The long dark lashes were twisted and wet. Behind them did he see the wisdom of the girl as well as the fish?

"Don't look at me like *that*," she made a face.

"Why not?" He turned to glance out the porthole. A boat, crowded with Wandervogel, coughed a smoke that glowed in the deck lights.

"You weren't really looking at *me*, that's why." He did not deny it. "What *were* you looking at?"

"Something out of this world," he replied. Was she curious? She took a step toward him as if he saw it through the porthole.

"Far out?" she asked, hopefully.

"Far, farther, farthest." She waited and he added, "A real cool mermaid—all fish below the thighs." Did she like that?

"Just so it's not *all* fish," she turned back to the mirror. In one fragment she flashed him an eye, as the *Hephaistos,* leaving the harbor, made her first pitch. When she reached for support the piece of mirror cracked on the bowl, she spread her fingers to let the glass splinter on the floor. One hand on the bunk post, Soby reached out to swoop one arm around her, wheeling slowly so that they fell on the lower berth. She did not speak, nor release the grip she had on him. A pair of cool fish, scared of drowning, but no longer so scared of each other, they crouched in the dryer corner of the berth. Soby managed to drag a piece of wet blanket over their legs. On the roll that seemed to splinter the sleeping arm that supported her head, he was able to see and exchange glances with the cat, Aschenbach. Over one petrified eye, like a masked bandit, he had lowered the lid.

twenty | Such a day—the lady guide explained—windless and bright as a new penny, would erase the memory of that unfortunate day they had spent in the gale on the Acropolis. But what if they didn't want to? Erase the memory, that is. Soby tipped her, explaining that the memory, such as it was, would have to do, since more urgent problems had presented themselves. Could she be of any help? The day was not so windless her voice was not strident and hoarse. Her dark eyes dilated to fix Soby with a bold stare. A film of the girl's face powder ill concealed the bump on his forehead. She glanced to see if he had given the girl as good as he had got. Soby thanked her; with the girl by the arm they walked around the bus loaded with Madame Sambar and her staring daughters, Damen und Herren, but no Fraulein Kretschmar. She was back on Mykonos, living with Herr Holzapfel the life of the Greeks. From the back seat of a cab Orien Reefy ran the window down to flap his hand, shout something Soby was mercifully unable to understand. The girl waved, swinging her plastic purse on its leather strap. On the corner they were stopped by the traffic and the back of a head that looked familiar.

"Hi!" said the girl.

"Hi, bebe," he replied, turned on Soby his marble gaze, then walked before them with his sockless feet loose in his laceless shoes.

On the opposite corner Soby paused and said,

"Let's see now—toothbrushes, toothpaste, soap, pajamas, a mirror." He had put up his hand to count on the fingers.

"Mother said I need a mirror like a hole in the head," she replied. What did Soby have to say to that? He tried to think. She reached for the hand that he held before them and took a grip on three fingers. "She's crazy," she said, "you'll love her."

By the hand she led him along the row of shop fronts. They paused to face a family dressed in matching pajamas.

"Just pajamas for *you*," she said. "You can wear the bottoms and I can wear the tops." When he said nothing she added, "The house is just full of Daddy's bottoms. All mother wears are the tops."

They bought a mirror, nevertheless. The glass was loose, but dolphins held the frame of a golden color to the nickel-plated handle, which contained an orange stick, a nailfile, a lipstick, a pair of tweezers for plucking the eyebrows. Pajamas? Never mind about the tops, but the bottoms were inclined to run short on Soby. Held to his waist, they resembled something new in swimming trunks. One pair was sufficient, plus a small zipper bag stamped with a view of the Acropolis to conceal them. Into it also went some panties, cold cream, aspirin, Dentyne gum, a safety razor, two boxes of tissue, a glass ball with a miniature of the Parthenon for Miss Throop. For Miss Kollwitz a book of pictures, *Immortal Greece*, all windless and bright as a new penny, to erase the memory of that memorable day on the Acropolis.

The apothecary clerk who had bandaged Soby's hand stopped him in the street to ask him about it. Had he yet symptoms of rabies? No? In that case he should have a new dressing. At the rear of the shop, while he applied it, he entertained them with photographs of his grandchildren, in white shirts without faces, all well known in the state of Illinois. Surely Soby had seen them? He would write and tell them to look out for Soby, lover of Greece, and if he and the Missus should stop in Bloomington they would get a free meal.

He and the Missus? They drank bottles of warm Coca Cola while a young man snipped out of black paper the silhouette of Gary Cooper smoking a pipe. And who was it? The spit and image, she said, of Soby. If fit snugly into the lid of her new compact. They were back on the *Hephaistos* when the busses returned from another windy day on the summit, Damen und Herren freshly powdered with marble dust. A Frau Gunther had fallen and sprained her wrist. A tripod had disappeared while Herr Knoedler had loaded his camera. Nevertheless, one sensed that this day on the Acropolis had been a good one, now that the small bat-like shadow of Herr Perkheimer had passed.

Accompanied by two policemen, his left arm in a sling, a gentleman in a seersucker suit, without lug-

gage, came aboard just before they sailed. Neither
Dr. Hodler nor Orien Reefy appeared. The sea was
calm. Soby and the Missus sat in steamer chairs,
under a rain of soot, eating the last of the peanuts in
the pockets of his coat. Her hand in one of them, she
dozed off. The sea darkened, the gulls swam like
goldfish in the windstream, and the coast of Greece
resembled Arizona flooded, thanks to Miss Throop.
But to whom did Soby owe thanks for the private
advice? It came unbidden, and was not the voice of
a stranger—

My dear Soby do you not think—for I leave the
point to you—that this is a path of perilous sweet-
ness? May I ask your intentions? Do you consider
them respectable? What good is a teacher who knows
he is headed for the pit? One would think, to hear
you talk, that the word *pit* belongs at the base of a
column, preferably broken, in the cool wing of a
library. Unless libraries have changed. I see you
smile. Getting back to the Greeks has its hazards,
doesn't it? If it's something immortal you're after
look behind the eyes, not at them. But that can be a
strain. We're men after all, not fish. However, if it's
something mortal you're after—and I take it that it is
—what you see before your eyes can be good enough.
In your case, if not in hers, eminently satisfactory, but
don't offend the Gods by ignoring your luck. On the
Orphic side, which is mine, the beloved is both named
and nameless, a charming Oberlin freshman, a Nau-

sicaa by the sea, a Lolita selecting a new popsicle. *Im*-persons, rather than persons—if you know what I mean. We have no name for what is fish below the thighs. Could that be why it is the lasting personality? Such things as terror and grief, love and desire, as well as the reverse side of the coin—but I leave the point to you. Who was it that said, *what a way to go?* A quite satisfactory—don't you think—way of putting it? You'll have time to think it over, in any case, there's nothing like a voyage by water, is there? A sea-change is the first and last change, isn't it? After all it was the sea, as you may remember, from where—

The voice trailed off since for some time the listener had been asleep. Another head rested on his shoulder, breathing upon him a vapor of gum and peanuts. Did he dream of mock-eyed sirens with gold tipped breasts, all fish below the thighs? Or did a train of weirdly clad night creatures file through his head? They went in pairs, as Adam and Eve, one with the tops of the pajamas, the other with the bottoms. Among them were two, their eyes bright with torchlight, who went hooting with the drawn out *u*-sound bearing between them a zipper bag with the gleaming replica of the Acropolis.

They were up at dawn to see the sun rise on Venice, but a mist-like rain shrouded the sea. They saw no more than a few funereal hooded gondolas. Fog delayed their arrival for several hours. Just before noon, slightly tilted from the Damen und Herren lining the rail, the *Hephaistos* docked from where she had departed just a week before. In the drizzle on the pier faces peered from beneath the umbrellas like sea urchins. Madame Sambar wept in the arms of Monsieur Sambar. Dry-eyed, her daughters looked on.

"Aunt Winnie!" the girl shrieked, and there she was. At her side, a sad-eyed immigrant child, the sleeve wrapped face of Miss Kollwitz.

"Look!" she cried, "where is he?"

This time Soby was equal to the question. The zipper bag, with its Acropolis stencil, he held up so the ladies could see it. Where the zipper did not close gleamed the eye of Aschenbach. He mewed.

"We flew," Miss Throop said, in answer to no question.

"You will not believe it!" Miss Kollwitz barked, "to fly is worse!"

"Your luggage follows by steamer," Miss Throop observed, "—if that is the right word."

Gripping the fingers of his sore hand, the girl led him down the gangplank. Was it the smell of Venice that excited Aschenbach? Hoarsely, he mewed.

"I must say—" Miss Throop paused to grope on her bust for her glasses, clip them to the bridge of her nose. "I must say," she continued, her eyes on the girl, "that the face looks familiar but the name escapes me. Or is it names?"

A tongue to his dry lips Soby said, "With your permission, the name is Mrs. Soby." He bowed.

"Even without your permission, Aunt Winnie." The girl did not smile.

The cheeks of Miss Kollwitz filled like a sail, then collapsed. Miss Throop exhaled a sigh that shifted the shawl, like a flynet, on her broad shoulders: the hand of Miss Kollwitz plucked at one of the tassels, as if adjusting a blind.

"You wired your mother, my dear?" Miss Throop inquired.

"From Corfu," put in Soby, "—as you suggested."

Out of the mist a gondolier called, Soby replied. Water trickled down the sleeve of the arm he waved in the air.

"How's Miss Winifred?" asked the girl.

Miss Throop signalled for silence, but Miss Kollwitz missed it. One hand gripping Soby's sleeve she cried, "You will not believe it! She is expecting!"

Miss Throop's resigned smile showed the color was running on her mask. One could not tell if it was tears, drizzle, or merely perspiration tinted with mascara. "We don't know what—" she said, then paused as if to add that she couldn't care less. But she did not. No, she merely repeated, "My dear, we don't know *what*."

Did Soby detect, behind her bloodshot eyes, the glint of great expectations? Out of the sea, a helmeted apparition, wagging slowly like the head of a sea serpent, the gondola thrust toward them its dripping snout.

"My child," Miss Throop said, "don't say *what a way to go*. I'm sure we are *all* in full agreement." She wheeled to include Soby in the shelter of her parasol. There was time enough for Soby to exchange glances with the girl, standing on the pier, but his eyes were on the smiling face of the gondolier, who had leaped forward, the boat rocking, to exchange his oar for an umbrella, hoisting it to keep the drizzle from falling on Soby's bride.

Wright Morris

was born in Central City, Nebraska, in 1910, and though he has lived in many parts of the United States and traveled extensively abroad, his home country has remained central to his work. His critical reputation has grown steadily since the publication in 1942 of his first novel, *My Uncle Dudley*. This was followed by *The Inhabitants* and *The Home Place*, two books primarily concerned with the fusion of photographs and text. *The Deep Sleep*, published in 1953, was runner-up for the National Book Award, and that prize for a year's most distinguished American novel went in 1957 to *The Field of Vision*. His other books are *The Man Who Was There, The World in the Attic, Man and Boy, The Works of Love, The Huge Season, Love Among the Cannibals, Ceremony in Lone Tree* and *The Territory Ahead*, a critical examination of American literature. Wright Morris has been the recipient of three Guggenheim Fellowships and a grant from the National Institute of Arts and Letters. He now lives in California.

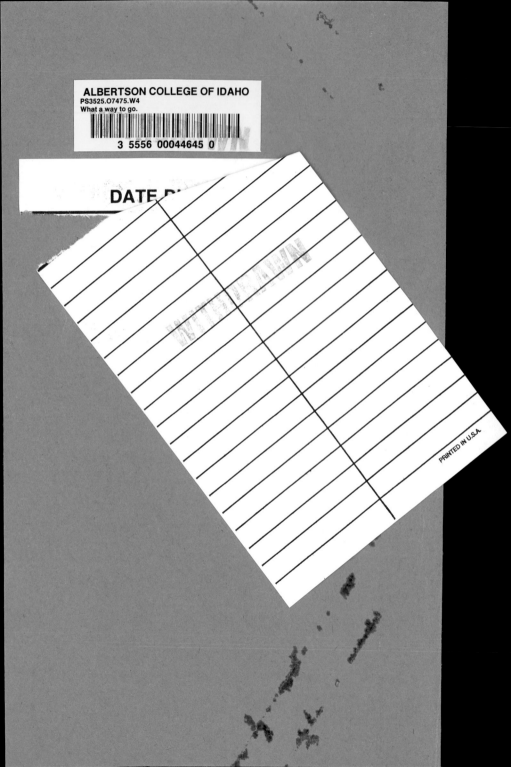